ROB THE VATICAN

Also by Robert Gallant: *Jericho's Trumpet, Satan's Stronghold, The Armageddon Virus,* and *God's Domain*

Rob the Vatican

A Novel

Robert Gallant

iUniverse, Inc.

New York Lincoln Shanghai

Rob the Vatican

Copyright © 2007 by Robert W. Gallant

All rights reserved. No part of this book may be used or reproduced by any means, graphic, electronic, or mechanical, including photocopying, recording, taping or by any information storage retrieval system without the written permission of the publisher except in the case of brief quotations embodied in critical articles and reviews.

iUniverse books may be ordered through booksellers or by contacting:

iUniverse
2021 Pine Lake Road, Suite 100
Lincoln, NE 68512
www.iuniverse.com
1-800-Authors (1-800-288-4677)

This is a work of fiction. All of the characters, names, incidents, organizations, and dialogue in this novel are either the products of the author's imagination or are used fictitiously.

ISBN: 978-0-595-43924-9 (pbk)
ISBN: 978-0-595-88247-2 (ebk)

Printed in the United States of America

PROLOGUE

▲

Halfway down the alley, Craig Reynolds shoved back into a doorway alcove and listened. Sirens pulsing in the distance told him the police were rushing in the wrong direction, searching for a quarry already vanished. A solitary lighted window on the second floor at the far end of the alleyway left the blackness of midnight undisturbed. Across the Seine River, mist dissipated the Eiffel Tower lights into a hazy silver glow.

Craig's ears sensed a new sound. Running footsteps approached the alley entrance.

A figure ran past the alley and disappeared. The thud of footsteps on cobblestone began to fade.

The footsteps stopped. When they began again, the sound was moving back toward him.

A form appeared at the alleyway entrance, momentarily silhouetted by city lights reflecting off clustered clouds. A weapon hung from the right hand. The figure shuffled sideways to the opposite wall and paced into the alley, becoming almost invisible.

Craig eased the .44 Magnum from his belt. How could Von Meier know he had come this way? The son-of-a-bitch must be half bloodhound. He watched the nebulous form prowl step by cautious step along the alley wall. Now he could discern the lanky body and sharp facial profile. It was definitely Inspector Von Meier.

Craig lined up the revolver sights on the face. His finger slid around the trigger. The hunter became the prey.

There was no quivering of Craig's hand, no blinking of eyes, no dots of perspiration on his forehead, not even a faster heartbeat. Drops of rain splattering onto brick surfaces dominated the silence in the alley.

Craig's finger tightened on the trigger. Everything disappeared into the background, leaving only the face of his adversary. At this distance, he could put a bullet through Von Meier's eye. One shot and the only hunter he feared would be dead.

He hesitated, eased the finger pressure on the trigger, shifted the gun downward, and lined up the target again.

The roar of his gun shattered the silence. The figure cried out in pain and grasped his leg as he fell.

Craig sprinted past the dark myriad of doorways, exited the alley, crossed through a small park, and melted into a maze of dark streets.

He chided himself as he ran. He should have killed him. Inspector Von Meier would be back to hunt again.

C H A P T E R 1

▲

A lone man, thin and erect, the gray of his thick hair the color of his suit, slowed his pace along the great columns encircling St. Peter's Square. The limp in Inspector Von Meier's left leg, distinct in his longer strides, became almost indiscernible. Splinters of bone lodged in his upper leg remained a permanent legacy of that split-second confrontation one year ago.

Von Meier's dark eyes assimilated every detail. Rays of afternoon sun slithered past gathering clouds and sliced through narrow openings between statues adorning the colonnade roof. Like a giant, mute sentinel, the granite obelisk in the plaza center towered above the scene. Originally a centerpiece of Nero's Circus Coliseum, it now hoisted aloft the Christian cross, commemorating the place where a pagan Roman Empire crucified St. Peter two thousand years ago. A sea of people, enclosed by the facade of the basilica and massive colonnade pillars, bobbed and shuffled across the plaza. The drone of their voices drowned the sound of water bubbling from the multi-tiered Bernini fountain.

Men and women crowded the basilica steps, appearing and disappearing through massive arched doorways. Awe filling the faces of those leaving conveyed the reverent splendor of what they experienced inside. An endless parade of priests swirled in and out of the basilica, clothed in a menagerie of apparel ranging from flowing frocks and dark clothes to bright patterned garb and turbaned hats. For many, this represented the culmination of journeys from all corners of the world. They came to fulfill a lifelong dream of conducting mass, often with no one in attendance, at one of the ornate altars inside the magnificent basilica constructed over a four century period under the combined genius of Michelangelo, Bernini, and other illustrious artist-architects of the Renaissance.

Serious business, not religion, brought Von Meier here today.

Two Swiss Guards watched him approach. One examined the identification papers and talked briefly on the telephone, his accent betraying the quasi-German harshness of the Schwyzerdütsch spoken by natives of Central Switzerland.

The Bronze Door, entryway into the Papal Palace, swung open. Von Meier walked with a guard along the glistening hallway to the long Scala Regia Staircase, following the route taken by groups attending audiences with the Pope. Each footstep echoed off vaulted walls embellished with vivid frescoes in a building beautiful beyond description.

The Swiss Guard paused, knocked on a gold encrusted wooden door, and pushed it open. Von Meier stepped into a room with a marble floor, draped windows, and ornate furnishings.

"Inspector Martin Von Meier," the Swiss Guard said, "Chief Investigative Officer of the International Criminal Police Organization." He closed the door as he left.

Von Meier gazed at four solemn-faced men. The tall one beside the window stood erect like a Prussian military officer. His tightly set jaw, protruding chin, and broad shoulders portrayed a man disciplined by years of military service. The uniform bore the same markings and color as the Swiss Guard, but exquisite hand-stitched patterns and jeweled medals conveyed the rank of a senior officer.

The other standing man had a uniform even more elaborately bedecked with braids and medals. A black mustache dominated the square, fleshy face. The countenance suggested Italian nobility lineage.

Two men sat in plush upholstered chairs at a marble-topped, engraved wooden table. The older man, heavyset to the verge of obesity, wore a black robe. It was the other man that drew Von Meier's attention. Garbed in the traditional red of the Church cardinal, gaunt by comparison with the older man, he had a large, perfect Roman nose. His deep-set black eyes riveted on the visitor like a hawk contemplating its next meal.

"Good afternoon, Inspector," the intense man said. "I am Cardinal Lastavis, Director of Administration and Security. My schedule today is rather demanding, but your telephone call indicated a sense of urgency."

The sonorous tone reinforced Von Meier's initial impression that Lastavis was a man accustomed to wielding power. Lieutenant Palermo of the Rome Police Detective Division had described Cardinal Lastavis as the Vatican's most influential man, other than the Pope himself. Always prominent, often dominant, in Vatican policy debates, Lastavis was an essential ally for any bishop or cardinal aspiring to a leadership role in Vatican affairs. People who spoke about him men-

tioned the attributes of intelligence, knowledge of Church doctrine, and a commanding demeanor. No one mentioned warmth or compassion.

As Lastavis introduced the others, Von Meier confirmed his earlier judgements. Captain Borgan, the man at the window, commanded the elite corps of Swiss nationals dedicated to protecting the Pope. They had fulfilled their obligation without blemish for five hundred years, sometimes at a high price. In the sixteenth century, a hundred and forty-seven of them sprawled in bloody pools from the colonnade plaza to the center of the basilica. The Captain himself, bloodied by a dozen wounds, had finally fallen beneath the magnificent baldachino soaring above the high altar of St. Peter's. Strewn in all directions were bodies of four hundred Spanish and German invaders. The carnage of Swiss Guards had allowed Pope Clement to escape through a secret passageway to the safety of the nearby Castel Sant'Angelo fortress. Without hesitation, every Swiss Guard would do the same today.

The second man was Colonel Guista, Commander of the Papal Gendarmes, the specialized army assigned responsibility for safeguarding the Vatican. Drawn from aristocratic families of Italy, the Gendarmes carried the stamp of Italian politics and position rather than the military regimen of the Swiss Guards. But beneath the pompous exterior of lavish uniforms lay the same unflinching loyalty to the Vatican monarchy.

Monsignor Pompa, the older heavyset man, had been Custodian of the Vatican Treasury for the past twenty years. Among three such strong men, he appeared tense.

Cardinal Lastavis completed the introductions and shifted his probing eyes back onto Von Meier. "You expressed concerns to Colonel Guista when you telephoned yesterday, suggesting that the Vatican may be the target of a robbery attempt."

Von Meier sensed disbelief, almost sarcasm in the voice. Lastavis made no gesture to offer him one of the other upholstered chairs. Both military officers remained standing. Lastavis obviously intended this to be a short meeting.

Von Meier chose to ignore the tenor and focus on the facts. "Two days ago, a supervisor at the Bratius Company here in Rome fortuitously discovered that wiring diagrams for their vault protection systems had been stolen from the files and replaced with fake drawings. With this knowledge, a thief might successfully abort even the most sophisticated vault alarms."

Monsignor Pompa rubbed his hands together. "We use the Bratius system on our vault. The Bratius system also safeguards the libraries and museums housing many of the Holy Church's most sacred treasures."

"The vault," Colonel Guista injected, "is buried in an underground cellar located beneath the center of the Vatican. It would be inconceivable that any person could rob the vault undetected, even if they knew how to silence the alarms. The vault locking mechanism is unrelated to the alarm system. No one could open the vault without prior knowledge of the combination. The Bratius files do not contain information relative to the vault combination."

Von Meier sensed that Lastavis would make the decision, and so focused his attention on him. "We are not dealing with an ordinary thief. Interpol is convinced that the robber of the Bratius files is an American who has burglarized chateaus and jewelry establishments throughout Europe. He aborts elaborate alarm systems, unlocks the most intricate vaults, and eludes massive manhunts. A seeming magician who appears, steals, and evaporates into thin air. He leaves only the telltale signs of ingenious planning and flawless execution."

Guista scowled. "Your jewel thief is certainly not an apparition who can walk through walls and vault doors. The Vatican is a walled city patrolled continuously by my Papal Gendarmes. Swiss Guardsmen and Church officials are always on duty. No thief could enter or leave undetected. Why would he attempt to rob a protected fortress like this when he has other lucrative, less hazardous choices?"

"Our master thief has overcome seemingly insurmountable obstacles before," Von Meier replied. "His past exploits suggest a man fascinated by the challenge of impossible robberies. He's like a moth drawn to the flickering flame, but a moth whose wings have never been singed."

Von Meier noted Monsignor Pompa patting his perspiring forehead with a linen napkin. Unlike the others, Pompa appeared alarmed by discussion of a possible theft. Perhaps his routine involvement with the vault and museums made him aware of potential deficiencies.

"The vault contains many priceless treasures given to the Holy Church," Pompa said. "We also keep negotiable securities and large amounts of various national currencies there for special needs. We still store gold bullion in the vault."

Von Meier wrinkled his face. "You have gold bullion stored here in the Vatican?"

"Benito Mussolini and the Church concluded the Concordant Treaty in nineteen twenty-nine, restoring the Holy Catholic Church to its rightful place as the nation's official religion," Pompa replied. "The government reimbursed the Church for Papal property confiscated by earlier Italian governments. The Church used some of the money to buy gold from the United States government. Today that gold is worth over forty million Euros."

Guista waved his hand as though chasing away a meddlesome fly. "No thief could carry away heavy bars of gold unnoticed."

"I've chased that elusive fox all over Europe," Von Meier said. "So close sometimes that he could surely feel my breath on his neck. But always he vanished. Not knowing that we are aware of his Bratius security system theft, our thief may err this time. The purpose of my visit is to alert you to the danger and recommend that you immediately modify the alarm system."

Colonel Guista opened his hands, palms up "The Vatican is walled and all access controlled. The vault is sealed underground. The museums and grounds are patrolled continuously by my men. How could any man rob this holy place?"

"Only a master thief could do it and then only if he had help from someone on the inside," Von Meier said. "Someone you trust."

Colonel Guista's body stiffened. His facial skin wrinkled and tightened around his eyes.

Cardinal Lastavis rose from his chair. "The Vatican is not a corporation or government where men toil for a salary, often caring little for their employer. Those working here are ordained by God to serve his Church. They are incorruptible guardians of the Vatican and its treasures. No priest and no soldier could endure the spiritual torment of betraying his sacred responsibility."

"I'm not suggesting such betrayal is possible," Von Meier replied. "My intent is only to comment as a police officer that your greatest vulnerability may lie in that very trust. I recommend that you modify the present alarm system as quickly as possible."

Cardinal Lastavis glanced toward the door.

Von Meier saw another man in a black robe with a red sash standing in the doorway, nervously rubbing his hands together.

"I'm finished here," Lastavis said to the man. He looked at Von Meier. "Thank you for your concern, Inspector. However, the expense and inconvenience of changing the protection system seem unwarranted. Now I must attend to other business."

Von Meier nodded toward Lastavis and the other men. "Thank you for meeting with me on such short notice. If I can be of further assistance, please do not hesitate to call."

Lastavis walked briskly past him and through the doorway, motioning to the waiting man to walk with him.

Von Meier followed them into the corridor. He heard the man speaking to Lastavis.

"Bishop Baccalete insists on a personal Papal audience concerning funds that were denied him for restoration of the Bernini fountain at Granople. The serious illness of His Holiness will not deter him any longer."

Lastavis's voice receded as they moved down the corridor. "Baccalete feels strongly about the Granople fountain. But his real purpose is to determine how incapacitated the Pontiff is and whether so much authority was delegated to me. As Secretariat to the Holy Father, you can quell those concerns."

The two cardinals disappeared through a doorway.

Von Meier followed the Swiss Guard down the Scalia Regia Staircase to the Bronze Door. He paused as he entered St. Peter's Square and lit his pipe. His eyes scanned the bronze door and massive stone walls encircling the one hundred-acre heartbeat of the Roman Catholic Church.

The Vatican contained the most magnificent collection of jewels, paintings, and treasures in the world. That would make it a tempting target for an adventuresome thief. But it did indeed appear to be an impregnable fortress. The American jewel thief was not foolhardy. He would rob a less secure place, almost certainly one that utilized the Bratius security system.

Gleaning through the Bratius customer list had identified fourteen potential targets. All had been notified by Interpol and regional police. Von Meier had personally visited four.

Maybe this time, the jewel thief would walk into a trap.

CHAPTER 2

▼

Three-hundred miles north of Rome, Craig Reynolds sped along a road twisting against cliffs and tree-lined slopes like a rope draped by a whimsical giant. The confining walls of a tunnel momentarily muted the roar of the Ferrari. Then the car flashed downward toward the rolling green and brown crosshatch of a sprawling plain dominated by an endless ribbon of water.

Eventually Craig turned onto a dirt road almost obliterated by entangled undergrowth and stopped among dense trees.

A husky man with a coarse beard and nicotine-stained teeth clenched around the stub of a cigar tramped up beside the Ferrari. "Bad day for doing business," he muttered.

Craig climbed out into the drizzling rain and walked to the edge of the hill. He wore a nondescript raincoat typical of workers in the Piedmont area of Italy. Rain pelted his sandy brown hair and dribbled down past sky-blue eyes. Despite being a lanky six foot, four inches, his movements suggested a tiger on the hunt.

His gloved hand pulled binoculars from the leather bag draped over his shoulder. He studied the clearing below.

A massive granite-walled chateau sat majestically on a sea of green grass, surrounded by sculptured shrubbery interspersed with decorative fountains and statues. Tall spruces stood like frozen sentries. Arched windows with billowing Austrian drapes partially obscuring glittering chandeliers transformed the granite walls of the chateau into a palatial mansion. A dozen chimneys pierced the slate roof. A curving stone fence encircled the entire estate.

"Is everything prepared?" Craig asked.

The husky man pointed with his large callused hand. "I dug the tunnel underneath the wall and into that grove of trees. It opens to the left of the tall oak tree, just like you told me to do. I had hell digging through tree roots."

"The stone fence is crisscrossed with alarms. So we have to burrow underneath." Craig shifted the binoculars to focus on a large dog with brownish-black hair and a face reminiscent of a wolf.

"I been watching those dogs," the man growled. "They prowl back and forth, sniffing everything. No way to get past them."

"The dogs are a unique breed developed by a kennel in Denmark, specifically for use as guard dogs," Craig said. "They're faster and more powerful than Dobermans, with a nose like a bloodhound. I owned one for two years. There isn't a guard dog in the world that compares with them."

"Then how are we going to reach the chateau?"

Craig pointed. "Watch the dogs. Every round, both dogs are together for about ten seconds, less than thirty feet from the trees. Over a period of time, they've developed the habit, like humans meeting and greeting. Guard dogs should never be in the same place at the same time. It's an oversight that makes our job easier."

"It don't look easier to me," the man groused. "I'd rather face two men with knives than one of those beasts."

"I'll take care of the dogs." Craig pulled his Magnum from the leather bag and attached the silencer. Even in the rain, the chrome skin of the gun glistened. Later today, he would tint the metal. The glint of a gun in semi-darkness had cost more than one man his life. Black pants, black headgear, black pullover, and muffled black shoes were standard wear for him during heists. His exceptional night vision and virtual invisibility in darkness gave him an advantage against guards and policemen. Success is in the details.

The bearded man eyed the weapon. "It's a tough shot with a pistol at that distance."

Craig zeroed in on the two dogs. He clicked on empty chambers as he targeted first one dog and then the other. "I won't miss from our position in the trees."

He pulled out odd shaped bullets and loaded them in the gun. "There's enough poison in each bullet to kill a bull. Any hit will drop a dog in its tracks without a whimper. Thanks to the carelessness of the guards, the dogs will die at the same time, side by side."

He put the gun in his shoulder bag and glanced at the billowing black storm clouds blanketing the sky. Thunder rumbled around them. "As soon as it's dark, we'll go in."

The husky man wiped mud from the lens of his binoculars with a rag already drenched. "The rain has turned everything into a quagmire. The rivers are all overflowing."

"Rain works to our advantage. The guards are making hasty rounds outside. When we blow the power transformer, they'll think the storm caused it. While they're switching to the auxiliary generator and resetting alarms, we'll go through the window. By the time they discover the robbery, we'll be across the Po River and headed into the Alps. Make certain you don't tear any of the sealed plastic bags holding electronic equipment. I can't open the vault with wet gear."

The man's yellowed teeth flashed a smile. "They say the Ducote Chateau has the finest collection of diamond necklaces in all of Europe. But the security makes it impossible to rob."

"The more secure they make a place, the easier it is to rob. They become careless. You concentrate on keeping the electronics dry and handling any guard who wanders in while I'm working."

The man pulled out a serrated knife and slashed into the tender green fiber of a young tree, slitting it open. With a hoarse laugh, he waved the weapon in front of the tall American's face. "I have the equipment that will handle any nosy guard. It works wet or dry and it's just as deadly as your fancy gun. You get us inside the chateau. I'll get us back out. There isn't a road in this region I don't know by heart, in daylight or pitch black."

"That's why I picked you. But I want any intruding guard incapacitated, not killed. So don't use the knife."

Craig focused the binoculars again on the chateau. "Did any one visit the chateau today?"

"A delivery truck came and went early in the morning. A man and woman came in the afternoon and spent two hours inside. They drove a fancy car and acted like they were either old friends or buying jewelry. An older man showed up about mid morning. He went inside for awhile and then walked around outside in the rain with a guard."

Craig frowned. "What did he look like?"

The man spit out the remaining nub of his cigar. "He was wearing an overcoat, but he looked kind of thin, with gray hair. Not quite as tall as you. I seen him light up a pipe while they stood underneath the overhang."

"Did he limp?" Craig asked.

"Not that I noticed."

"It would be a slight limp, especially when he walked fast or after he'd been standing still."

The man rubbed his beard with his muddy hand. "Now that I think about it, he did limp. They stood near the stone fence a few minutes. When they started back, he kind of stumbled. Yeah, he did limp."

Craig's fist tightened. He mulled the implications in his mind. Why would Von Meier come to the Ducote Chateau? Maybe he knows about the theft from the Bratius files.

"Who is he?" the bearded man asked.

"He's a bloodhound with the tenacity of a bulldog and the mind of a computer." Craig paced back to the edge of the hill and studied the chateau again. "What about the guard schedule? Any extra guards added?"

"They're not doing anything different. I counted the guards just like I always do. Same number, same schedule."

"Anybody else other than the man and woman come after the gray-haired man left?"

"No."

"We'll be in and out before they modify the alarm system. Let's move my car to the other side of the Po River. I've already wired the transformer for blowing. I have a black Fiat that we'll use during the robbery."

The husky man shoved a new cigar between his teeth. "This time tomorrow, we'll have a king's ransom in jewels. Looking at the chateau and those dogs, it don't seem possible. You still think we can do it in this rain?"

Craig didn't reply. His mind methodically traced through each step in the plan. Inspector Von Meier would be on his trail in a matter of hours, sniffing every clue, sifting through the ruses that leave local policemen bewildered and galloping off in the wrong direction.

Von Meier's visit created a worrisome complication. But by the time Von Meier arrived, they would have disappeared into the vast foothills of the Po River Valley.

The bulldog would be left grasping at a wisp of smoke and sniffing for a scent already vanished.

CHAPTER 3

▼

Darlena Aldonzo paused on the muddy levee, one hand holding the reins of her silver-gray Lipizzaner horse. Mud-encrusted jeans and a violet ribbed sweater clung to her petite body, accentuating round full breasts and curving hips that flowed into a narrow waist. Despite pelting rain, raven hair draped flawlessly over her shoulders, framing a tanned face and hazel eyes interspersed with green specks that sparkled like emeralds.

Her eyes blinked away droplets of water as she studied the ragged wall of sandbags stacked up against the turbulent water. The deluge of rain had transformed the normally placid Cabor River into a ravenous torrent gnawing at saturated earthen riverbanks. Only thin lines of sandbags constantly stacked higher held the floodwaters back from Luguri, a small city nestled in the northeast region of the Po Valley, industrial and agricultural center of Northern Italy. Encircled by towering Alps on the north and west, cut off from the Mediterranean Sea by the high Apennines Mountains, the Po River had carved a broad fertile plain in its journey eastward to the Adriatic Sea. Farms reflected affluence generated by rich soil that yielded the highest harvest of grains in all of Italy.

Now the river waged war against the prosperous land. Unable to dump its water into the swollen Po River, the Cabor had breached its banks downstream, inundating low-lying farmland and towns. Sitting on higher ground, Luguri and its surrounding countryside had thus far been protected by levees reinforced with sandbags.

Darlena had come into Luguri to teach her gymnastics class, but leaks in the school gymnasium roof had soaked the exercise mats and floor. With half the students unable to attend because of flooding, she had canceled the class and come to help at the river by riding along the levee, inspecting soggy riverbank for signs of collapse, and reporting problems to the swarm of men stacking sandbags.

Pegasus whinnied and stomped the ground. She had named the colt Pegasus a week after his birth because he pawed the ground with his front hoof when hungry, reminiscent of the Greek mythology winged horse that caused the stream Hippocrene to spring from Mount Helicon with a blow of his hoof. Pegasus had become the surrogate younger brother that she always wanted and never had. Both were free spirited, sometimes defiant, and always ready to run with the wind. They melded into one entity as horse and rider galloped across fields and cleared fences as though gravity had been banished.

She reached up to reassure Pegasus by rubbing his head and saw his ears cocked forward.

Something had frightened him. Glancing around gave her no clue. Horses have exceptional hearing, she thought. Something Pegasus heard alarmed him.

A dull rumble spread toward her from upstream. It diminished and then returned, louder and continuous, the rumble intermingling with a shrill grinding that sounded like a thousand claw hammers scraping on metal.

Darlena stared upstream, trying to see in the darkening mist. Where were the bridge lights? A few minutes earlier, she could still see the dim glow from the bridge spanning the Cabor River.

Her eyes darted back to the levee bank. The water level began receding.

A shiver spiraled down her body. The bridge must have collapsed into the river, partially blocking water flow. When the trapped water broke loose, the surge would sweep away anyone stacking sandbags on the riverbank.

Darlena leaped into the saddle.

Mud and water spewed from the hooves pounding into wet ground as she bent low against the neck and used her knees to urge Pegasus into a faster gallop. Her eyes scanned muddy terrain ahead, searching for washed out areas that would trip the horse. In the distance, she saw figures moving across the top of the levee, carrying sandbags to the riverbank.

A gutted-out trench loomed immediately in front of her. Her knees and voice shouted to the horse. The steed's powerful legs propelled them over the trench, landed on muddy ground, and regained the gait.

Fifty yards away, she began yelling and waving, hoping to attract someone's attention. No one saw her.

Twenty yards away now. A man spotted the onrushing horse, dropped his sandbag, and scurried out of her path. Darlena reined in Pegasus and yelled as she reached the men. "The bridge has collapsed! It's blocking the water. Warn everyone to get away from the riverbank."

Men shouted and scattered from the sandbagged levee.

Darlena urged Pegasus into a gallop again. A mile downstream, a group worked at the water treatment plant, buttressing the inlet piping station superstructure with sandbags. They would be the most vulnerable.

She heard a grating rumble. A continuous roll of thunder, growing louder, surged downstream toward her.

She spotted the hazy silhouette of the water storage tank and urged Pegasus faster. The pants of the horse and its heaving ribs accelerated. Mud spewed behind the pounding hooves.

The roar of onrushing water raced after them.

Darlena reached the piping superstructure and saw five men out on the gangway above the river inlet piping, dropping sandbags into the water swirling around the footings of the support girders.

She yelled and waved her hands. The noise of the river drowned out her voice. She jumped up, grasped a support girder, and catapulted onto the catwalk.

A man turned to come back for more sandbags and saw her sprinting toward them.

Darlena pointed upstream and shouted. "Water surge! Water surge!"

The man glanced upstream and yelled to the others. They scrambled onto the catwalk and ran toward her.

She whirled and raced for the water storage tank. Its elevation would provide a safe refuge from the water surge.

Where was Pegasus? She glanced toward the ground and saw the horse on the levee top, snorting and stomping in the mud. Darlena leaped from the catwalk to the muddy ground, somersaulted to ease the impact, and ran to Pegasus. Her hands grabbed the bridle and pulled the horse away from the riverbank.

She heard a crashing roar directly behind her. Water cascaded over the sandbags and swept toward them.

Darlena urged the horse onto the sloping backside of the levee. Water exploded over the levee, yanking the reins from her grasp and sweeping her underneath cascading froth.

She gasped for breath, but swallowed mostly water. Her body slammed against a piling of the catwalk. She grabbed the piling.

The force of water ripped her hands away. Darlena tried to breathe. Water poured into her mouth, choking her. Pain hammered her chest.

She grasped at another piling. Her slippery hands couldn't hold on.

The surge swept her out from underneath the catwalk. She fought to push her head above churning water.

Her face broke above the surface. She gasped for air but choked on water in her mouth.

The surge yanked her under again. Fists of water pounded her lungs.

Which way to the surface? Her body slammed into a tree. She wrapped an arm around it, thrust her head upward, coughed water out from her lungs, and sucked in air.

The current swept her away from the tree and submerged her beneath the deluge again.

Darlena resurfaced, gasped in a mixture of water and air, grabbed a partially submerged tree branch, wrapped both arms around the branch, and clung there as her lungs heaved to replenish oxygen to her depleted body. Mud in her eyes blurred everything around her.

The rush of water began to subside, swirling past now in a muddy froth. She clung to the tree, coughing out swallowed water and gasping in wet air.

"Darlena!"

She looked toward the sound of the voice. A figure scrambled down from the water plant superstructure and into the water and mud. Even in the twilight, she recognized the priest's garb. It was Thad Raphano.

When he reached her, she wrapped her arms around his neck, clinging to him to support her rubbery legs.

"Are you hurt?" he asked.

"I'm okay," she gasped out between breaths.

His concern shifted to a frown. "Going after Pegasus was foolish. You could have drowned."

Darlena stuck her face nose-to-nose with his. "I helped deliver Pegasus. I bottle fed him after his mother died, raised him, and trained him. I couldn't let Pegasus be swept into the river." She pulled back from him and looked around for the horse. A man was leading Pegasus to high ground beside the treatment plant.

Thad clasped her hand. Together they sloshed through muddy water toward the levee. Her five foot, four inch body bogged down in scoured-out holes. Thad hoisted her up, his muscular six-foot frame freeing her feet from the grasping mud.

Two men met them as they struggled up the embankment to the water treatment plant. One put a blanket around her shaking shoulders. She sagged down onto the concrete foundation of the large tank, clasped the cup of coffee poured from a thermos by the other man, and smiled to acknowledge their praise of her bravery.

Thad plopped down beside her and pushed disheveled black hair away from his eyes. "We would have been killed if you hadn't warned us. But your Papa will be furious when he learns you've been patrolling the levees."

The warmth of coffee trickling down her throat rejuvenated her. "I told Papa I would stay in town tonight with friends after I finished teaching my gymnastics class. So he doesn't have to know. Water leaked through the gymnasium roof and soaked the equipment. I canceled my class and came out here to help." She tilted her head to give Thad a jaunty grin. "Canceling class was also a reward to the team for winning the silver medal in regional competition last weekend."

"Congratulations. I hadn't heard. I've been here at the river since Sunday afternoon."

Darlena gazed into his face. Mud coating his face and matting his luxurious black hair couldn't detract from the sheer beauty of his brown eyes and perfectly shaped face. Beard stubble reinforced his masculinity. "Tradition requires rewarding the gymnastics coach with a kiss when you first hear the news."

He flashed a suspicious smile. "I've never heard of that tradition."

"That's because you spend your time either in the Church or on the soccer field, instead of coming to my tournaments."

Thad kissed her lightly on the cheek and held up his coffee cup in a salute. "This is the first time a Luguri team placed in a regional tournament. They didn't do that even when you won the individual gold medal two years in a row. You're as talented at coaching as you were at competing."

"That's not much of a kiss for such an achievement." Darlena puckered her lips, wrapped her arms around his neck, and gave him a lingering kiss on the lips.

He didn't try to stop her, but neither did he reciprocate.

She sagged down beside him and folded her arms. "I hate you for becoming a priest."

"Do you ever regret not joining the national team in Rome?" Thad asked. "You could have represented Italy at the Olympics."

"I didn't want to dedicate my life to gymnastics training. I'm not a perfectionist and that's what it takes to win at the national level or make the Olympic team."

"You didn't have to be a perfectionist," he replied. "You have a grace and electrifying presence that captivates the audience and judges. When you perform on the balance beam, you are the most elegant creature that ever walked on the face of the earth."

The cold chills and throbbing bruises in her body vanished. "Why didn't you tell me that back when I was competing?"

"I couldn't say that to a teenage girl who offered to marry me every year since she was six years old."

Darlena stuck her lips out in a pout. "You betrayed my love by becoming a priest. You knew I planned to marry you."

"Those were the fantasies of a young girl."

She shoved her face nose-to-nose again. "I'm not a young girl anymore. I'm nineteen and I'm still in love with you. I haven't been to confession in a year because I don't want to ask forgiveness for trying to seduce a priest into breaking his vows and leaving the Church."

Thad shook his head. "Serving the Holy Church has always been my life's dream. I'll never leave the priesthood."

Darlena scrambled up and put her hands on her hips. "Then you'll have to live with the consequences. The Regional Director of Gymnastics at Turin has offered me the opportunity to be assistant coach for the girls' team. It's the largest training school for gymnasts in northern Italy. I'm going to take the job, go to Turin, and become the mistress for twelve men. One man for each year that I asked you to marry me and you refused. I'll die estranged from the Church and burn in the fires of Hell, because you became a priest. It's on your conscience."

She sloughed through the mud to Pegasus, swung up into the saddle with an effortless motion, and looked back at Thad. "I have a terrible premonition that the priesthood is going to destroy you. I will never forgive the Church if it hurts you."

Darlena Aldonzo trotted away into the darkness.

CHAPTER 4

▼

Thad Raphano climbed from the truck, gestured in appreciation to the driver, and walked up the curving gravel road toward the farmhouse, enjoying the warm breeze and first hint of sunshine in a week. Wheat stretched away to the left. On the other side, plush rows of garden vegetables rolled to the edge of a pasture dominated by a large barn.

He smiled as he surveyed the farm. The Aldonzo farm was renowned throughout the Po Valley for the tastiest vegetables, most prolific dairy cows, freshest eggs, tallest grain, sturdiest fences, and immaculately painted barns. Not even the deluge of rain could lessen the farm's glow of perfection.

The front door swung open and Dominic Aldonzo strode onto the porch steps, the agile movements giving no hint of his fifty-seven years. He embraced Thad in a bear hug that squeezed breath from the lungs. Although three inches shorter, his large-boned body and bulk made him twenty pounds heavier. Gray hair ruffled in the breeze. Thick eyebrows and a large nose dominated the round face tanned and leathery from years of work in the fields.

"It's good to see you," Dominic said. "I thought you had returned to Rome."

"I've been helping strengthen the river levees," Thad replied. "But I have to leave this afternoon. There's a meeting at the Vatican tomorrow for all the young priests serving there."

"Have you seen Darlena?" Dominic asked.

"Not since last evening. She said you knew she was spending the night in town."

"A neighbor stopped last night to assure me she stayed at the Gardols. I expected her home this morning." Dominic thrust his hands toward the sky.

"Darlena is as wild as Pegasus. I urge her, even threaten her. She thanks me for my advice, kisses me, and does whatever she chooses. Only God in Heaven knows where she is now."

Thad smiled. "She's not a little girl any more. You have to allow her the freedom to explore life. She won't disappoint you."

"She takes her freedom whether I allow it or not." Dominic put a callused hand on Thad's shoulder. "You look tired from the struggle with the river. Come sit on the porch. I'll have Maria bring us a bottle of wine and some cheese."

"I need your counsel. After Papa died, you became an older brother to me. You made it possible for me to graduate from the seminary."

"Darlena has never forgiven me for that," Dominic muttered. "She refuses to even look at another man. Am I right when I say that Darlena is the most desirable, most beautiful young woman in all of Northern Italy?"

Thad followed him onto the porch. "I would agree with that."

"Yet she rarely accepts invitations from any man. Since graduation, she's immersed herself in gymnastics instruction. The son of Aldo Ducote came here to this house and begged her to attend a dinner party at the chateau. He had met her during a gymnastics exhibition and became captivated by her. She refused his invitation. Darlena refused the son of Aldo Ducote, the wealthiest family in the Po Valley."

"I heard that someone robbed the Ducote Chateau last night," Thad said.

Dominic paused. "Officer Lorenzo called. He said they killed the dogs and somehow aborted the security system and vault locks. The entire collection of diamond necklaces was stripped from beneath the guards' noses. The robbers would have disappeared into the night except the collapse of the Cabor bridge closed the route to the Po River crossing and the expressway. Police stopped them at a roadblock when they attempted to escape on the highway west toward Turin, but they eluded pursuit in the early morning fog. Half of the roads are closed by flooding. Police have sealed off the others. Lorenzo is certain they'll be caught. But it was such an amazing robbery. I've been to the Ducote Chateau. It's impossible to imagine that someone could rob it."

They sat down in chairs and gazed toward the pasture fields. A heavyset woman brought wine and cheese.

Dominic handed a glass of wine to Thad. "So what's troubling you?"

"Bishop Baccalete's trip to Rome was a failure. The Vatican committee refused to approve funds for restoration of the Granople fountain."

Dominic Aldonzo's bushy eyebrows hung over his narrowed eyes "Father Domus said Cardinal Lastavis blocked it. Since illness incapacitated His Holiness, Lastavis has exercised dictatorial power, using Vatican funds to curry favors and punish opposition. He intends to be the next Pope and few cardinals or bishops will openly oppose him. It's a terrible dilemma for the Church. I pray every night that God will restore His Holiness to health. Once healthy again, he will strip Lastavis of his ill-gotten power and assure that he doesn't ascend to the Papacy."

Thad took a sip of wine and set the glass on the table. "That's why I need your counsel. A dozen priests, plus two bishops in Northern Italy, are proposing an open challenge to Lastavis on funding the fountain restoration. They plan to send a letter to Cardinal Sangore, Secretariat to the Pope, detailing the obvious political implications in Vatican decisions since Lastavis assumed control. They'll ask Sangore to present their petition directly to His Holiness and send copies of their letter to all the Italian cardinals and bishops. I'm naive about political wars waged in the Vatican. I don't know whether it's right for me to join with them."

Dominic put his hands behind his head and leaned back in his chair to look toward the sky. "Bishop Baccalete would counsel all of you to refrain from such an overt attack on a high member of the Vatican. He would say that God will provide a way if it is right. My personal approach would be different. Remember that Darlena inherited her beauty and boundless energy from her dear departed Mama. She inherited her fiery temper and impertinent audacity from me. I would go to the Vatican, drag Lastavis from his office, and throw him into the Tiber. The correct action is somewhere between those two approaches."

Thad munched on cheese. "That's a rather diverse range of choices."

Dominic stood up, looked out toward the road, shook his head, and shouted through the door of the house. "Maria, prepare our lunch. Don't fix anything for Darlena. She knows I expect to eat promptly at noon."

He turned back to Thad. "Never go to war unless you intend to win. You will occasionally skirmish with someone because you want that person to know that any attempt to dominate you carries a substantial risk. Most people will choose not to force you into a fight and certainly not go to war with you."

Dominic sipped wine and continued. "A man like Cardinal Lastavis will always turn a fight into a war. So do not pick a fight with him unless you intend to go to war and you intend to win. Battlefields are littered with the bodies of brave, young idealists who rushed heroically into the wrong war at the wrong time. You can defeat a man like Lastavis only if you pick the time, the place, and the weapons."

"Maybe the Granople fountain is the time and the place," Thad replied. "Church leaders revere Baccalete. This is the only fountain designed by Bernini outside Rome. I pray for God's guidance. No answer comes."

Dominic placed his arm around Thad's shoulder. "Do not count on divine intervention. God is too patient, too willing to allow evil to fester in this world. God is often content with providing punishment years later in the distant eternal bowels of Hell. Here on earth, we suffer the consequences of God's procrastination. You know how deeply I revere the Holy Church. But remember, despite their vows and sacred callings, these men are subject to the same passions, ambitions, and angry reprisals as those in the secular world. This battle will not be fought or won in the spiritual realm. All the repercussions of victory or defeat will fall on the shoulders of the participants. So concentrate on the earthly ramifications."

Dominic glanced again toward the road. "Darlena will send me to an early grave. She knows I expected her home for lunch."

CHAPTER 5

▼

Darlena leaned down from the saddle, latched the fence gate, and urged Pegasus into a trot along the wagon path in the pasture. Impulsively, she had decided to check fences on the way back to the house. The small stream, swollen by the deluge of the past week, may have washed away posts, allowing cattle to wander from the field.

Her concern had been well founded. Rounding up stray cows and moving them into this secure pasture had occupied her for the past two hours. She coaxed the horse into a gallop, sending her silky black hair flowing out behind her like a spraying fountain. Here in the pasture fields, she lived unfettered in a world all her own.

So why would she leave this tranquility for the tumult of a big city like Turin? For the challenge, she told herself. To fulfill her dream of coaching gymnastic teams competitive with the best in Italy. She would do it to assert her independence and emergence into womanhood.

Her eyes spotted tire tracks in the muddy ground. Darlena slowed Pegasus to a walk. Fresh tire tracks stretched away toward the old barn, now used only to store hay. It now occurred to her that the chain had been loosely draped over the gate to keep it from swinging open. Papa had trained field hands to always securely fasten gates.

Darlena followed the ruts. The tracks continued around the side of the barn, ending at the large wagon doors. Probably a young man had brought his girl here last night. They parked inside the barn, preferring the spacious hayloft to the cramped backseat of a car. Their sloppy replacement of the gate fastener suggested indifference. If they smoked, they might have left smoldering cigarette butts.

She dismounted, led Pegasus to an area of plush grass, and patted the sweating steed on the neck. "Graze awhile, my winged stallion," she purred into the horse's ear. "You've earned an extra ration of oats for your work at the river last night and here this morning."

The horse nuzzled the pocket of her jeans. She rubbed the thick silvery mane. "Yes, you also deserve sugar cubes, but our sousing in the floodwater last night ruined my supply. You'll have to wait on that."

Darlena sauntered to the small side door of the barn and strained to press down the iron latchkey. Papa believed every barn latch should clamp closed with authority. Her gymnastics-strengthened hands could barely open it. She swung the door outward and stepped inside, sniffing for the aroma of hay, hoping for the absence of any hint of smoke.

The pungent odor of paint and the faint smell of cigar smoke filled her nostrils.

What had they done in here last night? Her irritation increased as she paced around the board wall separating the small entry room from the large wagon loading area.

A green Fiat sat in the loading area. Empty paint buckets cluttered the floor. Darlena touched the door panel. Her finger left a slight impression. The paint wasn't quite dry yet. How dare anybody have the audacity to use an Aldonzo barn without asking permission. How dare they smoke cigars with all the hay stored here.

The Ducote Chateau robbery!

The thought leaped into her mind. People in Luguri had talked this morning about the robbery. The thieves wounded a policeman at the roadblock and escaped in a black Fiat. That Fiat was now painted green.

A muffled noise made her whirl around. A husky bearded man stepped into the opening from the entry room. His lips curled upward in a half grin, half snarl. The stub of a cigar was clenched between his yellow teeth. The glare of cold, harsh eyes added to his sinister appearance.

Darlena's knees almost buckled. The thief blocked her escape route to the small door she had come through. She swallowed saliva draining into her throat and tried to keep her voice firm and angry. "You have no right to use this barn. Papa and the field men will be here in a few minutes. They will be very angry when they see what you've done to the barn."

The bearded man sneered. "I watched you coming. You're alone."

His face and eyes said he would kill her. Adrenaline stormed into her bloodstream. Her muscles flexed, driving out the inertia of fear. She had to somehow distract him and escape. "Please don't hurt me," she begged. "I won't tell anybody."

He moved toward her, still blocking the path to the door. "You're a pretty one. You do what I say and I won't hurt you."

His eyes leered at her firm breasts heaving against the blouse and the sculptured shape of her waist and hips outlined by tight jeans. Darlena felt violated, as though he had already stripped off her clothes and begun raping her.

The man stepped closer. The stench of his cigar and foul breath assaulted her nose. His huge hand reached out toward her.

She scooped up a handful of chaff and threw it into his face.

He grabbed for her as he blinked to clear away the irritating chaff.

Darlena jumped sideways and darted past him into the entry room. Her outstretched hands slammed into the outside door, expecting it to swing open.

The door wouldn't open. He had bolted it closed. She clawed at the latch, rammed it back, and plunged out the door.

The man caught her from behind and grabbed her arm. Darlena whirled around and kicked him below the knee, wrenched her arm free, and spun away as he pounced at her. She ran for Pegasus, twenty yards away.

His steps pounded behind her, so close she could hear his breathing. She reached Pegasus and leaped upward for the saddle.

He caught her in midair, with her leg halfway over the saddle.

Darlena teetered there, fighting to swing astride the horse.

He was too strong. He pulled her backward as Pegasus shied away, dumping her into the grassy mud. His heavy body jammed her against the ground, crushing breath from her lungs. A sweaty, smelly hand rubbed across her face and clamped over her mouth and nose.

Darlena couldn't breathe. His other arm wrapped underneath, clamping her arms against her body in a steel vise.

She kicked at him with her legs but his bulky body weight immobilized her.

The man yanked her upward, lifting her feet off the ground without even grunting, and slogged toward the barn. Darlena pummeled him with her feet. The man seemed impervious to her attack. He reentered the barn and hauled her into the large wagon area, keeping her arms locked in his bear hug. His smothering hand over her face stifled her breath, leaving her lungs gasping for air.

Darlena twisted her head, freed a side of her mouth, and bit into the skin of his finger. The man yanked his hand away amid an angry howl of profanity.

Her lungs gasped in air. He clamped his hands on her arms and slammed her backward against the wall of a feeding stall. The jolt exploded air from her lungs.

Darlena kicked, trying to reach his vulnerable groin area. The man yanked her forward toward him, pulling her off balance, and slammed her against the wall again. His hand shoved beneath her chin and locked around her throat. Thick fingers clamped her windpipe closed.

She pounded at him with her hands and feet. He blocked most of her blows with his body and other arm.

Her lungs expanded in a desperate search for oxygen. His fingers dug deeper into her windpipe. The barn and everything in it blurred.

Darlena's glazed eyes spotted a horse bridle hanging from the wall. She stretched out, straining to grasp it. Her fingers clutched leather and yanked the bridle off the nail. She twisted it to expose the sharp metal clip on the harness, rammed the clip against the hand on her throat, and slashed down across it.

Again and again she slashed.

The man's hand jerked away from her throat. With a roar, he lifted her off the floor and flung her into the back area of the stall.

Darlena crashed into the wooden wall and tumbled onto the floor. Her gymnastics instincts cushioned the blow, allowing her to maintain the precious new supply of oxygen being sucked into her lungs. She rolled over and scrambled on her hands and knees toward the back of the stall.

The bearded man glared at his hand where small streams of blood oozed from shallow, jagged gashes. The serrated blade of a large knife flashed out from his belt.

She grabbed the low boards of the hay manger, pulled herself upright, and sucked in breaths to replenish her lungs. The hayloft flooring loomed ten feet above her. The boards on the walls ran up and down. No handholds to pull herself up with and no opening in the hayloft flooring.

He had her trapped. She vaulted over the low board wall of the manger and backed up against the wall.

"I'm going to cut you good," the man growled.

What could she do? He could reach across the low front wall and slash her without climbing in. Darlena shuffled through the shallow layer of hay to the center of the manger, flexed her knees and bounced on her toes, preparing to jump either way when he reached her. Spitting breaths out between her teeth summoned up fierce anger to blunt the paralyzing impact of her fear. What he would do to her before she died terrified her more than the looming certainty of death itself. Somehow, she would reach his eyes, gouge and inflict pain before she died.

Her foot bumped something. She ran her foot along the wooden handle and felt steel prongs. A pitchfork lay partially buried in the hay. Darlena crouched with her back against the wall and grasped the handle with one hand, trying not to make him suspicious.

He moved closer, waving the serrated blade back and forth, taunting her.

Her hand burrowed through the hay, wriggling the pitchfork handle, maneuvering the metal prongs to face him. She blinked away the blur of chaff irritating her eyes.

Let him come a little closer. He leaned against the manger railing now, his cruel eyes gloating, the knife gleaming in her face.

Wait another second. He stretched forward, his chest and upper abdomen rising above the manger railing, the knife blade inches from her breasts.

Now! Her hands brought the pitchfork slashing from the hay. Darlena threw all her strength and weight into the thrust. The prongs thudded into his body.

The man let out an anguished howl and stumbled backward. Two pitchfork prongs impaled in his stomach, inches below his chest.

His face distorted in a snarl. Both hands grasped the pitchfork and yanked it out. Red blots stained his shirt, spreading outward like ripples from a rock tossed into a pond. One of his hands threw the pitchfork away. The other shook the knife at her. He staggered toward her, panting, his face turning more grotesque with each gasp.

Darlena darted back and forth in the manger, utilizing the railing between them, jumping and ducking away from the serrated blade.

He leaned lower, reaching deeper, forcing her toward the corner with each slash. Her back banged against the side wall as she retreated from the knife. His arm dropped lower, positioning the knife where she couldn't scramble beneath it to the other side.

"Got ya," he snarled.

Darlena flexed her knees as the blade flashed toward her. Her flexed knees propelled her upward and over the slashing blade. She landed on her hands, somersaulted to the opposite end, grabbed the front board, and vaulted over it, landing on her feet beside the wall on the opposite side of the stall.

The man lurched backward to block her escape from the stall. She grabbed the discarded pitchfork and positioned it in front of her, the prongs pointed at him. She had more maneuvering room now and a weapon.

He plodded toward her, one hand gripping the knife, the other pressed against his bloodied shirt. His bulging eyes raged at her.

Darlena bounced sideways, feinting left, springing right, unable to sprint past him. But her movements forced him to lurch back and forth to block her escape from the stall.

The man lunged at her.

She thrust with the pitchfork.

His knife arm knocked the prongs aside. His other hand clamped onto the handle at the prongs. With a heaving grunt, he ripped the pitchfork from her hands.

Darlena jumped away from his slashing knife and retreated toward the opposite side.

Using the pitchfork as a crutch, he stumbled after her, slashing wildly with the knife. His breath spewed out in gurgled snorts. Blood trickled out the corners of his mouth and down his chin.

Darlena back flipped over the low board railing into the manger, raced to the far end, and vaulted out into the stall area.

The man's knees buckled as he staggered sideways to block her escape. The outstretched knife hand trembled. Blood vomited from his mouth. He tumbled forward and fell face down onto the floor. Blood oozed from beneath his body, staining the thin layer of hay.

"Oh God, please let him be dead," she muttered to herself. Darlena shuffled along the stall siding, afraid he would jump up and come after her again.

The man still hadn't moved. A circle of crimson spread outward from his body. He must be dead.

What if he wasn't dead? Should she retrieve the pitchfork and stab him again? Or try to yank away the knife still clamped in his outstretched hand?

No. Run to Pegasus and ride for home. Papa would know what to do.

Darlena turned to run.

Another man stood at the front of the stall!

Her breath locked in her throat. Every nerve in her body screamed. Her legs became rubbery.

The man gazed at her in silence. An open leather jacket covered his black pullover. He was tall, taller than the assailant, with thick wavy brown hair. His face and eyes displayed no emotion. No sinister glare, no hatred, not even surprise. He glanced at the man in the pool of blood on the floor and then focused on her. With no change of expression, he reached inside his leather jacket and pulled out a gun. Without a flicker of emotion, without a word, he swung the gun upward and pointed it at her heart.

Darlena stared at him, hypnotized like a bird facing a swaying cobra. He was the other jewel thief.

Darlena knew he would kill her.

CHAPTER 6

▼

Thad walked out onto the porch with Dominic Aldonzo.

The older man let out an irritated sigh as he stared toward the road. "What am I to do about Darlena? God has cursed me with a daughter too much like my own youth."

Thad smiled. "Encourage her to go to Turin and fulfill her dream of coaching a major gymnastics team."

"She is too young," Dominic protested.

"The traits that make her rebellious are the same traits that will enable her to cope with the rigors and seductions of the city. We have to trust her."

Dominic nodded. "I know part of my reluctance is because I'll miss her so much. She brightens the house and keeps me young, just as her mama did for so many years."

"You can visit her often and ..." Thad stopped in mid-sentence. "That's Pegasus."

Dominic turned to look toward the pasture. The horse trotted up to the fence.

Dominic's face paled. "He's saddled. She must have fallen off and injured herself."

Thad bounded off the porch and ran toward the pasture. "I'll try to backtrack where he came from."

"I'll take the truck and check along the road," Dominic shouted. "If she's hurt, we can use the truck to carry her to the hospital." He yelled to two men working in the garden and motioned for them to join him at the truck.

Thad swung onto the saddle and urged Pegasus into a gallop. Once clear of the first pasture, he slowed to a trot and moved in a zigzag pattern, pausing often to rise up in the saddle, scan the fields, and shout her name.

No response. No sign of her. What could have happened to her?

In the back pasture, he slowed Pegasus to a walk. There were lots of cow and horse hoof prints here. He noted the washed-out fence in the adjacent pasture and cows bunched near the far fence. Darlena must have rounded up cows and moved them here.

The old barn partially blocked his view. Thad circled along the fence to where the cows grazed. Pegasus is easily spooked. Maybe the horse ran off while she was working with the cows. Hopefully Dominic will find her trudging down the dirt road toward home.

Thad scanned the field again. The old barn seemed an unlikely place for her to go if she was hurt or stranded. But the barn had always been one of her favorite places. He dismounted beside the barn and saw hoof prints in the soft ground. Darlena had been here. He spotted tire tracks but took no special note of them.

Thad pulled open the side door and called out.

No reply.

His nose wrinkled at the pungent odor of paint. He stepped into the large wagon area. Empty paint buckets littered the floor. Dominic would never allow his laborers to leave an area so sloppy.

Thad shouted Darlena's name again as he walked toward the opposite end. Sweat peppered his forehead. None of this made any sense.

He heard the truck rumble up beside the barn and someone hurry into the entry room.

"Is she here?" Dominic called out.

"No," Thad shouted. "But somebody's been here."

Dominic frowned as he surveyed the paint equipment scattered around the wagon area. "Who could have done this? What were they doing?"

Thad finished searching the adjacent area and the stalls. "Hoof prints say she stopped here. She must have spotted something going on and checked the barn." His mind flashed back to an earlier observation. "I saw tire tracks outside. Someone brought a car or truck here. They may have forced her to go with them. But why would they be painting something here in the barn?"

"Oh God!" Dominic stared at a corner underneath the haymow.

The floor glistened from red soaked into the soft hay. On the haymow flooring above, a drop of crimson formed, grew, broke free, and dropped into the hay.

Thad scrambled up the ladder, plunged across the loft, and dug into the mass of hay.

His hands struck something. A body!

"It's not Darlena!" Thad shouted. "It's a man. A stranger."

He clambered back down the ladder to the floor. "Someone killed him with a pitchfork."

Dominic's face blanched. "When Darlena discovered him, he attacked her. She fought him with the pitchfork. But where is she now?"

"Someone buried that man in the hayloft," Thad replied. "Darlena wouldn't do that. There had to be others."

Dominic sagged back against the wall. His shoulders slumped. "They'll rape and kill her," he mumbled in a voice barely audible.

He stared up at the vast hayloft. "Perhaps they already have."

CHAPTER 7

▼

Craig Reynolds slowed the green Fiat as it approached a line of cars waiting at a police barricade. One policeman checked cars. Another leaned against a parked police car off to the side. Two others manned the roadblock. A fifth policeman stood beside an Audi, talking to the driver.

Craig's hair was black now and a neatly trimmed mustache had been added. His eyes were brown rather than the earlier sky-blue. Plastic rimmed glasses, a sport coat, and an open neck dress shirt suggested a businessman relaxing. Once again, he practiced saying words with an accent identical to the Italian spoken in the Piedmont region. His right hand held the steering wheel and his left grasped a gun, lowered out of view between the seat and the driver's door.

He glanced toward Darlena, sitting in the passenger seat with her right arm tied to the frame below the visible front seat. "If you try to warn the policemen, I'll kill them all. With you as a hostage, they'll hesitate to shoot." He lifted the gun up high enough for her to see it. "This is a fifteen shot automatic. I never miss what I aim at."

When she didn't reply, he shifted to look straight at her face. "Do you understand what I just said?"

She nodded. "I won't try to warn them."

"Then get that frightened look off your face. You're my wife. We're driving over to your parent's home to see if they had any flood damage."

The policeman at the Audi waved it through the barricade and walked over to relieve the officer checking cars.

Craig saw Darlena bite down on her lip. "Why are you staring at that policeman?"

"He lives in Luguri," she replied. "I was two years behind Marc in school. We dated a few times."

"You have to convince him everything's all right. Tell him I'm a relative visiting the family."

The green Fiat moved forward, now one car away from the policeman.

Craig saw her breathing escalate and softened his voice. "I don't want to kill anybody. Not you, not the policemen. So concentrate on getting me past this roadblock."

The other car passed through the raised barricade. Craig pulled the Fiat up beside the young policeman.

"Sorry for the delay, but I must ask you for your identification and ..." Marc stared in the window. "Hello, Darlena."

A nervous smile played across her face. "Hello, Marc. This is a friend of Papa's. I'm taking him to see the Bernini fountain ruins at Granople. He's an architect. Photographing distinctive structures is his hobby."

"The road to Granople is impassable because of flooding," Marc replied.

Craig saw her glance toward him, obviously searching for how to reply. The silence seemed to go on forever, but he knew it was only a few seconds.

Craig shifted his attention to the policeman. "Are the roads open to Corlona and Piasta?"

"Neither town has any flooding," Marc replied.

"Architecturally," Darlena said, "the church and town square at Corlona are more interesting than the Granople fountain. Why don't we go there? They also have a small restaurant that serves some of the best food in the region."

Craig nodded. "I'd enjoy that. We can visit Granople on my next trip."

Marc pointed toward the policeman leaning against the police car. "We're required to confirm the identification of anyone that isn't from this immediate area. If you'll park over there by the police car, they should be able to clear you in less than ten minutes."

Craig shifted his shoulder, almost imperceptive, but it positioned the gun just below the top of the doorframe, lined up with the policeman's chest. His eyes surveyed the scene as his brain figured the sequence of action. Shoot to wound, but he had to hit all five policemen and disable the police car.

"Please, Marc," Darlena blurted out. "Let us go through. If Papa finds out, he'll never forgive me."

Marc stared at her, then at Craig, and back at her. "His identification will have to be verified."

"Please, Marc, I don't want to hurt Papa." Her trembling lips almost garbled the words. "I'm begging you, let us pass through."

The young policeman blew out a deep breath. "Okay, I won't record the car." He glared at Craig. "Get out of here." He motioned to the policemen at the barricade.

The gate swung open. The green Fiat passed through the barricade and quickly distanced itself from the police roadblock. The Po River Bridge loomed ahead.

"That was a clever subterfuge," Craig said. "Thank you."

Darlena glowered at him. "I didn't do it to help you. I did it to save those policemen."

Craig sped across the bridge and intermingled with traffic on the expressway.

They rode in silence.

Eventually Craig turned off onto a local highway winding through the Alps foothills. A few houses dotted the hills. He slowed and swung off the highway onto a bumpy rural road.

In another few miles, he turned onto a dirt road. A derelict house loomed ahead.

Craig noticed Darlena grappling to free her wrist from the rope. "Struggling only increases the pressure," he said. "Relax. I'll untie your hand when we stop. I'm a jewel thief, not a killer."

The Fiat swung past the house and continued through a cluster of trees into a field overgrown with weeds. The car stopped.

Craig came around to her side, opened the door, and untied her hand.

Darlena climbed out and put her free hand on top of the open door. Her breathing had escalated and her knees appeared wobbly.

Craig reached out to steady her.

Her body suddenly sprang upward, catapulting her onto the roof of the car. She rolled across it, leaped to the ground, and sprinted for the woods.

Craig raced after her. He caught up with her thirty yards from the woods, grabbed her shoulder, and yanked her backward.

Her feet flew out in front of her, dumping her on the ground. But she bounced off the ground in a back somersault, her rotating feet slamming into his chest. Her kick more surprised him than hurt.

She was up and running again. Chasing her was like trying to corner a squirrel. Craig caught her again, grabbed her upper arm, and twisted her around to face him.

Darlena tried to claw his face.

He grabbed her wrists, swung her off balance, came down on top of her, and pinned her arms to the ground. Her foot struck a glancing blow on the backside of his head.

Craig scowled. "Don't you have any bones in your body?" He slid backwards over her upper thighs, immobilizing her legs.

Darlena spit out breaths between her teeth and kept struggling.

He yanked her partway up and dragged her by the arms across the field to within twenty yards of the car.

When he stopped, she grappled to her feet and swung her leg, trying to kick him in the groin. Craig caught her foot, hoisted it into the air, and dumped her on the ground with a force that knocked breath from her lungs. He moved five feet away and pointed the gun at her. "If you run again, I'll shoot you."

Darlena struggled into a sitting position, gasped in breaths, gritted her teeth, and glared at him. "I'll wait in purgatory for you. I want to see you condemned to Hell."

"God and I have an agreement," he replied. "I don't have to visit purgatory. I can go straight into Hell."

"Then I'll wait in Hell for you!" Darlena yelled.

"I'm sure you will. But this isn't your day to die." Craig lowered the gun to his side. "Don't move from that spot."

Craig walked back to the car, opened the trunk, and lifted out a shoulder bag from a hidden compartment. His eyes glanced back at her. Darlena had slowly shifted her legs into position for springing up and running.

"If you run again, I'll put a bullet through your leg," he shouted.

He pulled out two gasoline cans from the trunk and doused the trunk, front seat, and area around the gasoline tank. Next he pulled off the Fiat's gas cap, jammed a long cloth down into the throat of the tank, soaked it with gasoline, and tossed the cans into the back seat.

Craig strolled back and squatted down to gaze into her face. "Do you know how to play hide and seek?"

"I'm not a little girl," Darlena retorted.

"Then listen very carefully, Darlena, because your life depends on it. I want you to turn your back and cover your eyes with your hands. No matter what you hear, do not open your eyes until you're absolutely certain that I'm gone. Do you understand that?"

Darlena nodded.

"Can I trust you to do that?"

She nodded again.

Craig turned to walk away, but paused to look back at her. "How did you jump over the car? That was amazing."

"I'm a gymnast," she replied.

"I've watched some good gymnasts in competition. None of them could have done what you did. You caught me flatfooted with that move. And it was hell trying to catch you."

"Why are you letting me live?" Darlena asked.

Craig looked down at the ground and then back at her. "I don't kill people, especially someone like you. Now turn around."

He walked to the Fiat, ignited the gasoline, and watched the fire rapidly begin consuming the car. A glance told him that Darlena had her face buried in her arms and turned away from him.

He hustled to the backside of the deserted house, climbed into the red Ferrari, and drove slowly away from the house and field to keep the engine from revving loudly. Once on the rural road, he shifted gears and let the engine roar to life.

Craig's mind mulled the day's events. He had the Ducote jewels and he was long gone from the crime scene. He would quickly disappear into the French Alps.

Darlena's face floated into his thoughts. Even when frightened, she had the most enchanting, beautiful eyes he had ever seen. They sparkled like emeralds. And a fighting spirit that refused to back down.

He had to let her live, even though she could identify him.

"That's not a problem," Craig told himself. "Our paths will never cross again. I don't need to come back to Italy."

CHAPTER 8

▼

Darlena slumped in the wooden chair. Her body was too weary to stay awake and her mind too tense to fall asleep. She stared at the oak desk in front of her. Scars from years of use marred the brown stain on the side of the desk facing her. Darkness peered through a window framed by bedraggled brown curtains. The round clock on the wall showed almost midnight. She grasped the ceramic coffee cup in both hands and sipped from it. The warmth soothed her parched throat.

She heard the door behind her open.

"The Luguri police are bringing your papa," a voice said.

Without turning around, she recognized the voice of Officer Saia, the Calmeta policeman who questioned her when she arrived at the police station. She vaguely remembered banging on the door of a farmer's darkened house and the trip here in his wheezing Fiat truck. Papa's sobs of relief had filled the phone when she blurted out the words, "I'm safe, Papa. He didn't hurt me."

Darlena sensed someone else enter the room. When she turned in the chair, she saw a thin, erect man with thick gray hair. His gray suit and vest gave him the appearance of a banker. But the intense dark eyes and gaunt cheekbones conveyed the image of a wolf on the hunt.

"This is Inspector Von Meier with Interpol, the International Criminal Police Organization," Officer Saia said. "He's investigating the Ducote Chateau robbery."

Von Meier pulled a chair up and looked directly at her. "I know you've been through a traumatic experience, but time is critical. I need to ask you questions about your kidnapping and escape. You're the only person who has seen the jewel thief's face."

His words swept the lethargy from her mind. Darlena shifted in the chair to a more alert stance. "I didn't escape. He let me go."

"Tell me everything you remember about him."

"He was almost a head taller than you. He had brown hair, but then dyed it black. Or maybe he washed out the brown and it became black. I don't know which. His eyes were blue like the afternoon sky, but devoid of emotion. I initially thought he was a predator without feelings. His eyes were hazel at the road block and he wore glasses then. So maybe the earlier blue eyes were colored contact lens." She set down her coffee cup and shook her head. "He kept changing. Even his accent changed at the road block. But he spoke fluent Italian. At the end, just before he let me go, he became much less intimidating."

She took a sip from her coffee cup.

Von Meier sat silently gazing at her.

"He had a handsome face, with no wrinkles," Darlena continued. "I judged him to be late twenties or early thirties. He seemed very confident and afraid of nothing. If the police at the road block had tried to stop him, I'm sure he would have killed all of them."

She paused. "Do you know who he is?"

"He's an American who has stolen jewelry and paintings from a dozen places in Europe. The robberies are always very methodical, daring, and ingenious. Even when we trap him, he somehow eludes us."

"He noticed every detail. I tried to escape, but he was too fast and too strong."

"Tell me everything that happened," Von Meier said. "Don't leave anything out."

For the next thirty minutes she talked. Von Meier mostly listened, occasionally asking a question. When she discussed the final confrontation in the field after her attempt to escape, she said only that he told her to turn her back and cover her eyes, then burned the Fiat, and disappeared.

"Did you hear any sounds? Like another car?" Von Meier asked.

Darlena hesitated. Even though the jewel thief had kept the car engine throttled back, she had recognized the quiet growl of a Ferrari. "I don't know what kind of car he had," she finally said. "I kept my eyes closed until I knew he was gone."

Von Meier's eyes told her that he knew she was lying.

"I can't tell you anything else," she continued. "He should have killed me. Instead, he let me live."

"He will rob again and perhaps kill someone," Von Meier replied.

Darlena sipped on her lukewarm coffee to avoid the penetrating gaze of his eyes. Should she mention the Ferrari? The jewel thief was a dangerous criminal and he would not abandon the Ferrari. The Ferrari and he melded together like she and Pegasus. The Ferrari symbolized his power, his charisma, and his invincibility.

But for reasons she herself didn't understand, Darlena had no intention of telling Von Meier about the Ferrari.

"He's quite an enigma, isn't he?" Von Meier's voice conveyed no irritation.

She looked back at him. "He let me live, even though I'd seen his face. Why would he do that?"

"He also chose to let me live and I don't know why." Von Meier shuffled up from the chair and grimaced as he put weight on his leg. "The jewel thief has momentarily eluded us. But I will find him. At some point, he will either miscalculate or overreach. When he does, I will be there."

Von Meier walked to the door, paused, and looked back at her. "The sound must have been very distinctive for you to recognize the car. Few cars have such a distinctive sound."

He disappeared through the doorway.

"You've met your match, jewel thief," Darlena thought. "No matter how clever you are, Inspector Von Meier will hunt you down."

CHAPTER 9

▼

Darlena leaned back against the upholstered fabric of the chair in the club car and watched the countryside sweep past. The train was south of Florence now, less than two hours from Rome. The rolling hills and low mountains of Tuscany were different from the plains of Luguri. Pastures rippling with sheep covered some slopes. Olive groves and vineyards beautified the landscape. Row after row after row of posts burdened down with grapevines flowed in all directions from a lake to the crests of the hill. Further away, red and yellow wild flowers spread up slopes toward distant low mountains shrouded in blue-gray mist, as if posing for a Claude Lorraine landscape painting.

Thoughts in her mind came and went like the countryside; appearing, flashing past, and disappearing. For the past three months, she had worked with the girl's gymnastics team in Turin. Now she would spend the next two months in Rome, practicing with the National team to learn the latest techniques and caliber of the competition. Then back to Turin to build a girl's team that could match, and eventually exceed, the best in Italy.

Training intensely again excited her. Her endurance and strength remained near her competitive peak, thanks to a daily exercise regimen. She wouldn't be competing for judges' points, but her competitive nature wouldn't allow her to simply learn the latest coaching techniques. Her personal performance on the uneven bars and balance beam must be as good as the best. In Rome, she would face the best every day.

Darlena would also have to deal with seeing Thad regularly. She had resolved not to fight the Church for him. That would be a challenge, but she wanted them to enjoy their time together without conflicts. Thad understood her better than anyone else.

The feeling that someone was watching intruded into her thoughts. Darlena glanced up and saw a young woman standing only a few feet away, her large azure-colored eyes staring at her.

A flush of embarrassment spread over the woman's face. "You argh so bee-oo-tiful," she said in slurred English. The woman's fingers twisted at strands of long brown hair that draped across her shoulders but became entangled and frazzled at the ends. Her flowered casual blouse tucked neatly into the blue slacks on one side but rumpled on the other. Her eyes darted like a nervous rabbit.

Darlena smiled, trying to ease the woman's feeling of awkwardness, and replied in English. "Thank you. That's a very nice compliment. If I seemed startled, it's because my mind was wandering in another world."

The woman's hand waved as though trying to help pull the words from her mouth. "I am sor-sorry I star-tled you." She turned away and bumped into another passenger.

The cup in the hands of the heavyset man tipped, spilling coffee across his coat sleeve. He shook his hand to relieve the burning pain of the hot coffee. "You clumsy fool! Look what you did to my suit," he growled in Italian.

The woman's eyes widened into saucers. "I di-did not s-see yough. I am sor-sorry," she said in English.

"People like you aren't allowed in here," he grumbled as he grasped her arm. "This is for first class passengers only."

Darlena sprang from her chair and yanked his hand away from the young woman. "Get your hands off her. It was an accident."

"She doesn't belong in here."

"She's with me." Darlena gently guided the woman to a set of chairs and helped her sit down.

The young woman blinked to stifle tears. "I am s-so sor-ry."

Darlena clasped her trembling hand and shifted again to English. "It's all right. It was an accident, as much his fault as yours."

"Cof-fee."

"Yes, it was coffee that spilled."

"Goo-od cof-fee."

"You want coffee?" Darlena asked. "You want a cup of coffee?"

The young woman smiled and nodded.

Maybe drinking coffee would relax the woman, Darlena thought. "Stay right here. I'll bring you some coffee."

The woman smiled again. "Th-ank yough."

Darlena hurried to the coffee urn. The man with the coffee stain on his coat sleeve stood beside the urn, preparing to fill a new cup. She grabbed a cup, used it to shove his cup aside, and began draining coffee into her cup. "Excuse me. I'm in a hurry," she said.

His pudgy cheeks flushed. "If you don't take her out of here, I'm going to summon the conductor."

Darlena finished filling her cup and turned to leave. Her anger surged. She whirled around and slapped the man's face.

He stepped back, more stunned than hurt.

Her motion shook her other hand, spilling a little of her coffee on her hand. She glared at him. "You clumsy fool. Look what you did. They shouldn't allow people like you in here."

Darlena sauntered back to the chair, grinned at the young woman as she sat down, and handed the coffee to her.

The woman's hands trembled as she took the cup. Darlena sensed that she had made a mistake bringing hot coffee to her. She re-established a grip on the cup.

"N-No." The woman tried to pull the cup toward her mouth.

"Let me help you," Darlena offered in a non-assertive tone.

The young woman relaxed slightly but kept a tight grip on the cup handle and pulled it toward her mouth.

Darlena steadied the cup and eased it to her lips. "Drink slowly. The coffee is hot."

The young woman took a small sip and smiled. "Go-od cof-fee."

Darlena set the cup on a small stand out of reach and tried distracting the woman's attention from the coffee. "What's your name?"

"Joan."

"Joan is a beautiful name."

"Th-thank yough. Yough argh s-so bee-oo-tiful."

"Is there someone here on the train with you?"

The woman nodded. "My bru-ther. I los my pu-r-se. He we-went to fin-d it."

"Your brother must be very nice."

Joan's face brightened as she looked past Darlena.

"I have your purse," a man's voice said.

Darlena caught only a glimpse of him as he pulled another chair up beside them.

"I spilled cof-fee. Sh-she hel-ped me."

He stepped around in front as he spoke. "Thank you for … helping her."

The flicker of pause before the final two words indicated he saw her face at the same time Darlena saw his.

The pleasant smile on his face didn't change and the eyes didn't blink. The hair was different. Still sandy brown but styled more casually. A neatly trimmed beard covered the lower part of his face. But the blue eyes and facial features were unmistakable.

Darlena knew her shocked expression told him she recognized him.

Darlena was staring into the face of the jewel thief.

CHAPTER 10

▼

Craig Reynolds forced himself to maintain a pleasant smile as he slid into the chair beside Darlena. How in the hell could he end up on a train with the woman he allowed to walk away three months ago? Having Joan with him closed out a lot of options. He needed to gamble that Darlena would be too frightened to force a confrontation. His hand clamped firmly onto Darlena's wrist. He looked at Joan as he spoke slowly in English. "Your new friend and I are going to get a cup of coffee. Stay right here. We will be back quickly."

Joan smiled.

Craig pulled Darlena upward from the chair and brought his face close to hers, speaking Italian in a low voice as casual as if he was asking her whether she used sugar in her coffee. "I have a gun with me. Don't make me have to use it."

He guided her to the coffee pot, poured half a cup of coffee, and handed it to her. "If you throw this coffee in my face and run, I'll shoot you and everyone in this car." This time, his tone shifted to ominous.

She handed the cup back to him. "Then I don't want a cup of coffee."

"The three of us are going to walk back to my compartment."

Darlena shook her head. "I'm staying here in the lounge car with these people."

Craig turned his head toward Joan and smiled. Joan smiled brightly. He focused his attention again on Darlena. "If you want to live, you'll do exactly what I say."

She glared into his face. "You could intimidate me in a deserted field, but not on a crowded train." Her glare shifted to a slight smile. "Do you still own a Ferrari?"

When he didn't reply, she continued. "I can recognize a Ferrari engine with my eyes closed. Even with the engine idled down, even when it's a kilometer away. But I didn't tell the police you left in a Ferrari. You let me live, so I owed you that. I don't owe you anything on this train."

Craig's mind ran through a half-dozen options and didn't like any of them. She was going to be as combative here as when they battled at the deserted farm. Maybe softening his rhetoric would lessen the confrontation. He eased his grip on her wrist. "I don't want to hurt you or anyone on this train. I don't want Joan caught in the middle of a confrontation. Please give me your word that you won't tell anyone about this."

"I read about a jewel robbery in Belgium last week," Darlena retorted. "The paper said you did it and two people were killed. That's murder."

"Those robbers were sloppy amateurs. It wasn't me."

"You shot a policeman at the roadblock the night of the Ducote Chateau robbery. He could have died. You would have shot others if I hadn't talked you through the roadblock going to the Po River bridge."

"The policeman didn't die because I shot to only wound him," Craig replied. "I always hit what I aim at, but I don't kill people."

Darlena glanced toward the young woman. "Because of Joan, I won't do anything while we're on the train. But I'll tell the police everything I know because what you're doing is wrong."

The sudden jolting of the train broke the intensity of their confrontation. Craig frowned. Why had the train braked heavily? They were an hour away from Rome.

The train continued to slow. Craig heard a clattering sound, like hailstones hitting a tin roof.

A brick crashed through a club car window!

Craig bounded over to Joan, grabbed her arm, and pulled her into the center of the car.

"A mob is blocking the tracks," a passenger shouted. "There's a dispute between railway workers and the government. They must be striking."

The drumbeat of rocks hitting the sides of the railroad car escalated. Another window shattered.

A conductor hustled into the lounge car. "Everyone come this way. The police have cordoned off the front of the train. You'll be safe there."

Craig guided Joan toward the motioning conductor. Darlena crowded in ahead of a businessman, positioning herself between Joan and the shoving passengers. They passed through the connecting doors and hustled down the aisle through one car and into the next car.

The connecting section ahead suddenly filled with two husky men. The conductor backpedaled.

Craig released Joan's arm and called back to Darlena. "Watch her."

He pushed past three passengers and the conductor and stopped in front of the two men. One waved a heavy wooden club. "Let us through, please," Craig said in Italian. "There are women with us."

The one with the club smirked. "Sit down. We'll tell you when you can go."

Craig's foot flashed upward into the man's crotch. As the man doubled over with a groan, Craig plowed into him, driving him backward. In the same motion, his hand caught the other man by the shirt and slammed him into the wall of the connecting section between the cars.

A third man standing on the boarding steps crowded into the car. Craig's rush sent the three men tumbling backwards out the exit door into the arms of strikers milling on the side of the tracks. Before anyone could react, Craig slammed the door closed and laid his weight against it, barring their re-entry.

"Move!" he yelled at the passengers.

His command sent the conductor scurrying into the next car. Men pounded against the railroad door, trying to force it open. Craig glanced back to see how close Joan and Darlena were. As soon as they got past, he would join them and leave the rest of the passengers to impede the strikers.

Joan and Darlena were gone!

What had happened to them?

CHAPTER 11

▼

Darlena battled past onrushing passengers and finally managed to get a hand on Joan's arm. "Joan!" she shouted. "Come back this way."

"Pur-se. I los my pur-se." Joan yanked her arm free and continued toward the club car.

Darlena lunged after her. A man shoved Darlena out of his path, sending her tumbling into the seats. Joan disappeared into the lounge car.

Darlena vaulted over the seats and into the lounge car entry. A man blocked her path. Ten feet away, Joan screamed as she struggled for control of her purse with a husky, unshaved man.

The big man put a hand on Joan's breast and shoved her away. Joan stumbled and fell against a lounging chair. "My pur-urse!" she screamed.

The man waved the purse in his hand in a taunt. Joan clambered toward him.

"Don't hurt her!" Darlena yelled as she grappled with the smaller man. "She doesn't understand what's happening. I'll pay you money for the purse."

The husky man swung his arm. His open hand caught Joan across the side of her head, knocking her against the rear door of the car.

Darlena grabbed the coffee urn, yanked the top off, and threw the contents onto the burly assailant. He screamed as hot coffee splashed onto his face and chest. She threw the remaining contents and the urn into the smaller man coming at her, yanked the purse from the hands of the big man, and scrambled over to where Joan cringed against the wall, sobbing. She pushed Joan through the door onto the lounge car rear balcony and wrestled her down the steps and into a group of surprised strikers.

They half-ran, half-stumbled along the side of the train, brushing past men pounding on the railroad cars. Joan tripped and fell. Darlena bent down to help her up.

"Wh-wh-ere is Crraig?"Joan cried out.

Darlena grappled her to her feet. "Craig is waiting for us at the front of the train." She clasped Joan's arm and urged her into a fast walk.

A milling crowd of men blocked their path. Darlena searched for a route through them and found none. "Please let us through," she said.

The men stared sullenly at her. No one moved.

"Please let us through," Darlena pleaded. "She needs medical help."

A middle-aged man in coveralls stepped from the group. "We don't want to hurt anybody. I'll take you to the front of the train." He reached for Joan's arm.

Joan staggered back from him.

"It's all right," Darlena said to Joan. "He's going to help us reach Craig." She turned back to the man. "Lead the way. We'll follow you."

"Stop those women!" The husky man lumbered down off the train platform, one hand clasped to the reddened side of his face, the other hand pointing toward them. "They scalded me with coffee."

"He tried to steal her purse," Darlena pleaded to the middle-aged man.

He stepped back. "I can't help you. You better run to the town square. You'll be safe there."

Darlena looked to her left. It was at least fifty yards to the edge of the town. They had to cross two railroad spurs and a field of packed gravel. She clamped onto Joan's hand. "We have to run."

"Rr-un?"

"Run fast."

The gravel made running difficult. Joan stumbled. Darlena caught her before she fell. They made it across the first spur. On the second, Joan tripped and went down on her knees. Darlena yanked her up. They started running again.

The husky man and two others were already across the tracks, running diagonally on the gravel, aiming to cut them off.

Joan stumbled and went down. They were only halfway across the field. The men had them blocked from reaching the town square. Darlena knelt and cradled Joan's head in her arms.

"I..I..sor-ree," Joan gasped.

"It's all right," Darlena consoled.

The men stopped a few yards away. The husky one with the scalded face stepped closer and pulled off his leather belt. "I'm going to make you bitches hurt like you made me hurt."

Darlena kept Joan's head cradled against her shoulder. "Don't hurt her. She doesn't understand what's happening. I'm the one that threw coffee on you."

"Then I'll give you enough for both." The husky man motioned to the other two men. "Get that moaning bitch out of the way."

They yanked Joan up and dragged her off to the side. A group of men ringed them in a semi-circle.

Darlena scrambled up to face her assailant. Her instincts yelled to fight with rocks and whatever other weapons she could lay her hands on. But that would only enrage the man more. She had to get Joan to the safety of the town square. To do that, she would submit to the beating.

The husky man shifted the belt to hold it by the end, leaving the large metal buckle dangling. "I'm going to put my mark on you, so you'll remember how to treat a working man. You hear me, little rich girl?"

"Don't touch her with that belt!" a voice called out.

Darlena glanced toward the voice.

Craig pushed through the crowd and stalked toward the husky man.

CHAPTER 12

▼

Six feet away from the three men, Craig stopped. "These women are going to the hotel in the town. If you have a problem with that, you settle it with me."

"You gonna fight twenty men?" the husky man snarled.

Craig reached into the belt covered by his jacket, pulled out a gun, and pointed it at the man's face. "I'll fight as many men as necessary, but you and your two buddies won't be alive to see it. You get the first bullet."

The snarl disappeared from the man's face. His eyes widened.

Craig pointed the gun at the other two men. "Take your hands off that woman."

One of the men shoved Joan in front of him as a shield.

"I can put a bullet through your eyeball from twice this distance," Craig growled. "Get your damn hands off her."

The man released Joan and shuffled backwards. Darlena clasped Joan's arm and brought her over beside Craig. Joan reached for Craig, but Darlena blocked her hand and pulled Joan up against her.

Thirty men crowded around them, blocking their path to the town square. Some held bricks. Others grasped wooden clubs and crowbars. One rested a sledgehammer on his shoulder.

Craig lowered the gun to his side. His finger remained curled around the trigger. "We have no quarrel with any of you. Let us pass through to the town square."

No one spoke. No one moved. Joan's stifled sobs and the noise of the train being ransacked across the tracks became the only sounds.

"It would be unwise to kill any of these men." The husky voice came from behind.

Craig turned toward the voice. A big man, almost his height, with massive arms and a barrel chest, stepped in front of the others.

All eyes shifted toward the big man.

"Your man stole a purse from these women," Craig said. "They fought to get it back. My only intent is to take the women to the safety of the hotel."

"That gun won't help," the huge man replied. "It'll get you, and maybe the women, killed."

Craig stepped back from the scalded man with the belt and focused his attention on the big man with heavily tattooed, massive arms and a square face marked with two scars. Thick black hair scattered in disarray across the man's head and over his ears. Beard stubble added to the grizzled, powerful appearance.

Craig flipped the gun around in his hand to hold it by the barrel and tossed it through the air toward the man. "Then you take the women to the hotel."

Darlena let out an audible gasp.

The big man's face registered surprise as he caught the gun in his huge palms. He held the gun in one hand, pulled out the ammunition magazine, studied it, and reinserted it. "A Beretta automatic with a modified stub barrel is a very impressive weapon. How many rounds are in the clip?"

"Fifteen," Craig replied.

"You could kill quite a few men with a weapon like this," the big man said.

"Fifteen to be exact."

The big man laughed and spread his arms open. "Well said. I'll take the three of you to the hotel." He shoved the Beretta inside his belt. "The gun will be a memento of our meeting." He scowled at the crowd of men. "Why are you standing here? You have a train to plunder."

They scattered like straw in a heavy wind.

As the man with the burned face plodded past, the big man pointed at him. "You ever strike a woman this beautiful and I'll kill you."

The scalded man ran toward the train.

The big man strode over to where Craig stood with his left arm wrapped around Joan. He grasped Craig's right hand in a bear clamp. "I'm Romano Pantel."

"I'm Craig."

Romano peered into his face. "What business are you in, Craig with no last name and a gun that will kill fifteen men?"

"I'm in the business of going to Rome today."

Romano grinned. "Ah. I live in Rome. If you're ever in need of special services, come to the Paesada Casino in the Dipanico District. They'll know where I am. You can judge for yourself the caliber of my work." He swept his hand toward the train.

The mob swarmed over it, smashing windows, throwing seats onto the ground, and looting baggage. Policemen were nowhere in sight. Behind the train, another group began tearing rails from the track.

Craig smiled. "I suspect you're not a railroad worker."

Romano shrugged. "I sometimes do jobs for unions still controlled by the Communists. No job is too big or too difficult. I can provide a hundred men or a few men who are very discrete." He stepped up close to Darlena. "I envy your friend. He has plucked the most beautiful flower in all of Italy. What's your name?"

Darlena folded her arms and stood her ground. "My name is Darlena Aldonzo. And no man has plucked me."

His hoarse laugh, with its cigarette stench, blew in her face. "Your spirit matches your beauty. Do you live in Rome?"

"I'm only visiting."

Romano leered at her, making no pretense as he ogled her breasts pressing against the sweat-drenched, soiled ivory sleeveless linen blouse, and studied the perfectly proportioned waist, hips, and legs snugged inside her pleated pants. "How long will you be in Rome?"

Darlena planted her hands on her hips. "May we go to the hotel now?"

Romano grinned, displaying yellowed, uneven teeth. "I am at your service, now and at any time during your stay in Rome. Ask for Romano Pantel, at the Paesada Casino in the Dipanico District."

"Right now," Darlena retorted, "it would be a great service if you could retrieve my luggage before your friends loot it."

"Consider it done." Romano signaled with his hand. Two men hurried over.

Darlena dug out the ticket from her belt purse. Craig pulled tickets from his jacket pocket and handed them to Romano.

The big man glanced at the tickets. "Mr. Reynolds. So you do have a last name." He handed the tickets to the men, with words that amounted to, "don't come back without their luggage." Then he pointed toward the town. "I will show you the hotel and arrange rooms for you. Your names will not be listed." His toothy grin indicated he suspected Craig would prefer that.

Craig put his arm around Joan's waist and guided her toward the square. Darlena slipped in between him and Romano.

Craig glanced at Darlena. Romano had pegged Darlena right. She was both beautiful and a spirited fighter who had risked her life to protect Joan. She was sandwiched between a brawling hoodlum and a jewel thief. Yet, she refused to yield an inch or be intimidated by either.

Tomorrow Darlena would continue on to Rome and he would disappear into his furtive world. He should be breathing a sigh of relief.

Instead, that realization bothered Craig.

C H A P T E R 13

▼

Craig sat on the edge of the bed, watching Joan in the semi-darkness of evening. The room contained a bed, a square lamp table, one rickety wooden chair, and a scarred two-drawer chest. The rumble of boisterous men and occasional shattering of glass drifted through the open window. Rioters continued to plunder the train. Except for confiscating the local bar, their rampage had not spread into the town. True to his word, Romano Pantel had delivered their luggage undamaged, presenting it with the flair of a knight bringing the head of a slain dragon to King Arthur's Round Table.

The hotel room door eased open and Darlena entered, carrying a tray of food. "I thought you'd be hungry," she said. "The hotel staff disappeared when the rioting began, but the proprietor allowed me to raid the kitchen. I hope you like hard bread stuffed with meat and cheese. How is Joan?"

"The injection I gave her put her to sleep," Craig replied. "She'll have a severe headache and voracious appetite when she wakes up. So your choice of food is excellent." He slid his hand from Joan's clasp and sat down beside Darlena on the floor.

She handed him a sandwich and poured a glass of wine for each of them. "Why did Joan become so upset when you brought her into the room?"

"She thought it was a confinement room at the sanatorium. They were locking her in, sometimes strapping her to the bed, when she had one of her attacks. That's why I'm moving her to a new place. This one promised to be tolerant of her outbursts."

"You're amazingly patient with her. What happened to her?"

Craig took a sip of wine, set the glass down, fingered it, and debated how to reply. This was something he had never talked about to anyone except doctors.

"I'd like to know what happened," Darlena persisted.

He looked up from the wine glass. "There were serious complications during my mother's pregnancy. She died giving birth. Joan suffered permanent brain damage. She's twenty-two now. Her violent outbursts have increased significantly over the past two years."

"I'm so sorry." Darlena squeezed his hand. "That must have devastated you and your father."

Craig took a heavy gulp of his wine. "Dad never forgave himself for not insisting on an abortion, even though we were Catholic. He spent all his money on medical care for Joan. When his money was gone, the government put her in an institution of marginal quality. When I could, I took over the financial responsibility and we put her in a specialized care clinic."

"Is that why you became a jewel thief?" Darlena asked. "To pay for giving Joan specialized care rather than confining her to a government institution?"

Craig chomped off a large piece of sandwich and chewed it. "Don't be naive." He saw her lips pout and smiled thinly. "I became a jewel thief because I enjoy the lifestyle that the occupation provides. Pulling off an impossible robbery exhilarates me, especially when the victim is pompous and grandiose. The Ducote Chateau robbery represents the pinnacle of my career. I'll have to stretch to top that one."

Darlena reached over to touch his hand again. "You must have enough money now to provide Joan with whatever help she needs. Stop before you're captured or killed. Take Joan back home and help your Dad care for her."

"Dad died a year ago. That's why I have Joan here with me." The conversation had aggravated Craig's headache. He wanted to close off this discussion. "I need now to prepare for Joan's travel tomorrow." He walked over to the luggage.

Darlena followed him. "You said earlier that Joan would be frightened to travel again on the train. Are you going to drive her to the new place?"

"I used to take her for long drives in the Ferrari. She loves the roar of the engine and sense of freedom. The last time, she almost killed us by grabbing the steering wheel when I told her we had to go back to the sanatorium. That's why I brought her on the train. I've arranged for people at the sanatorium to pick us up here tomorrow morning. I don't know how she'll react to them. It may become very confrontational."

He clasped Darlena's hand and guided her over to the door. "Thank you for what you did for Joan. Defending her when she spilled coffee in the club car and risking your life to protect her during the riot. No one has ever been so kind to her."

"My bus to Rome leaves at noon," Darlena said. "I'll come say good-bye to Joan in the morning." She opened the door and started to leave.

Craig caught her shoulder and turned her around to face him. "Not killing you in that deserted field complicated my escape from Italy. I spent a couple harrowing days maneuvering my way through southern France. Von Meier almost nailed me. But I never doubted my decision to let you live. You are the most amazing, fascinating woman I have ever known."

Even in the dim light, he saw the sparkle in her mesmerizing eyes and a flush of warmth fill her face. She stretched up and kissed him lightly on the cheek. "Thank you for telling me that."

Craig watched until she disappeared into her room down the hallway. Tomorrow morning they would say good-bye to each other. She would go to Rome. He would deliver Joan to her new treatment center and disappear into his clandestine world.

His logic told him that they would never see each other again. But deep inside, he sensed that perhaps that would not be true.

Craig couldn't decipher whether that premonition was a wish or a foreboding.

CHAPTER 14

▼

The first rays of daybreak painted the scattered gray clouds with hues of orange and yellow when Darlena hustled down the hotel corridor to the bathroom. The night had been long and restless. Her mind kept replaying the events of yesterday. The shock of meeting the jewel thief on the train, the pathos of his sister, the riots, the odor of Romano Pantel's breath and sweat as he crowded in on her. But mostly, her thoughts centered on Craig. Diverse emotions churned inside her. How could she possibly be attracted to a jewel thief? Why did she dread saying good-bye?

Darlena relaxed in a hot bath for fifteen minutes, forcing herself to concentrate on the gymnastics training awaiting her in Rome. She returned to her room, let the morning air wafting through the open window cool her body, and combed her hair. She dug out a pair of blue jeans and a cotton blouse, put them on, and checked her appearance in the mirror.

The outfit was comfortable and practical apparel for riding on a bus, but not the appearance she wanted to convey when saying good-bye to Craig. Rummaging back into the suitcase brought out a silk crepe blouse with long sleeves and a high neck. The ivory color accentuated her tanned complexion and black hair. She added a pair of worsted wool pants. The black color with shadow stripes made her appear taller.

She surveyed herself again in the mirror. Still not quite the effect she wanted. A sleeveless rose vest with covered buttons, plus a narrow black belt cinched around her waist added the proper air of relaxed sophistication. Glancing at her watch told her it was too early for breakfast. Sitting in the room would escalate her nervousness. A walk would be refreshing. She put on tennis shoes, smiling at the contrast with her other clothes.

Darlena strolled through the deserted hotel lobby and stepped out onto the street. Across the field, railroad cars sat as abandoned derelicts beside the station. Several cars had been upended. She sauntered in the opposite direction, toward the back of the hotel. The aroma of red blossoms on two sprawling oleanders caressed her nostrils. Orange marigolds clustered in a narrow strip along one side of the street. Grass behind the hotel hung heavy with morning dew. Walking in the fields would soak the legs of her wool pants. She would content herself with strolling on cobblestone streets.

Her eyes spotted a low fence built with mortared-in rocks. It was relatively smooth on top and four times as wide as a conventional balance beam. Darlena vaulted up onto it and walked the length, checking for protrusions that would be tripping hazards. On the return trip, she did simple warm up exercises, enjoying the cool breeze in her face and the tangy smell of freshly cut pasture hay intermingling with the fragrance of oleander blooms.

Her thoughts disappeared into the world of the balance beam. It had always been her place for meditation, relaxation, and reflection. The longer she stayed on the stone fence, the more vigorous her exercise became. Her lungs sucked in deep gulps. She paused, purged her mind of all other thoughts, and positioned her feet. A backward somersault would be easy on this wide stone fence. She glanced backward to be certain of adequate distance. One backward somersault; followed by a second; and then a third. She landed flawlessly.

The sound of a voice made her look toward the hotel. Joan stood beside Craig in the hotel back doorway, her face glowing, clapping her hands together and calling out. "Ooooh. Bee-oo-ti-ful. Ooooohh. So bee-oo-ti-ful."

Craig also applauded. "She saw you from the window and wanted to watch."

Darlena jumped from the stone fence and replied in English. "I'm sorry I didn't notice you. When I'm doing an exercise routine, everything else vanishes."

"You had a captivated audience," Craig replied. "We didn't want to interrupt you. We came to say good-bye." He shifted to Italian. "The car from the sanatorium is waiting for us."

Darlena glanced toward the corner of the hotel beyond the stone fence. Two men in white hospital uniforms leaned against a black limousine. She wrapped her arms around Joan and hugged her. "Craig will take good care of you."

"Yough argh Joan fri-end."

"You are my special friend," Darlena replied.

"Good luck in Rome." Craig took Joan's hand and walked her toward the limousine.

Darlena's mind churned. This was it? There had been no special emotion in his voice, no personal dialogue, not even a simple farewell hug. But what was there to say? They would never see each other again. He was a jewel thief, dangerous and indecipherable. But despite that, he was the most fascinating man she had ever met.

"We go ba-ack?" Joan stopped walking and stared at the men beside the limousine.

"It's a new place," Craig said. "You'll like it."

"Joan st-ay wih yu. Joan w-won go ba-ack. Not go! Not go ba-ack!"

"This is a good place," Craig said with a calm voice. "You'll like it. We must go there."

Joan wrenched her hand free and stepped away from him. "No!" she yelled. "St-ay wi yough!" Her breath seethed between tensed lips. Her face distorted.

Darlena had never seen anger explode so rapidly. She mulled how to help defuse the spiraling rage. "Joan, walk with me on the balance beam," she called out.

Joan turned toward her.

Darlena vaulted onto the stone fence, crouched down, and extended her hand. "Walk on the balance beam with me."

Joan shook her head. "Sca-red of be-em."

"We'll do it together. Trust me."

Joan shuffled nervously up to the fence.

Darlena reached down, grasped Joan's hands, and helped her scramble onto the stone fence. They stood there, Joan's hands clamped onto her hands like trembling steel vises.

"Together we can walk the beam," Darlena encouraged.

"Sca-red to fall."

"I won't let you fall. Watch my feet. I'm going to take this foot and move it backward to here. You take your foot and move it to where my foot was."

Step by step, Darlena guided her, moving backward along the fence as Joan followed her. She felt the tightness in Joan's grip begin to loosen. Still tense but not terrified. "You're walking the beam. You're a gymnast."

Joan laughed and turned to look toward Craig. "Joan wal-king the be-eem."

He smiled. Joan's shift in position tilted her balance. She teetered on the verge of falling.

Darlena pulled her back upright and steadied her.

Joan's breathing accelerated. Her eyes widened.

"You're very good," Darlena said. "You didn't fall. Almost everyone falls the first time they walk on the balance beam."

Fear lessened in Joan's eyes. Her face glistened. "Joan no fa-all," she said.

Step by step, they continued along the fence top until they reached the section of stone fence near the limousine. Darlena eased one hand free and reached up to her neck to pull off the chain necklace with a medallion hanging from it. "This is the first medal I won in competition. Not first place, but still a medal for doing the best I could." She slipped it over Joan's head and arranged it to hang against her breast. "This is your medal for walking the balance beam. For walking the beam even when you were scared. You are now a gymnast."

Joan blew out breaths of delight. She turned toward Craig as she clasped the medal in her hand. "My me-dal. I wa-alk the be-eem."

Darlena debated what to do now. Joan had calmed, but whatever happened next could trigger a new outburst. She glanced toward Craig, looking for guidance.

His eyes were focused on her, not on Joan. She hadn't seen this expression on his face before. His face conveyed the glow of a man who meets a woman for the first time and likes what he sees.

"Would you come with us?" Craig asked. "Just long enough to settle Joan into her room. I'll take you to Rome this afternoon."

"Co-uld yu?" Joan begged. "Pl-eese?"

Every nerve in Darlena's body tingled. "Yes. But you have to help me pack. And Craig has to get us down off this balance beam."

Craig lifted Joan off and hugged her.

Then he clasped his hands on Darlena's ribs, his thumbs touching the edges of her breasts, and swirled her effortlessly to the ground.

"Thank you," he said.

Darlena remained in his grasp, luxuriating in the feel of his hands on her body, not wanting to pull away, uncertain how to react.

Joan grabbed her hand. "I he-elp yu pack."

Craig released her.

Darlena and Joan ran toward the hotel back door. Joan laughed with the excitement and joy of a child going to the circus.

Darlena felt the same surge of excitement, triggered by emotions of a woman happy to not be saying good-bye yet to a man who had become important to her.

He's a jewel thief, her mind cautioned.

Darlena chose to ignore the warning.

CHAPTER 15

▼

Craig clasped Darlena's hand as they stepped into St. Peter's Square. It bustled with clustered, confused tourists straining to hear tour guides shouting amid noise generated by a sea of people. Some stared in silent awe at the architectural spectacle. Others moved from spot to spot, photographing every detail. Couples strolled hand-in-hand among the melee, oblivious to the tumult. Immaculately attired businessmen clutching cellular phones sat beside shabbily dressed laborers munching on bread filled with cheese and olives. People flowed in and out of the six towering bronze doors of the basilica, women pausing to cover their heads before entering. A young man in a sleeveless shirt and a blonde in walking shorts argued with the uniformed usher on the steps of the basilica. They were denied entry.

Craig paused at the narrow alleyway between the steps of the Basilica and the massive pillars of the colonnade. "I assume your prince charming turned priest is waiting at the gate for you." He hesitated before continuing. "So I guess it's time to say good-bye." He immediately disliked the bland words.

Darlena squeezed his hand. "You remain such an enigma. I've told you all about me. You know I'm excited and also apprehensive about leaving the security of Luguri to embark on a gymnastics coaching career. I'll be in the gym early tomorrow morning familiarizing myself with the equipment so I won't look bewildered on my first day. I'll have to bite my lip to keep from telling Thad about the past twenty-four hours because he's always been the one person I could tell everything. You probably sense that I care enough about you to dread picking up a newspaper and reading that the American jewel thief was killed during a daring robbery." She blew out a breath. "You also realize that I'm chattering semi-coherently because I don't know how to say good-bye."

Craig kissed her softly on the lips. "You are a difficult woman to walk away from."

She flashed a come-hither smile. "If you really feel that way and you have a couple hours, Thad and I could tour you through the Vatican. It's the most fascinating hundred acres on earth."

Craig frowned as he gazed down the passageway at a cluster of Papal Gendarmes dressed in dark blue caped uniforms with silver buttons. They stood watch like soldiers reincarnated from Napoleon's army. "High walls and armed guards make me nervous. Besides, why would I want to meet a man stupid enough to choose the priesthood instead of you?"

"Thad is not stupid," she retorted.

Craig smiled at her pursed lips, which he suspected were intended to convey a little irritation mixed with a hint of demure sensuality.

"He's an idealist," she continued, "and, like you accused me, often naive. He's also a superb soccer player. You said soccer was your favorite sport. If soccer conversation and a tour of the Vatican, plus a couple more hours with a woman who is difficult to walk away from, doesn't interest you, then please leave. I'm not going to ask you again to stay."

He took her hand. "Your logic is irrefutable. Why don't you introduce me to your naive, but not stupid priest?"

They waited at the Arch of the Bells gate while Thad talked with two Swiss Guards to approve entry of businessman Craig Reynolds. Craig leaned down and whispered in Darlena's ear. "I expected Thad to be a mousy guy who walked around with his hands clasped in prayer. He looks like a Roman god. No wonder you had the hots for him. Why would he become a priest? Did he get kicked in the head by your horse?"

She stuck her finger in his face. "If you make fun of Thad, I'll turn you over to those two burly Swiss Guards."

"If you do, talk slow. They speak terrible Italian. Their language is Schwyzerdutsch, spoken in some sections of Switzerland. It's the toughest dialect in Europe. As best I can tell, the dialect is one-third German, one-third ancient Swiss, and one-third hacking cough."

Darlena laughed. "I like it when you're warm and funny. How many languages do you speak?"

"I speak as many as necessary. Six fluently and I can survive in most others. But I hate Schwyzerdutsch. The accent is so difficult to master. I almost got killed in Switzerland because of it."

Thad led them into a small piazza and paused beside a marble disc buried in the courtyard. "The Egyptian obelisk in St. Peter's Square originally stood here as a centerpiece of Nero's Circus. We call this the Square of the First Roman Martyrs."

They strolled along a narrow passageway dominated on one side by the massive walls of St. Peter's Basilica, under two archways, and emerged onto a huge plaza containing a sculptured fountain. Ahead of them spread the grounds of the Vatican.

Thad turned to Darlena. "Bishop Baccalete is meeting this evening with the priests who signed the petition protesting Lastavis's usurpation of power during the Holy Father's illness. I apologize for reneging on taking you to dinner, but I have to be at the meeting."

"That's okay. I need to unpack and get settled in my apartment. This will be a hectic week." She spread her hands open, palms up. "I want you to fight Lastavis. Maybe they'll kick you out of the Church."

Thad didn't smile.

Darlena squeezed his hand. "I'm sorry. That was inappropriate."

"Bishop Baccalete has a private meeting with His Holiness tomorrow," Thad said. "It's a follow-up to a personal letter that he wrote. Hopefully, the Holy Father will clarify specific lines of authority to follow during his illness when he speaks to the Conclave of Cardinals next week. Some senior priests believe he will also privately tell key cardinals that Lastavis should not be a candidate to succeed him."

Thad shifted his attention to Craig. "Bishop Baccalete could have been a cardinal. He chose instead to leave the Vatican and return to his former diocese in Northern Italy. He's one of the most revered men in the Church and more influential in Italy than most cardinals. When Lastavis blocked funds for completing the restoration of the Granople fountain, many saw it as a covert effort to force Baccalete to support him. The Granople fountain is the only fountain that Bernini built outside of Rome. Bernini also designed the great canopy over St. Peter's altar and the fountains in St. Peter's Square. Lastavis's decision to oppose the funds may be his undoing."

Darlena motioned toward the buildings. "We're here to give Craig a tour of the Vatican. We are not here to discuss its political intrigues."

"This issue has totally consumed me for the past week," Thad said. "And now it's spoiled our plans for dinner this evening."

"I know a little ristorante nestled beside the river," Craig said. "The view and cuisine are superb. It's a perfect place for a gymnast to relax after unpacking and before tackling the beams and bars tomorrow morning."

Darlena smiled. "I would really enjoy that."

Thad grinned at her. "It sounds like Bishop Baccalete did you a favor by making me cancel our dinner for this evening."

She put her hands on her hips. "Could we have our tour now? I don't want to hear Baccalete or Lastavis mentioned again."

Thad motioned toward two brown brick buildings on the left. "The smaller one is San Carlo palace. That's where I stay."

"Priests stay in a palace?" Craig asked. "Isn't that a violation of your pledge of piety?"

"It's a palace in name only. My room has no amenities."

"All these buildings look rather drab," Craig commented. "I thought Vatican City reigned as Catholicism's showplace."

"Most of these drab-looking buildings are spectacular on the inside," Darlena said. "The basilica and Vatican Museums are absolutely awesome."

Craig pointed toward a pink, green, and yellow marble building with a columned entryway sitting atop a small hill. "Looks like a different architect designed that one."

"That was Mussolini's gift to the pope," Thad said. "Mussolini built a railroad station as a symbol of goodwill after the signing of the Concordant Treaty in nineteen twenty-nine. The station has a fancy waiting room specifically for the pope. But it's never had a passenger."

Craig laughed. "I don't think Mussolini ever got anything right. But the railroad looks like a busy freight yard. The Vatican must ship in a lot of stuff."

"The Vatican doesn't pay any taxes. So churches in Italy have their large purchases shipped to the Vatican. The Vatican then ships the materials to the church, which means the churches avoid paying taxes. The Vatican also gets a big discount on freight rates."

Craig grinned. "You Catholics sound adroit at financial matters."

"You're not Catholic, are you?" Thad's tone conveyed casual curiosity, not irritation.

"I used to be," Craig replied. "But I'm a great admirer of fine art. If I was God, this is where I'd live."

For the next hour, they strolled around the Vatican, passing through narrow corridors between buildings, following twisting paths within ornate gardens, and lounging on grassy plazas surrounding fountains. Thad did most of the talking, but commented several times about Craig's excellent knowledge of European history and art.

Eventually Thad led them through an archway onto a massive grassed square adorned with flowers and dominated by a large fountain. "This is the Giardino Quadrato. Beneath here are the underground garage for papal carriages and the vault. The vault was placed underground to protect Church records from the possibility of a nuclear holocaust. The written records of the Church, dating back to its earliest years, and important Vatican treasures are stored there." He walked them toward the basilica. "I'll show you Vatican village. Then we'll come back here to see if the carriage garage is unlocked. The carriages of past popes are magnificent beyond description."

Craig glanced back at the area surrounding the Giardino Quadrato. Buildings bordered it on two sides, with the sprawling papal gardens on the other sides, and the massive stone walls further away. He remembered glancing at the Bratius security system for the Vatican vault among the drawings he stole and noting that it had an outdated and unsophisticated alarm system. But with the vault buried underground in a walled city, they didn't need anything elaborate. He followed Thad into a courtyard totally enclosed by buildings.

"This is Belvedere Court," Thad said. "Straight ahead is the entry leading to Via di Belvedere, the main roadway for workers and vehicles entering through the Porta Sant'Anna gate. Over a thousand people live in Vatican Village adjacent to the via. Off to the right, that small portico entry is for cars bringing dignitaries to the Papal Palace. Cars go through there to the San Damascus courtyard. They either walk up the Scala Nobile stairway or take the elevator to meet with the pope and other high Vatican officials."

Thad stopped talking. His attention became focused on two men walking on the nearby statue-lined walkway. "That's Candalio," Thad muttered. "What's Candalio doing in the Vatican?"

Craig watched the two men with idle curiosity. One man wore a Papal Gendarme uniform. The other was a short man in a business suit. "Who's Candalio?"

"The Devil's physician," Thad replied. "Candalio was a doctor at the Turin hospital. He secretly worked for the Red Guard, the leftist terrorist group. He eliminated political opponents by drugging them into a demented stupor or killing them with a heart-attack-inducing poison. The police arrested him but didn't have enough evidence to convict him. I attended Candalio's trial in Turin during a summer assignment for the Luguri newspaper. After his release, he disappeared. He's shaved off his beard and changed the color and styling of his hair, but I recognize the walking cane he always carried with him and the stiff way he holds his head because of an automobile accident. I want to see where he's going."

Craig caught Thad's arm and pulled him back. He pretended to ignore the two men on the sidewalk. "Wait until they go through the archway. Otherwise, Candalio may notice you. I suspect that's a cane knife. Yank off the lower part of the cane and you have a dangerous weapon in a fight. The hollowed out handle is an ideal place to carry poison or secret messages. The cane knife was a fashionable accessory for adventuresome gentlemen a hundred years ago. It is still very effective."

When the two men disappeared through the archway, Craig pointed toward the roof of the building beside the archway and walked in that direction. "That's an interesting architectural style. Let's have a closer look."

They intermingled with a half dozen priests and passed through the archway to the other side. As soon as they entered the adjacent plaza, Thad glanced around the crowded area. "I don't see them."

Craig pointed toward the building housing the Sistine Chapel as though they were discussing it. "I have them spotted. Relax."

"I've lost them completely." Thad rubbed his hands together.

"Trust him," Darlena said. "Craig has eyes in the back and side of his head."

Craig acted preoccupied with the building architecture. "They just reached the archway to your far right."

"That leads into the Courtyard of San Damascus," Thad said.

Craig led them across the plaza and into the archway. He paused before entering the courtyard. "The Gendarme is unlocking a wooden door. They're going into that building."

Thad stared at the closing door. "That's the Papal Palace, where administrative leaders of the Vatican work. The Holy Father's apartment is in the front section. That's not a place where outsiders visit, except by invitation. I'm going to see where that door leads."

Craig put a hand on his shoulder to restrain him. "Based upon the fact that the Gendarme unlocked the door, plus the effort he used to pull it open, I don't think it's a heavily traveled route into your Papal Palace. When you walk through that door, you may become very conspicuous. Why do you care what this Candalio is doing here?"

"Candalio has left a trail of death everywhere he's been," Thad replied. "It scares me to see him here."

"That's all the more reason for you to stay away from that door," Craig cautioned.

Thad ran his fingers through his hair. "I can find out where the door leads by looking at Cardinal Sergio's drawings. He documented all the old passageways when he hid the Vatican treasures in the catacombs."

Craig glanced at him. "Why did they hide treasures in the catacombs?"

"Toward the end of World War Two, the Italian army collapsed as the Allies advanced through Italy. Hitler sent German troops in to fight the Allies. Pope Pius feared the Germans might loot the Vatican to help finance the war. So he told Cardinal Sergio to hide the treasures in catacombs underneath the Vatican. Sergio was a very methodical and cautious man. He documented exactly where he hid everything and the access routes from Vatican buildings into those sections of the catacombs. He put the documents in the Vatican Archives where no outsider would find them. When the Germans were defeated, Sergio brought the treasures back out of the catacombs."

Craig mulled that information as he glanced back toward the heavy wooden door. "Is it appropriate to eat lunch here in the Courtyard of St. Damascus?"

Thad's forehead furrowed. "Priests do it. Why?"

Craig pulled Euros from his coat pocket and handed them to Darlena. "Grab us some food. We'll relax here and see how long the Devil's physician stays. I don't imagine he'll be in there very long."

Darlena pointed a finger at Thad. "Don't do anything foolish. For once in your life, act like a pragmatist rather than an idealist." She glanced at Craig. "Please don't let him do anything stupid."

Craig smiled. "We're going to sit here and talk about soccer."

As soon as Darlena disappeared through the archway, Craig motioned for Thad to join him on a bench. "Can a person come through catacombs into the Vatican buildings?"

"They can't from outside. The wall foundations seal off all the catacombs. But inside Vatican City, a person could reach most of the buildings from the catacombs. These buildings contain dozens of old passageways and hidden rooms, giving access between buildings and down into the catacombs. Hidden passageways and the catacombs saved the lives of popes on several occasions."

Craig's interest increased. "Have you seen the drawings that this Sergio did?"

"Cardinal Sergio was from northern Italy," Thad replied. "Bishop Baccalete has been campaigning to have him eulogized for his service to the Vatican. I was documenting his noteworthy accomplishments when I found his comments about hiding the treasures. Not even Baccalete knew about it. I tried to trace out a few of the routes, but the passageway doors were locked."

"And these drawings are in the Vatican Archives?" Craig asked.

"Right now, most of them are in my room. I have Cardinal Sergio's files from the archives."

Craig saw Darlena hurrying back through the archway. "Darlena said you're a very talented soccer player. I played soccer in high school and college. Now I settle for buying a ticket and watching it as a spectator."

Thad smiled. "I play every week. My dream is to attend a European World Cup match."

Darlena sat down beside them. "Is Candalio still inside?"

Craig nodded. "Yes. We've been sitting here talking about soccer."

She grimaced as she handed each of them a stuffed pita. "Don't let Thad get started on soccer. He's as much a fanatic on soccer as I am on gymnastics."

Craig bit into his pita. "Stay relaxed and disinterested. The door into the Papal Palace is opening."

The Papal Gendarme and the short man in the business suit came out the door, walked to an adjacent archway, and disappeared.

Thad jumped up.

Craig pulled him back down. "Don't follow him. He's probably on his way out of the Vatican. Whatever he came here for has already been accomplished. So let's relax and finish the tour. You have an important meeting later today and I promised Darlena a delightful evening."

Thad stared toward the wooden door and the Papal Palace. "I know that was Candalio. Wherever Candalio goes, people die."

"Then don't let Candalio know you recognized him," Craig said. "Or you'll be the one who dies."

CHAPTER 16

▼

Craig accelerated and the red Ferrari swept past other cars along Via Tiburtina east of Rome. Suburbs and drab industrial buildings flashed by and eventually became replaced by forests and vast marble quarries gouged into hillsides. He glanced toward Darlena. With the windows rolled down, the wind billowed her hair into a raven fountain splashing around her face. The wildness of her hair only enhanced the beauty of her facial features and luminous eyes.

"When you said a ristorante beside the river, I thought you meant the Tiber," Darlena said.

"I want to show you my favorite place in all of Italy," Craig replied. "We're going to the Villa d'Este adjacent to the Aniene River."

Her face brightened. "I've read about the villa of fountains, but never seen it. I'd much rather visit the villa than sit beside the smelly waters of the Tiber and listen to cars honking."

"You have to thank your Roman Catholic Church for Villa d'Este. Ippolite d'Este was a cardinal and grandson of a pope. In keeping with the traditions of spiritually-inspired Church leaders, he confiscated a Franciscan monastery and used Church wealth to build his villa. He diverted the Aniene River into a channel to provide water for the fountains." Craig pointed toward the rolling terrain off to the right. "A Roman emperor built Hadrian's Villa during the second century. What barbarians didn't plunder, d'Este stole for his villa. The ruins scattered among trees and hills still conjure up the aura of Rome's power and glory. The Ristorante Adriano is nearby. We'll finish out our evening there."

An hour later, they strolled along the mossy green walkway of fountains at Villa d'Este. Water gushed from a hundred fountains on the roadway and from a myriad of other fountains spread around the grounds of d'Este's palace. Fountains had been created in every conceivable shape, including boats, owls, lilies, and lion heads. Some sprayed skyward, some trickled over marble flowers, and others cascaded down embankments. Reddish-brown nightingales fluttered among chestnut tree branches, their cooing adding melody to the gurgle and splash of the fountains. Crocus and purple spikes of snapdragons sprouted from algae-covered alcoves.

Darlena paused beside a fountain where slender maidens frozen in time poured water from sculptured vases. "Power is such a mixed blessing. If the world had no powerful men, then nothing like this would have been built. No Egyptian pyramids, no Greek Parthenon, no Roman coliseum, no Michelangelo Sistine Chapel paintings, no cathedrals, no China Wall, no Taj Mahal. For better or for worse, powerful men build personal legacies that symbolize the pinnacles of their civilizations."

Craig put his arm around her shoulder and pulled her up close beside him. "When you get tired of coaching gymnastics, you can teach philosophy. I'll be one of your first students."

She smiled. "I'll always be a gymnastic coach. That's been my dream for years." She shifted to look into his face. "What's your dream?"

"Someday," he said, "I'm going to find a wooded hillside overlooking a stream with crystal-clear water bubbling across rocks, and build a house. I'll do some fishing, go hiking, and run an investment business from a screened-in oak porch jutting above the water. Bring Joan there and let her wander around. Unlike people, nature is very tolerant. She would be okay."

Darlena snuggled her head against his shoulder. "Will you build it in Europe or America?"

"I'll build it in the Smoky Mountains of Tennessee or North Carolina."

"We have beautiful mountains and crystal-clear streams here in Italy. The low Alps north of the Po River valley are magnificent."

"The United States is home," he replied. "Plus, Joan needs to be where people speak English."

Darlena gazed up into his face. "Then go back home now and take Joan with you. Do it before something destroys your dreams."

"You're getting too serious," Craig admonished. "I like you best when the enthusiastic, starry-eyed girl tempers the overly serious woman."

"You like the fun-loving girl side of me?" She sprinted toward the steep rock steps running upward beside a series of gushing waterfalls. "I'll beat you to the top," she called back as she pounded up the steps.

When Darlena reached the top, she sagged against an elm tree and gasped in breaths.

Craig staggered up beside her. "I thought I was in superb physical condition. But you ran up these stairs like they were level ground."

Darlena grinned. "In Luguri, I ran up hills every day to build strength and endurance in my legs for gymnastics. So that's the fun-loving girl side of me. Here's the woman."

She stretched up and kissed him on his lips.

He wrapped his arms around her hips, lifted her feet off the ground to bring her face level with his, and massaged her lips with his open mouth.

She clasped his head in her hands and locked her legs around him.

He felt her inner thighs pressing against him. Her body and lips sent sensual emotion surging through every part of him.

"God, I wish you weren't a jewel thief," she blurted out. "First a priest captivates me and now you. The only two men I've ever cared about and both of you are impossible dreams. Life can be very cruel."

Craig's body urged him to escalate the moment, but his mind warned against it. What he was contemplating doing would destroy any possible future relationship. He eased her feet back to the ground, clasped her hand, and led her along a curving, downward pathway toward the Ferrari. "Hadrian's Villa closes at sunset. We'll only have time to see a few sections of it."

A midnight moon perched high in the night sky when Craig walked Darlena to the doorway of her apartment building.

"I'm leaving Rome tomorrow," he said.

"Write me occasionally. Just a handwritten note so I'll know you're safe and thinking of me." Darlena dug into her purse and scribbled her Rome, Turin, and Luguri addresses and phone numbers on a scrap of paper. "I'll burn the envelope and letter the day it arrives. That way, no one can know where you are."

He caressed her hair with his hand. "I'll do that."

"Would it be okay if I visited Joan before I go back to Turin?" she asked.

Craig nodded. "Joan would enjoy seeing you as often as you could come. Don't take her anywhere. There's no way to predict her reaction outside the sanatorium."

Darlena stretched up, wrapped her arms around his neck, and nuzzled her face against his. "The first time I met you, I feared and hated you. On the train and that night in the hotel, I wasn't sure how I felt. Now I dread never seeing you again."

"The man that wins your love will be very fortunate. Don't settle for anything less than what you want." He kissed her lightly on the lips and pulled away.

Craig climbed into the Ferrari and sped away without looking back.

An hour later, Craig handed a wad of Euros to the night guard at the library and began searching for information on the Vatican. He now knew his next target.

CHAPTER 17

Craig rotated his arms to relieve stiff muscles as he paced around the table. Books, sketches, and pages of notes covered the table in his three-room apartment. One book was entitled, "Treasures of the Vatican". Others were "A Visitor's Guide to Vatican City"; "History of Vatican City"; "The Catacombs of Rome"; "The Vatican Museums"; and "Architectural Perspectives of Vatican City Buildings". Additional books lay open to various pages.

After leaving Darlena last night, he had scoured the Rome library for reference books. A substantial bribe to the night watchman allowed him to spend the night in the library reference section and use their duplicating machine to copy information. If asked, the guard would describe him as a bespectacled, gray-haired man. His demeanor and speech suggested a university professor frantically rushing to complete a scholarly presentation scheduled later in the week.

Earlier today, he had joined a public tour of the Vatican Museums and purchased ten books at various shops. Four of the most useful books had come from the Vatican's own bookstore.

Craig poured a glass of white wine, the first he had allowed himself today, walked onto the balcony overlooking the Tiber River, and gazed toward the magnificent Dome of St. Peter's Basilica. How many times had he seen that dome, indifferent to the hundred acres around it? He had not slept for thirty-four hours. Yet, he never felt more alert. His mind churned through a dozen possible scenarios. It sorted, discarded, rearranged, and discarded again.

He had the Bratius security system information for the Vatican vault and museums. Von Meier would have already warned them. What if the Vatican had modified the security system? His mind reran words from a reference book. The statements confirmed Thad's comment that "The Vatican vault is underground, designed to protect the most important Vatican documents and treasures from the possibility of nuclear holocaust." He remembered noting the lack of sophistication and modernization in the Vatican vault security system. They don't expect to be robbed. Probably the vault locking mechanisms are equally antiquated. Vatican officials probably ignored Von Meier's warning.

Craig paced back and forth on the balcony. Reaching and opening the vault may be possible. Looting the Vatican Museums may be possible. But how could he carry treasures out from a walled fortress that never sleeps and has no escape routes? Anyone attempting to rob the Vatican will almost certainly be trapped inside.

Only an insane person would attempt to rob the Vatican. By any line of logic, those treasures are impossible to rob. But what if the robber is a master thief with fortuitous access to the myriad passageways and catacombs? Robbing the greatest collection of treasures in the world from an impregnable fortress would stamp him as the greatest thief of all time. It would be the perfect finale.

Craig glanced at his watch. It was four-twenty in the afternoon. He had left a message for Thad, saying he would call him at four-thirty. He dialed the number and heard a voice answer on the second ring.

"This is Father Thadeus."

"Hi. This is Craig. I need to visit with you this evening."

"I'm leaving shortly for Turin. It'll have to be when I return."

Craig hit his fist on the table. Thad leaving would force him to delay the robbery plans. "You sound upset," Craig said in a sympathetic voice.

"His Holiness suffered a relapse last night, leaving him mentally incapacitated again." Thad replied. "I'm positive that Candalio drugged him. The door we saw is an old entryway to the Pope's living quarters. The Papal Gendarme was a man named Perrin. He reports to the Director of Security for the Vatican, which is Cardinal Lastavis. Because Bishop Baccalete couldn't see the Pope, he returned to Turin this morning. He's the only one I trust enough to tell what I know."

Craig let out a low whistle. Lastavis planned to incapacitate, maybe eventually kill the Pope and succeed to the Papacy. He assessed the implications and concluded this might work to his advantage. But it accelerated the timing of the heist dramatically.

"Meet me at the Porta Sant'Anna gate and check me in," Craig said. "You and I need to talk."

"I have to tell Baccalete what I know tonight," Thad replied.

"You and I have to talk first, at your place."

"Why?"

"Trust me. I think I know how to protect the Pope. Meet me at the gate. I'll personally drive you to Turin afterwards."

Craig heard Thad breathing heavily, probably debating how to respond.

"All right," Thad finally said.

"I'll be at the gate in twenty minutes."

Craig hung up and mulled the new information as he opened a small case and pulled out a digital camera. Lastavis would kill Thad if he found out that Thad knew about the conspiracy. That would scuttle the heist. So he needed to make copies of Sergio's drawings of the catacombs and buildings, delay Thad talking to Baccalete, and figure out a logical-sounding scheme for protecting the Pope. The timing had become more urgent. But these new events may have provided some other options.

His mind swirled through various possibilities as he reached the street and hailed a taxi. Only Thad and he knew about the drawings. He needed to smuggle out the original drawings, not simply photograph them. But how could he do that without Thad knowing? If Thad warns Baccalete about Candalio and Lastavis learns who tipped off Baccalete, Lastavis will kill Thad. It's important to keep Thad alive. He can provide access into Vatican City for reconnoitering everything. Thad knows that place like an Indian knows the forest.

His mind shifted to Cardinal Lastavis, the man who was Director of Security and obsessed with becoming the next pope. That was an interesting combination. Letting someone rob the Vatican would be an embarrassing, fatal incident for Lastavis's papal aspirations. In a showdown, Lastavis would negotiate and probably let a trapped thief escape in exchange for not destroying important Vatican documents or publicizing the heist.

Craig made a mental note to reread the book on Vatican treasures and determine which items were worth a king's ransom to a Director of Security campaigning to be pope. He also mulled the value of the Director of Security being distracted by an aging Bishop Baccalete and an idealistic priest.

The more he mulled the new scenarios, the more possible the impossible became.

But first, he needed the drawings of the Vatican and he needed to orchestrate the next actions by the crusading young priest. He preferred methodically casing a robbery target and meticulously carrying out each step in the plan. But to rob the Vatican, he would have to plan and execute at breakneck speed and expect changing events to alter actions at the last moment.

Craig leaned back against the taxi seat and gazed at the dome of St. Peter's basilica looming ahead. Snatch the ultimate hoard of treasures from an impregnable fortress while an arrogant cardinal preoccupies himself with his own treacherous conspiracy.

Life doesn't get any better than that.

Thad closed the door to his room and motioned toward the solitary chair. Craig chose to stand. The small room contained only a narrow bed, an armoire, and the wooden chair pushed up against a desk.

Thad ran his hand through his already disheveled hair. "Since the Pope's relapse doesn't appear life threatening, they're keeping him at his residence rather than at a hospital. That lets Lastavis control access to the Pope. The Conclave of Cardinals scheduled for next week has been delayed. When the Pope recovers enough to issue edicts, Candalio will drug him again. I tried to contact Baccalete, but he had already left for Turin."

"What do you expect Baccalete to do?" Craig asked. "Walk into Lastavis's office and accuse him of drugging the Pope because a young priest saw a man that looked like an evil doctor going into the Papal Palace with a trusted Gendarme? Candalio probably entered through the Vatican gate without being signed in or out. Baccalete may believe you, but he has no proof."

Thad paced in the small space between the bed and armoire. "Baccalete can have trusted colleagues watch the two gates. That will keep Candalio from coming back inside. They can also maintain a vigil outside the Papal living quarters."

Craig batted that idea away with a wave of his hand. "Lastavis controls security. He has a dozen ways to bring Candalio back in. I have an idea that might save the Pope. Show me Sergio's drawings and how he planned to move treasures out of the Papal Palace into the catacombs."

Thad opened the armoire, lifted out a stack of papers, and unfolded the top one. The heavy paper sheet covered most of the desktop. Protected in folders in the temperature and humidity controlled Vatican Library, the ink drawings showed only minor fading and fraying except in the fold creases.

"There is a small room with a door connecting into the Papal living quarters," Thad said as he pointed. "I saw the living quarters during a tour for new priests assigned to the Vatican. They didn't show us that room. Sergio documented it as part of an escape route for Pope Pius, and for carrying works of art into hiding places if the Germans entered the Vatican. A trapdoor under the rug leads down into a passageway on the lower floor. I suspect only a few people today know about that old passageway." He moved his finger along the drawing. "Near the far end of the passageway is a side doorway into a room with stone steps descending into the catacombs. That's where Sergio planned to hide the treasures."

Craig studied the drawings. "Was Sergio this detailed on all his drawings?"

"Sergio documented everything in meticulous detail. Thanks to him, volumes of information exist on Vatican policies, procedures, and building activities in the nineteen thirties up through the fifties. These drawings were filed separately. I discovered them while following up on an obscure note Sergio made in one document concerning discussions with Pope Pius on the German threat to the Vatican."

The drawings exceeded Craig's wildest expectations. A complete blueprint of Vatican buildings sat at his fingertips, including hidden passageways and entries to catacombs. He pushed back his surge of exhilaration and maintained a serious demeanor. "Gather up Sergio's drawings, plus any details related to them that he wrote down. We'll set up in a hotel and do some heavy work tonight. The drawings may give us a way to protect your Pope from Candalio and Lastavis."

Thad shook his head. "I have to go to Turin. And these drawings are originals from the Vatican Archives. They can't be taken outside."

"You don't have to travel to Turin to talk to Baccalete," Craig replied. "You can do that on the telephone. But don't call him from here. These phones aren't secure. Someone could listen in. Maybe Lastavis monitors phone calls. We'll call from the hotel. Since we're trying to save the Pope's life, I think he'll give you a Papal dispensation for smuggling out Vatican Archive material. You're already packed for traveling. Put the information in your bag and let's go."

"That's a good idea on telephoning Baccalete." Thad glanced at his watch. "He should be in Turin by now. I'll telephone him as soon as we reach the hotel."

"No, you can't call Baccalete tonight."

Thad glanced up from packing papers in his travel bag. "I need to call him."

"As soon as Baccalete starts contacting people concerning this, someone will either intentionally or accidentally tip off Lastavis. When that happens, Lastavis is going to kill you. I know you don't mind being a martyr, but Lastavis will look in the visitor roster at the Gate of the Bells and see that you brought in two people with you on the fateful day. One was named Craig Reynolds, which isn't a particular problem, because I can disappear out of Italy tomorrow. The other name was Darlena Aldonzo."

Thad's face paled. "I hadn't thought of that."

Craig's face remained solemn. "We have to protect Darlena. So don't let her know anything about what we're doing. Don't even let her know that you and I are working together. And don't tell anyone, including Baccalete, what you know until you and I agree that it's the right time. If we do this right, the Pope will be safe and Lastavis will be discredited."

Craig helped Thad finish packing the papers in his travel bag. Step one in the robbery plans had been completed.

CHAPTER 18

▼

Craig followed Thad through the Papal Gardens and past the summer house of Pius IV. His eyes photographed the layout and every detail, matching up what he learned from Sergio's drawings during the all-night session with Thad at the hotel and his previous night's work in the library. Thad had told him that patrolling Gendarmes did not use sentry dogs. The maze of shrubbed pathways and secluded nooks with statues and fountains would provide cover for surreptitious movement at night.

They paused beside the wall of the Vatican Museum.

Thad pointed to the adjacent sprawling green lawn dominated by a massive fountain in the middle. "This is the Giardinao Quadrato Garden that I told you about during your first visit. The vault and the Raedis Ponificum Servandis, where they store cars and carriages used by previous popes, are located underneath. Cardinal Sergio used the underground garage for moving treasures into the catacombs."

Thad led the way into the underground garage. Vaulted ceilings gave the appearance of a king's court, filled not with people but with relics of past popes. Elegant vehicles lined both sides of the wide corridor.

Craig paused in front of one with solid gold lamps, grille, and door handles. Embroidered lilies decorated the red and gold throne chair. "Popes apparently didn't embrace austerity and humility."

Thad gazed at the car. "Unfortunately, that's true. But this is nothing compared to the great carriage built in the eighteen twenties for Pope Leo XII."

They strolled over to admire it. The mammoth wheels, taller than either of them, elevated it above other vehicles. Ornate life-size carvings of cherubs gave it a regal flair far surpassing any of the other carriages and automobiles.

"This carriage," Thad said, "elevated Pope Leo above the heads of his subjects as he traveled through the streets of Rome, and provided him a view of the entire Vatican grounds during summer afternoon rides. It's the most elegant, commanding carriage ever created and symbolic of a man obsessed with his own grandeur."

They turned into a side alcove. "This is where the cars and carriages are cleaned and polished," Thad continued. "When the Vatican began a massive building program in the nineteen thirties, workers digging the drainage system for the garage exposed extensive burial grounds. The laws of the Roman Empire forbade burying people inside the city. Consequently, lower class citizens were buried along vast underground burial corridors around the periphery of Rome. All of Vatican Hill is interlaced with ancient underground catacombs. Cardinal Fantelli, in charge of the building program in the thirties, explored the catacombs discovered by the workers. Then he ordered them sealed off to prevent desecration of the tombs. When Pope Pius asked Cardinal Sergio to hide the treasures, Sergio remembered this drain adjacent to the museums, reopened the entrance into the catacombs, and hid the treasures here beneath the Pope's Garage. He replaced the stones above the bottom of the drain when the treasures were returned to the museums. But he didn't cement the stones, in case Russia overran Europe and they needed to hide the treasures again."

"Watch the alcove while I take a quick look." Craig seized the heavy steel grating, wrestled it from the drain, and lowered himself into the seven-foot deep hole. He pressed against the bottom wedge of stones. No movement. Bracing himself against the opposite side allowed him to apply more pressure with his feet. Stones slid backward and tumbled into the void behind, spewing musty air into his face.

Craig gazed into vast darkness that swallowed the small beam of his pocket flashlight. His mind visualized a secret subway running in the dank foreboding underground world beneath the Vatican. He lifted himself from the drain and carefully repositioned the grating. "How far do these catacombs extend?"

"Cardinal Sergio's notes said they open into a huge burial roadway lined on both sides with tombs," Thad replied. "The only catacombs he explored led toward the Ethiopian Seminary near the back of Vatican City. But I'm certain these catacombs are part of the burial complex discovered under St. Peter's Basilica during excavations for the remains of St. Peter's tomb."

Craig collated what he had learned in the past few days, pressing each piece of the puzzle into place. If the catacombs extended underneath the Ethiopian Seminary and St. Peter's Basilica, then they almost certainly stretched beneath the railroad station.

The final piece of the puzzle fell into place. Craig knew now how to remove the treasures from the Vatican.

Thad's voice interrupted his thoughts. "I still don't understand why you're so interested in this area of the Vatican?"

"Let's walk toward the Pope Pius summer house," Craig replied. "Right now, the Pope is incapacitated again. Lastavis will keep him alive until he can finish lining up votes to make him the next pope. As soon as that happens, or if the Pope recovers enough to call a Conclave of Cardinals, Lastavis will send Candalio in to kill him. Given the Pope's health problems, no one will suspect foul play. You can't protect the Pope in the Papal Palace from a surreptitious visit by Candalio. No matter how hard Baccalete tries, Lastavis, as Director of Security, holds all the high cards. But Lastavis can't kill the Pope if he doesn't know where he is."

Thad grimaced. "You're suggesting we hide the Holy Father in the catacombs? In his health condition, he wouldn't survive."

"That's not my plan. Step one is for Baccalete to insist on a private meeting with the Pope even though he's incapacitated. You and a few trusted priests will come through the catacombs into the Papal Palace, use the abandoned passageway to reach the Papal living quarters, and carry the Pope back through the catacombs to the carriage garage. From there you take him to the Pope Pius summer house, where you'll have secretly assembled some doctors. When they revive the Pope from his drugged incoherence, he'll issue both a call for a Conclave of Cardinals and an edict stripping Lastavis of his powers."

Thad stared at the summer cottage. "You think we could do that?"

"I think you could do that."

Thad wiped perspiration beads from his forehead. "But we can't get through the passageway in the Papal Palace. The doors are locked."

"Those doors were not designed to be difficult to unlock. You and I are close enough to the same size and build for me to wear some of your priest garb. Two priests are going to check out that route."

An hour later, Craig and Thad strolled down the service corridor in the Papal Palace. They paused beside a heavy wooden door emblazoned with a large gold-leaf medallion.

Craig traced across the medallion with his left-hand fingers. "The Borgia family plastered these all over the Vatican when they controlled the Papacy." He continued talking casually while his right hand inserted metal probes into the keyhole.

Clerks carrying paperwork and other paraphernalia ambled past, paying no attention to the two priests.

Craig heard the click of the lock opening. He grasped the handle, twisted it, and pressed against the door. It creaked loudly as he forced it open. Hot, musty air puffed into the corridor.

Two clerks paused to watch them.

Craig pointed inside the dark corridor and spoke to Thad in a loud voice. "The cardinal insists that the bishop's chair and desk were stored here after his death in nineteen ninety-one. The family certainly waited a long time to ask for them." He stepped inside and turned on a large flashlight. "Let's see if we can find them. And close the door. We don't want this smell and dust in the corridor."

The clerks continued down the hallway.

Thad helped Craig close the door. Craig locked the door from the inside.

"How did you unlock the door?" Thad asked.

"I paid my way through college working for a talented locksmith who opened safes and doors for people who lost the keys or combinations. What I learned comes in handy sometimes." He motioned with the light. "Let's go this way first and locate the trap door into the Pope's closet."

Thad's footsteps cast dull echoes in the passageway. Craig padded silently, noting the marble floors, stained paneling, and occasional frescoes. Chairs, their cloth now torn and rotted, sat in jumbled stacks. Dust and cobwebs covered everything. His nostrils rebelled at the moldy, stifling air. No one had been in this corridor for decades.

Craig's flashlight beam picked up a door in the wall.

"Think this is it?" Thad asked.

"We haven't come far enough," Craig replied.

They continued walking, Craig silently counting his footsteps. Another door glittered in the light. Craig crouched in front of the door. Thirty seconds later, the bolt clicked away from the door jam. Thad pulled the door partway open.

Craig squeezed through into a small room with wooden steps leading upward toward the high ceiling. He climbed the stairs and pressed his ear against the wooden door in the ceiling. No sound of movement above him. No glint of light in the thin cracks of the door. But a comment on Sergio's drawing indicated a rug covered the trap door. Hopefully no one had stacked furniture atop the door since Sergio set it up as an escape route.

He pushed against the trap door with his shoulder and felt it move upward. The edge of a thick rug fell over the corner of the trap door, exposing complete darkness in the room above him. As Craig rose higher, he saw a glimmer of light protruding underneath a door in the wall.

That must be the entry to the Pope's apartment. He squirmed through the trap door, padded silently to the door, and put his ear to it. No sound of movement on the other side. He slid a thin plastic card between the door and doorframe. The lock wasn't engaged.

So far, everything looked good. Craig slid back through the trap door, repositioning the rug to cover the trap door as he lowered it.

"The door to the Pope's apartment isn't locked," he said to Thad. "Let's go back the other way and find the entry to the catacombs. I'll leave all the doors in the passageway unlocked, including the one opening into the service area corridor. Everyone expects that door to be locked, so they won't check it."

They hurried down the corridor. Sweat peppered Craig's forehead, intermingling with dust to create a salty irritant dribbling into his eyes. Stale air parched his nose and throat.

At the far end of the passageway, Craig found an unlocked door. They descended marble steps to a lower floor. This level had brick walls and a stone floor.

"We're going underneath the Apostalic Library now," Thad said. "There should be a door on our left that leads down into the catacombs."

"I see it." Craig positioned the light to illuminate the door. "It's padlocked."

Thad grimaced. "Is that a problem?"

Craig laughed as he inserted two metal keys. "You could pick this one with a screwdriver."

The padlock popped open. The air shifted to cool and dank when they opened the door.

They followed a twisting, crude stone stairway downward. At the bottom, Craig swept his flashlight back and forth. Clods of dirt from partially collapsed walls and small piles of bones littered the earthen floor of a wide corridor disappearing into darkness in both directions. Cavities with exposed bones pitted the walls. Multiple layers of tombs lined the walls, some sealed with stones, most closed off with packed dirt.

Thad studied a sketch on a sheet of paper and pointed down the passageway. "I need to check out the route to the drain in the garage to make certain that cave-ins or construction haven't blocked the tunnel since Cardinal Sergio used it."

Craig caught his arm. "We need proper equipment down here or we may become permanent residents. You don't want to step back out into the service corridor looking like you've been rolling in dirt. I'll return later and mark the route for you. Let's go back to my hotel room."

They sat in the hotel room, reviewing drawings. Craig leaned back in his chair. "We're missing some of Sergio's drawings and notes."

"They're still in the Vatican Archives," Thad replied. "I didn't see any value in having all of them."

"Bring all of Sergio's drawings and notes here. I want to study them."

Thad drummed his fingers on the table. "What we're planning is dangerous. I'm trying to save the Holy Father and protect the Church. You aren't Catholic. I don't think you're even religious. Why are you willing to run so much risk?"

Craig sipped his glass of wine. "I enjoy the challenge of beating a man like Lastavis. The ultimate victory would be to defeat him at his own game on his own playing field. There is a lot of satisfaction in bringing down arrogant manipulators who feed on innocent people. I like helping the underdog. In this situation, you are a distinct underdog. But I'm not foolhardy. So I need some commitments from you."

Thad ran his hand through his hair. Dust powdered down onto his priest's garb. "Tell me what you need."

"First, bring me the rest of Sergio's files related to the buildings and catacombs. Don't let anybody, not even Baccalete know that we have them. Second, don't talk to Baccalete without telling me first. One misspoken comment by Baccalete or his confidantes and we're both dead. Baccalete doesn't need to know until we're ready to move the Pope. That could be a week or more. Third, don't say anything to Darlena about this. Don't tell her that you and I have met again. As far as she knows, I've left Rome. I want to keep her totally insulated from any involvement, in case Lastavis learns what we're doing."

Thad wiped muddy sweat from his forehead. "I need to talk with Baccalete and get his counsel. The Pope's life is hanging in the balance."

Craig planted his elbows on the table and leaned forward almost in Thad's face. "Talking to Baccalete will get both of us and your Pope killed. Don't talk to him until you and I agree it's time to do it. I'll stay registered at this hotel room as Mr. Bartello. Don't come here again. If you need to contact me, call from a pay phone in Vatican Village and leave a telephone message at the desk. Call yourself Plato. If you leave a message under the name Dante, I'll know you're in trouble."

Thad's eyes blinked and his chest heaved. Finally he nodded. "Okay. You understand this game. I don't. It's still inconceivable to me that Cardinal Lastavis would consider killing the Holy Father and usurping the Papacy."

Craig grinned as he stood up. "Many of the popes in the Middle Ages got there by killing their predecessor and competition."

Thad frowned. "You actually have a low opinion of the Church. I don't understand why you're risking your life to save the Pope."

Craig put his arm around Thad's shoulder and walked him to the doorway. "As I said earlier, predators like Lastavis anger me. The current Pope symbolizes what's right about the Catholic Church. He's championed human rights and the dignity of man. The world needs his voice and influence." He paused at the door and faced Thad. "But most of all, I'm doing it for Darlena and you. Darlena is very special to me and you're very special to her." He grinned. "I'm glad you decided to become a priest."

Thad embraced him. "God must have ordained that you and Darlena would meet and that you would come here to help the Church. I'll call you as soon as I have the rest of Sergio's drawings." Thad disappeared through the doorway.

Craig gathered up the drawings and notes. He would keep them at his apartment. This part had gone well, but a lot of work remained to be accomplished in a short time frame. Hopefully God would keep the Pope alive long enough. As the scriptures say, God works in mysterious ways. In this case, so mysterious, even God's Church won't know what is happening until it is too late.

He looked out the hotel window and watched Thad intermingle with crowds on the street. He liked Thad. Unfortunately, after the robbery, Thad would realize that he had been conned and tell the police what he knew. Von Meier would quickly figure out how the robbery was accomplished. Craig mulled another possibility. Tipping off Lastavis about Thad's knowledge of Candalio's role would assure that Thad would be killed before he had a chance to talk to the police. Craig rejected that approach. Thad was a good person and Darlena's best friend. So, despite the risks of Thad giving valuable information to Von Meier, Craig would work to keep him alive.

Craig's mind shifted back to the robbery details. Timing would be critical on this heist. The clock was running at breakneck speed.

He needed to find the right accomplice to help him finish reconnoitering the Vatican and carry out the heist.

CHAPTER 19

▼

Craig wended his way along a street in the Rome Dipanico District, a crumbling array of tenement houses and drab shops backing up against the Tiber River. Horn-blowing cars and rattling pickup trucks crammed with boisterous men searching out their evening drinking place or a woman for the night jockeyed for position in the narrow cobblestone street. Small groups of men in undershirts and scruffy pants sat on doorsteps, smoking and debating nothing of substance.

Strangers assumed substantial risks when they invaded this lower class working man's territory. But Craig's size, coupled with the obvious air of self-confidence, made him an unlikely victim. Black hair, Italian features, and a middle class business suit suggested a moderately successful escapee from the tedium and poverty of their streets. People would assume he was coming back to visit family or a woman.

He spotted the glittering neon lights over a wooden and brick building. The final two letters were either burned out or broken, but what he saw confirmed that he had arrived at the Paesada Casino.

When Craig walked to the bar, he received only cursory glances from patrons. The carved designs in the heavy mahogany bar hinted at a more auspicious past. Scars, stains, and smell of spilled beer relegated it now to patronage by heavy-drinking local laborers. The mirror behind the bar had hazed and cracked in places. One shattered panel appeared to be the victim of an errant beer bottle. Wooden chairs and tables pushed up close together to accommodate the large crowd.

Noisy groups crowded around some tables. Solitary men hunched over other tables, clasping their alcohol glass as though they feared the drink might sprout wings and fly away. Women circulated among the men. Three women appeared to be carrying drinks to patrons, moving from table to table, pushing off pawing hands. One woman helped an inebriated man struggle through a door leading to the backside of the casino. The man's hand had burrowed inside her blouse to fondle the ample breasts. Her hand would soon burrow into his not-so-ample wallet.

Craig spoke fluent Italian, but his accent being devoid of the harsh colloquial Dipanico sound marked him as an outsider. That drew immediate attention from a woman sitting at the end of the bar. He had noted her eyeing him when he walked in, marking him as a stranger to this bar, but a man at ease in the rough Dipanico district. Her demeanor indicated she sat at the top of the pecking order among the women.

His eyes met her gaze. She maneuvered in beside him and signaled the bartender to bring her a drink. "I'm Rita," she said.

What Craig saw would interest any man. Rita possessed the dark features and flowing black hair of the Southern Italian. Her high cheekbones accentuated sizzling eyes and pulpy lips. Large breasts puffed upward on the verge of bursting from the confines of her lacy, multicolored blouse.

He smiled at her. "I can't consume a bottle of wine by myself. Want to join me?"

Her lips pursed sensuously. "There's a table near the wall where we can be alone."

Craig noted the unoccupied table shoved into a dim corner, obviously reserved for her exclusive use with handpicked clientele. He motioned to the bartender. "Bring a vintage white wine. Don't open it until you come to the table."

Rita's smile indicated his response confirmed her initial impression that he would spend money for what he wanted. She led the way, her large hips swaying as she serpentined between men and chairs.

Craig sat down with his back to the wall, where he could watch movement of people in the casino.

She gyrated into the chair beside him. "I've never seen you here before."

"This is my first visit. I'm looking for someone."

Rita shifted position, spreading open her legs and sliding her dress upward to expose fleshy, firm thighs. "I think you've found that someone."

Craig delayed answering until the bartender arrived at the table and began opening the bottle of wine. "I'm looking for Romano Pantel. Do you know him?"

The momentary pause in pouring the wine told Craig that the bartender heard his comment. Rita frowned, indicating that this was not the reply she had anticipated. "Romano is not here," she said, "but I could arrange for him to meet you another evening. It would be a shame for you to waste your trip tonight."

"I have no intention of wasting tonight." Craig appeared preoccupied with her, but his eyes noted the bartender stopping to talk with a group of men at a distant table. One of the men left.

Rita ran her fingers across his palm. "You have strength in your hand. It's not accustomed to laborer's work. The lines suggest a powerful man with strong desires." She sipped on her glass of wine. "A wine of this quality deserves better surroundings. My place is behind the casino. We could continue the discussion of your needs there."

"Not until I've talked with Romano."

"Romano knows where I live," she purred. "While you wait for him, we can become more intimately acquainted. I promise you won't be bored. I never disappoint."

The sound of a chair moving beside them interrupted their conversation.

A man sat down across from him, pulled out a large knife, and began scraping his fingernails. "Why do you wanna see Romano?"

"Personal business," Craig replied.

The man laid the large knife on the table, still gripping the handle, the blade pointed in Craig's direction. "I'm making it my business. What's your name?"

"Go drink your beer, Mario," Rita said. "I'll see that Romano gets the message."

The man's eyes shifted toward her as he opened his mouth to reply.

Craig's fist slammed down on top of the knife hand, moving so fast the man never saw it. Craig's other hand yanked the knife away from the pained fingers.

"Before you drink your beer," Craig growled, "deliver this message to Romano Pantel. Craig, the man from the train, needs to talk with him tonight. Here at the Paesada Casino."

The man rubbed his bruised hand and glared sullenly. "I'll give him your message."

"Ah," a voice said. "It is the man with no last name and a gun that will kill fifteen people."

Craig didn't look toward the deep, hoarse voice to his left. "Good to see you again, Romano."

Romano put his huge callused hand on Rita's bare shoulder and massaged it. "My friend and I have business to discuss."

She undulated up from her chair and clasped Craig's hand. "Would you prefer the privacy of my apartment? It's nearby and much more comfortable."

Craig turned toward Romano. "What I have to say is for you only."

"I can be very discreet," Rita replied. "My ears hear only what they are supposed to hear."

Romano nodded. "We will use Rita's place."

Rita picked up the wine bottle and led Craig through the back door, down a dark hallway, and onto the edge of a stone plaza reeking with the stench of garbage, beer, and vomit.

He followed her up a narrow stairs into the dimly lit hallway of another building. She maneuvered past dilapidated furniture cluttering the passageway and paused to unlock a door at the far end.

The room and furnishings contrasted sharply with the dowdy hallway outside. Luxurious upholstered chairs, a small kitchenette containing a modern refrigerator and stove, and an ornate lamp perched on a carved mahogany table gave the room an elegant appearance.

Rita smiled. "Some of my friends have been very generous."

"I can see that." Craig walked to the wall where four oil paintings hung.

"Personal gifts from the artist himself," she said.

"He's a very talented person," Craig replied.

"So am I." Rita opened a cabinet door, lifted out a glass goblet, filled it with white wine, and handed it to Craig. Then she pulled a beer from the refrigerator and tossed it to Romano as he rumbled into the room. She sauntered into the bedroom, still clutching the bottle of wine, and closed the door behind her.

Romano lifted his beer in a salute and took a deep swig. "So, Craig with no last name, what brings you here tonight?"

"I need a man who can drive a truck like it was a Jaguar and fight a small army if necessary."

Romano grinned. "You're planning something big. I knew you were that kind of man. What do you have in mind?"

"Let's talk about you first. Are you Roman Catholic?"

Romano laughed. "All Italians are Roman Catholics. But the Church means nothing to me."

"That's good, because I plan to rob the Vatican."

Romano stopped in midmotion of taking another drink. "You can't be serious."

"I'm absolutely serious."

Romano plopped heavily into an upholstered chair. "You're proposing suicide. I've been in Vatican City. Guards are everywhere. The high walls make it impossible to escape."

"I know the security system. I know every hidden passageway and how to open every locked door. I know a priest who'll get us inside and I know how to carry the treasures out."

Romano rubbed his stubby beard and pointed a finger. "You robbed the Ducote Chateau. You're the jewel thief who carried out the robbery that everyone said was impossible." He leaned back in the chair and took a deep gulp of beer, his face now ablaze with interest. "What do you intend to steal from the Vatican?"

"The coin and jewelry collections in the museums alone are worth over fifty million dollars. The vault contains jewelry, negotiable bonds, currency, and gold bullion. There are paintings, gifts to the popes, and religious artifacts that the insurance companies or the Vatican will eagerly buy back. All told, there are five hundred million dollars of treasures that could be carried out. That's four hundred million Euros."

Romano plunked his beer down on the table with a thud. "Four hundred million Euros?" he gasped.

"There's actually more than four hundred million, but we'll be selective. Selling at a discount to dealers, we should collect well over two hundred million Euros. I'm offering you fifteen percent of the take."

Romano sucked in breaths. "For that amount of money, I would fight my way barefooted through Hell."

"If they catch us, you may have to do that." Craig dropped a stack of Euros on the table. "Give me a way to contact you anytime day or night. When the opportunity comes, we must move quickly."

Romano lit a cigar. "Rita will know where to find me. Use her as the contact. If she's not available, the bartender can get a message to me."

"Tell Rita only that you and I are working together. Tell her nothing else. Otherwise I'll have to kill her." Craig said it to emphasize the need for secrecy, not as an actual threat.

Romano quit puffing on his cigar. "When this is over, Rita will become my woman. Do not mess with my woman, Craig with no last name."

"Then make certain you don't tell her too much. There's a trattoria near St. Peter's Basilica, called Tre Pupazzi. Do you know it?"

"On Borgo Pio," Romano replied.

"Meet me in front of it at ten o'clock tomorrow morning."

"And how do I contact you at other times?"

Craig handed him a piece of paper. "This phone sits in a deserted one room apartment. I can access the messages with my phone. Call the number only from a public phone, so that nothing can be traced to you. Your code name is Venice. If you need to warn me, your code name is Pisa. Code name for the robbery is Pompeii. All the information is on that piece of paper. So memorize it and destroy the paper. From this moment on, you work exclusively for me. Not one word to anyone else."

"I am the best at what I do," Romano said. "I deliver exactly what I promise."

"That's why I picked you." Craig paused at the door. "This robbery will be very complex and extremely dangerous. One small mistake or a careless comment will get us killed. But you and I will rob the Vatican."

Craig left.

CHAPTER 20

▼

Craig and Romano stood beside an ancient sarcophagus with three worn stone figures and gazed at the high walls on the northeast corner of the Vatican.

"We can't go over the walls," Craig said. "They're monitored and alarmed to pick up intruders. The museum entry for the public is on the north side. It's of no value to us."

They strolled under the overhead walled passageway leading from the Vatican to the Castel Sant'Angelo fortress. Craig pointed toward two cars and a truck lined up near the wall. "Daily workers and supplies for the Vatican come in and out of the Porta Sant'Anna gate. You'll enter through that gate as a laborer and remain in Vatican Village with families who live inside. Do you have any problem doing that?"

Romano spread his palms open. "That's easy to arrange. But it will be difficult to smuggle anything in or out through the gate. The guards search all vehicles."

"We won't be smuggling anything through the gate. When they discover the robbery, they'll immediately suspect any vehicle that passed out the gate. You need to give them a promising candidate. Perhaps a daily delivery truck could disappear after leaving the Vatican."

"No problem," Romano said.

They maneuvered through masses of chattering people and emerged on the south side of the soaring colonnade. There were still clusters of people but less noise.

"On this side of the Basilica is the Arch of the Bells gate," Craig continued. "No vehicles, only people enter here. Entering through this gate requires special permission or a helpful priest. That's how I'll come and go in the Vatican. There are no other gates for people or vehicles."

"So how do we remove the Vatican treasures?" Romano asked.

Craig led him back to the street and up onto a platform beside the railroad trestle that ran above city streets before passing through the stone wall into Vatican City. "See that massive iron gate in the wall? They open it three or four times a week to admit and disgorge a string of freight cars. The Vatican is exempt from all import duties, property taxes, and sales taxes. The Vatican also receives a substantial reduction in freight charges. So most of the freight cars come in, sit undisturbed for a few days, and then leave, headed for churches all over Italy. It's a clever little trick that eliminates taxes on supplies for Catholic churches. Does that intrigue you?"

Romano grinned as he pulled the cigar from his mouth. "That intrigues me. But the vault and museums are on the other side of the basilica."

"We move everything through the catacombs underneath Vatican City. The ground beneath the Vatican is interlaced with vast burial catacombs."

"Have you been in catacombs?" Romano asked.

"I visited a small catacomb beneath a church and I looked into a large one underneath Vatican City."

"You need to walk in a real catacomb," Romano said. "When I worked in Communist youth gangs, we sometimes hid from the police in catacombs along the Appian Way. It's easy to become lost. Once lost, it is easy to die in the catacombs."

"Can you show me one similar to what we'll find underneath the Vatican?" Craig asked.

"I could show you some that we hid in but there are larger catacombs open to the public that are probably more like the ones beneath the Vatican," Romano replied.

Two hours later, Craig and Romano joined a group of twenty people filing into a large stone building. Most people looked like tourists, a few of them American. Four Japanese clutched cameras. Two priests jabbered in French.

"Below us are some of the most extensive Christian burial grounds in the Rome area," the guide said. "Keep close behind me and don't stray from the group. The darkness quickly swallows a lone flashlight. A person may wander for days trying to find the exit. Those who become lost are seldom found alive."

One of the Japanese interpreted for the other three. All four quickly crowded close to the guide. Craig and Romano positioned themselves at the rear of the group. The words of the guide were obscured by the Japanese spokesman and comments by others.

They descended a steep stairway of crumbling rock and turned into a narrow corridor barely three feet wide. Craig ducked below an ancient, crude arch but found he could stand erect once inside the underground roadway. Total darkness engulfed them, pierced only by the narrow beams of flashlights carried by each person and the guide's glowing fluorescent lantern. The shuffling sound of feet moving cautiously on the dirt floor created a low rumbling echo. Hollowed out tombs lined each side of the underground roadway, some with bones exposed, others with nothing left in the cavities. Many had originally been enclosed in burial vaults long since desecrated by looters.

The musty odor of stagnant air irritated Craig's nose. He blinked away perspiration dribbling into his eyes.

They crawled into the next section and clattered down rock-strewn steps to a lower level. The air became cooler, almost chilly. Other passageways branched off from the narrow underground roadway.

Craig whispered into Romano's ear. "I see what you meant about becoming disoriented. I've lost all sense of direction. This makes a cemetery seem like a cheerful place."

Romano wiped his forehead with his sleeve. Dust accumulated on his shirt left a muddy splotch on his face. "Prominent families in ancient Rome had elaborate gravesites, but the cemeteries in Vatican hill should be similar to these. Over the centuries, they built one layer on top of another and burrowed new levels below. The main roadway often spread two meters wide and high enough to accommodate four to eight layers of tombs. The Vatican Hill catacombs are probably three, maybe four levels deep. Hopefully they haven't collapsed."

Craig coughed dank dusty air from his lungs. "Is there enough oxygen for a person to stay in these catacombs?"

"During the war, Communists utilized catacombs for concealing weapons used against the Fascists and later against the Nazis." He laughed hoarsely. "And then against the Italian government when the Communists were trying to take control. They sometimes lived for weeks in catacombs."

Craig glanced at the barely visible lights ahead of them. "Let's catch up with the others. I'm not interested in learning what it's like to be lost in catacombs."

Thirty minutes later, Craig leaned against his Ferrari and wiped grime from his face and neck with a towel. "You're going to spend at least two days in the catacombs under the Vatican. If you have to dig out a collapsed passageway to reach the railroad station, it could be four or five days."

Romano shrugged. "These tombs and passageways don't bother me, especially when I consider the rewards. But how will you arrange for a suitable freight car to transport the loot to the outside without drawing suspicion?"

"There's a famous Bernini fountain in northern Italy, in a town called Granople. It was damaged during World War Two. The Diocese bishop petitioned the Vatican for money to pay for bringing replacement marble in from a quarry. Vatican officials, playing politics, refused. This week, Bishop Baccalete was blessed beyond his highest expectations when a wealthy benefactor visited him and offered to pay for the marble. This benefactor has arranged for marble to be shipped at the appropriate time to the Vatican. You'll hide the treasures in crates containing the marble. When the freight cars arrive at Granople, we'll transfer the treasures to a truck and disappear into the French Alps, where my merchandise dealers will be waiting."

Romano shook his head. "It is so simple and yet so ingenious."

Craig smiled. "We have to thank Cardinal Lastavis and his obsession with power for providing the opportunity. He tossed our eager young priest and Bishop Baccalete into my lap."

"Baccalete and the young priest can identify you," Romano said. "We'll have to kill them after we have the treasures."

"Baccalete met a middle-aged, gray-haired, slightly stooped Frenchman." Craig replied. "I'll make the decision on the young priest."

"He'll know too much," Romano persisted. "We have to kill him."

"He'll never meet you or know your role," Craig said. "So he is my problem, not yours. Be sure you remember that."

Craig pondered their exchange as he climbed into the Ferrari. Romano's blunt macho mentality could make him react brashly in a confrontation during the robbery. Offsetting that, Romano would be fearless, brutally efficient, and loyal in a fight.

Romano clambered in beside him. "Join me for a drink and lunch. I know an excellent place near the casino."

Craig started the car. "I have something else already planned."

CHAPTER 21

▼

Craig followed the doctor down a long corridor. The doctor's bald head reflected the overhead lights. Small tufts of gray hair remained in shallow lines above his ears. He wore a blue coat with a badly mismatched tie. Horn-rimmed glasses and a goatee gave him a scholarly appearance.

"We transferred your sister to this section last night," the doctor said. "Earlier this week, she attacked the nurse who tried to bring her in from the garden terrace for dinner. Yesterday she was banging on her window with the chair, trying to break it out so she could go outdoors."

"Joan loves being outdoors with the flowers and trees," Craig replied. "I brought her here because you have a large outdoor area. I'm paying you to keep someone with her all the time so that she can stay outside. You can bring the dinner to her."

"Your sister has to come in at night. She has to stay indoors when it is raining or too cold. She becomes angry whenever we try to restrict her movements. She tried to climb the fence enclosing the sanatorium. We accommodate her wishes as much as possible. But we have to impose some rules." The doctor paused at a door and unlocked it. "For years, your sister made progress. She learned to speak, dress, feed, and bathe herself. Now that dexterity is lessening as brain deterioration continues. Her sensing of that loss fuels her growing anguish."

Craig followed him into a large room with a television, a sofa, a bed, a table and chair bolted down to the floor, a small refrigerator, and an adjoining bathroom. Two TV cameras in the ceiling allowed monitoring of the room. The window was protected by a crosshatch of metal rods.

Joan sat in an upholstered chair, staring out the window at the terrace and landscaped grounds. She glanced toward the door; and then jumped up from the chair, a smile blanketing her face. "Crraigg. Crraigg."

Craig walked over to meet her onrush, wrapped his arms around her, and hugged her. "I'm sorry I couldn't come back sooner. I've been very busy. Let's walk around outside."

"Ride. Peese, Crraigg. Ride."

He nodded. "Okay. I have the Ferrari."

Joan scrambled from the bed and yanked clothes from drawers, tossing them on the floor in her frenzy to find the right combination. She finally held up the same outfit she wore the day she walked on the stone fence with Darlena. "This? This, Crraigg?"

"That's good. I'll wait outside while you dress."

When he closed the door, the doctor caught Craig's arm. "You should not take her for a drive. She could be very dangerous in the car."

"I'll be careful."

"I don't think you realize how strongly her sense of deterioration is impacting her emotions," the doctor cautioned. "Her outbursts will continue to increase with time."

Craig ignored an emerging headache and turned to look into the doctor's face. "I'm paying you to give her as much freedom and enjoyment as possible, regardless of the difficulties. Make sure you do that."

Craig leaned against a tree, watching Joan kick at leaves accumulated on the ground. It was beautiful and peaceful here in the forest. She had always loved trees and flowers and the feel of breeze blowing her hair. Pine scented the air. Joan ambled around, stopping often to tug at a small plant or strip a leaf off a low branch. She mumbled and giggled, seemingly oblivious to his presence. Periodically, she would suddenly glance around, her eyes darting like a frightened antelope. When she spotted him, her face would brighten. Then she would become lost again in the tranquil world surrounding her.

He glanced at his watch. They had been here for two hours. He needed to leave. Critical details of the robbery remained to be finalized. He walked over to her. "Let's ride some more. Then we'll go back."

Anxiety swept across Joan's face. "Nooo. St-ay. St-ay here." Joan turned to run, stumbled as her feet tangled in tree roots, and tumbled to the ground.

Craig helped her up and guided her toward the car.

Incoherent words spewed from her mouth. The closer they came to the car, the more she fought. Her fingers clawed his hand grasping her arm. Even with her fingernails trimmed to nubs, she raked into his skin until blood came.

Craig grabbed her wrists and pinned her arms. "Joan, we have to go. I'll come back often. I promise."

"Noo!" She struggled to pull free. When she couldn't yank free, she began sobbing. "Peese. Peese, Crraigg. I ha-ate the ro-oom."

He released his grip on her. "You can stay awhile longer. But then we have to leave."

A smile swept away the torment on her face. She clapped her hands together and became immersed again in the plants and trees around her.

Craig trudged to the car and leaned against it, pondering the situation. Her anger would return when he insisted on leaving, forcing him to drag her back to the sanatorium crying and fighting. He paced back and forth in front of the car, watching her.

Joan bent down, grasped a flower, and fondled the pedals in her fingers.

His earlier headache returned, stronger than before. The forest and drives in the Ferrari were the only refuges she had known from cell-like rooms and people in white uniforms. The forest accepted her, tolerated her, and entertained her. Outdoors and the forest were where she wanted to stay.

"Lo-ook, Crraigg."

He watched Joan point toward a red cardinal perched on an evergreen tree limb. Its shrill call seemed to be serenading her. The bird soared upward and vanished among the maze of tree branches.

"Go-ood bye," she called after the bird and became engrossed again with the patch of yellow flowers.

Craig knew now what he had to do. He would take Joan back home to the United States, build his dream house along a mountain stream, bring in some full-time nurses to help him care for her, and let her run free in the forest. Robbing the Vatican would be his final job.

He walked over and gently placed his hands on her shoulders. "I have some work to finish up here in Italy. It will take me about a month. No more than thirty days. Then we'll go back home. I'm going to build a house next to a bubbling stream surrounded by forest. You and I will live there, plus a few people to help us. You won't be locked in a room. You can run around in the forest all day and sleep on a porch overlooking the water at night. Would you like that?"

Joan's face brightened. "Weally? Weally, Crraigg?"

Craig smiled. "I need time to finish up my work here in Europe. So you have to stay at your place for another thirty days. You have to be nice to the people and do what they ask. Can you do that for me for the next thirty days?"

Joan's face turned serious as she nodded. "I twy hard. I weally twy hard."

He squeezed her hand and helped her up. "I know you will."

An hour later, Craig swung the Ferrari onto the main highway and sped toward Rome. His mind churned through details and changes. The current plan to fence the stolen treasures through a variety of dealers requires staying in Europe for three to four months. So he would have to cut a deal before the robbery to deliver all the treasures for cash to one dealer. That means giving a large discount, but that's okay. Unfortunately, Karl Brauder is the only dealer who can handle it all and ante up the cash quickly. That son-of-a-bitch will pull a double-cross if he can.

Craig ran through the list of dealers again, trying to figure how to avoid cutting a deal before the robbery with Brauder. His mind drew a blank. There is no other way to keep his promise of one month to Joan. It's good to have Romano Pantel. Because at some point, they may have to face off with Brauder's henchmen.

CHAPTER 22

▼

Craig climbed from the taxi and hustled up the steps onto the porch of a sprawling wooden structure. Ornate woodwork adorned the wide porch that stretched the length of the building. He had been here numerous times, but still paused to admire the architecture. These old casinos on Lubeck Bay in Northern Germany had survived the saturation bombing by Allied warplanes during World War Two. Perhaps they survived because they were remote from industrial areas. Perhaps Allied generals chose to spare them, knowing they had been the preferred resorts for many political leaders and aristocrats of Europe and might be again after the war ended.

This building was the most elaborate of all, spanning a city block and accentuated by tall corner turrets spiraling above its Mediterranean slate roof. The enormous lobby radiated the same grandeur, with stained oak walls, seventeenth century furniture, and a floor-to-ceiling stone fireplace centered in one wall. A glittering array of cut-glass French doors decorated with billowing Austrian drapes filled the side facing Lubeck Bay. Chandeliers hanging from oak ceiling beams reinforced the resemblance to a palace grand ballroom.

Craig could almost see ghosts of past kings, princes, and nobles passing through the lobby on their way to the gaming tables. But the mix of customers had changed. Elegantly dressed older people, their mannerisms marking them as traditional Continental nobility, still clustered in polite conversation. The newly rich intermingled with them, less formally attired, although showy jewelry and designer dresses bedecked their women. There were very few Americans here. Americans preferred Mediterranean playgrounds like Monte Carlo. The Lubeck casinos smelled of old money, old traditions, teatime with crumpets, and afternoon promenades along the bay. From all appearances, the casino still thrived on old money.

He walked to the lobby desk and spoke in German. "Good afternoon. My name is Mr. Reynolds. I have a reservation."

"We've been expecting you."

Craig turned toward the feminine voice and saw a tall, slender woman with waist-length blonde hair surrounding a fair-skinned face and blue eyes typical of a Northern German. The ankle length dress clung tightly to her body, splitting open up to the thighs to expose lithe, perfectly shaped legs.

"I'm Tanya Schumann," she said. "I'll be your personal escort during your visit here, compliments of Herr Brauder."

Craig smiled. "Herr Brauder has excellent taste."

"I'll show you to your room. Where's your luggage?"

He held up his travel bag. "This is it." He could have added another comment. One bag makes it simpler to dispose of the location transmitter that Brauder will plant in his luggage.

Tanya clasped his hand and led him into the main gaming room, her soft fingers plying his skin. The hum of roulette wheels and dealers' voices provided background for shouts of winners and disgruntled sighs of losers. Women in low-cut gowns moved among the tables, replenishing drinks, bringing fresh stacks of chips, and pausing to cajole patrons into larger bets. Smoke engulfed the room, wafting up to chandeliers swaying overhead.

Tanya paused at an elevator secluded in a corner of the immense room. The door opened and they stepped inside. "Do you come here often?" she asked.

"I've visited in the past, but it's been awhile. Nothing seems to have changed."

"Nothing here ever changes," she replied. "Only the people change."

Craig glanced at her. Her accent and pronunciation had the ring of German aristocracy and wealthy schooling. Brauder maintained a cadre of call girls. Some were sophisticated and others were simply big tits and hot twats. All were trained to service, seduce, con, and compromise clients and high rollers. Anyone ensnared in Brauder's web, whether by debt or extortion, never escaped. Brauder sucked life out of his victims and left the shell to dangle and wither in the web. Tanya Schumann didn't fit the mold of Brauder's sexual marauders. Her softness and uncertainty appeared out of place. But maybe the demeanor adroitly hid a predator.

The elevator door opened, revealing a short dark-stained oak hallway decorated with a long marble-top table, two large oil paintings, and a life-size statue of a nude woman so meticulously sculptured that it would compete with the best in the Vatican. Craig recognized the Ming dynasty vase on the table as one of his first sales to Brauder. The polished marble floor gleamed. They were in the private wing where Brauder himself stayed. Brauder apparently sensed this would be a high stakes meeting.

Tanya punched in the combination at a closed door. Craig noted the numbers. She was not one of Brauder's elite. The professionals always blocked the client's view of lock combinations.

They stepped into a short hallway. Tanya paused at a door, inserted a computer card, and handed the card to him.

Craig stepped into a suite as richly furnished as the corridor, with a Persian rug, plush Queen Anne chairs, a velour love seat, and all the elegant accessories. A glassed liquor cabinet was amply stocked. Off to one side, a door opened into a spacious adorned bedroom.

Tanya lifted an already opened wine bottle from a silver ice bucket and sauntered out onto the balcony overlooking the shimmering water splashing against the brown, sandy beach of Lubeck Bay. Breeze ruffled the soft hair around her face as she poured two glasses of wine.

Craig sipped the wine. A dry Rhine Piesporter Riesling opened at the peak of its flavor. Brauder was an uncompromising wine connoisseur who would serve vintage wine to a man being tortured.

"So what brings you back here?" she asked.

"I like the sound of gaming tables and the tradition of promenading along the beach and long porches prior to afternoon tea and pastries in the dining room. The first time I came, people talked about how the East Germans used to have guard towers with machine guns poking out on the opposite shore, and patrol boats searching for defectors foolish enough to risk an escape from the workers' paradise." He raised his glass and lightly touched hers. "To the marvelous casinos created by Christian capitalism, ensuring that no inveterate gambler will go unsatisfied."

She reached out to gently caress his hand. "I'll be available to provide you with whatever services you need, both at the gaming tables and later tonight here in your suite."

"You look more like a woman completing her studies at the University of Vienna than a casino hostess."

Her face flushed. She glanced down at the ring on her finger that signified her attendance at the University. "You're very observant. Be assured that I'll satisfy whatever needs you have."

For the first time Craig studied her face closely. The dazzling blue of her eyes could not hide the weary spirit gasping for breath. Brauder had sunk his fangs into her and drained out most of the blood. Unfortunate for her, but it didn't make her any less dangerous. "Why would a young woman with your family pedigree and financial capabilities work as a casino hostess for Karl Brauder?" He wasn't sure why he asked the question. She would give him a reason unrelated to the truth. Maybe he did it to tell her he knew her role and she could drop the pretense and simply survive the evening. Maybe the smothered warmth he detected deep inside her made him curious.

Tanya extended her hand to him, a mechanical smile on her face. "It's time for your meeting with Herr Brauder."

They walked down the hallway and turned into an alcove. A husky man with short blond hair and a bulge beneath his coat unlocked a ten-foot high set of double doors built from black walnut planks emblazoned with carvings of Teutonic warriors. Tanya led him down a wide corridor covered with plush carpet. The stained ash wall panels, darkened over the years to a deep brown, provided background for oil paintings by Cézanne and other European masters. Craig spotted a Rembrandt that he had stolen from a French chateau. Brauder had a passion for masterpieces.

Tanya paused before another ornately carved wooden door and lightly struck the gilded gold doorknocker. "When you finish your business with Herr Brauder, I'll be waiting in your room. I promise you won't be disappointed with me tonight."

She kissed him tenderly on his lips.

Craig watched her hurry down the corridor. Tanya lacked the provocative strut of Brauder's typical hostesses. Her eyes portrayed anguished capitulation rather than lust. Brauder's bordello was rapidly consuming her soul.

He pushed the door open and stepped into a large room with upholstered chairs and massive marble tables. His eyes noted the absence of windows. A heavyset man with receding gray hair that magnified his large head sat in a leather chair behind an oversize antique oak desk. His immaculate suit included a glittering diamond stickpin and enormous gold cufflinks. Jeweled rings glistened on three fingers.

"Welcome back to Lubeck Bay, Mr. Reynolds." A strong German accent punctuated the speech, making the deep voice sound guttural. "It's been a long time. Your skills at the gaming tables need revitalizing."

Craig slid into a chair opposite Karl Brauder. After World War Two, Brauder's father purchased part ownership of the casino, using money stolen during his tenure as a Gestapo officer. Over the years, the Brauders eliminated their partners and competition, eventually creating a stranglehold on the gambling casinos along Lubeck Bay. From here, money furtively transferred in and out of their criminal operations.

"Judging by the crowds," Craig said, "your gambling business is flourishing without me."

"It's not like the old days. The aristocracy of Europe is poor. We tolerate them because they maintain the aura of historic pomp and wealth."

Craig glanced at the other man sitting nearby. The man had a large square chin, the body bulk of a Germanic Frank, and the cold, cruel eyes of a predator sniffing the blood of wounded prey. His black hair was sheared close to his skull. Craig already knew Gerhard Kusler. As Brauder's chief lieutenant, he closed most deals, collected overdue payments, killed competitors, and settled scores with anyone unfortunate enough to irritate Brauder. Like young lions roaming the same jungle, Craig and Kusler had studied each other, wary of the other's talents, each sensing that someday they would collide on a pathway too narrow to pass.

Craig turned his attention back to Brauder. "I have a business proposition. Because the merchandise is so unique and diverse and timing is critical, I'm offering you the opportunity to handle all of it."

Brauder's face remained emotionless. "You know I have the best distribution system in Europe."

"I also require a large down payment as collateral to provide the financing I need."

Brauder shrugged. "That can be arranged if the merchandise interests me. How much do you want in advance?"

"Fifteen million Euros."

Brauder's face furrowed. "I don't provide that amount of money until the property is in my hands. I never give more than ten percent of the value in advance, even to my most valued suppliers."

Craig relaxed in his chair. "I'm asking for less than ten percent, as good faith indication that you'll rapidly move the merchandise and give me full value."

"What exactly do you have in mind?" Brauder's voice conveyed heightened interest.

"You'll hear about it when it happens. All you need to know now is that it includes negotiable bonds, stocks, paintings by the masters, and a fabulous assortment of jewelry and antiques."

"This is too much money to risk on a speculative robbery of such magnitude," Brauder said. "The only way we'll participate is as a partner with knowledge of the plans. I can finance it and provide valuable assistance."

Craig stood up. "That's your decision to make, Karl. There are other groups out there who will risk the money to have a chance at replacing you as the premier merchandise fence. They may require more time to move it, but they will come up with the money. They like doing business with me. I didn't come here to bargain. This is a take it or leave it deal. You either trust me or we don't do business."

Brauder's fingers rubbed the knuckles of his other hand as he stared at Craig. Several times his eyes shifted toward Kusler.

Finally he nodded. "Your word is good enough for me. You're the ultimate thief and I'm the ultimate dealer. It would be foolish for us to not do business together."

"Timing is critical," Craig said. "Before my flight leaves at noon tomorrow, I need a credit voucher from a highly respectable bank to deposit in a dummy corporation account in Switzerland."

Gerhard Kusler scowled as he prowled up from his chair. "That amount of money is not available on such short notice."

Brauder raised a hand to silence him. "Mr. Reynolds is a young man in a hurry. We must not delay his plans. Gerhard will arrange for your money. Now you shall join me for dinner and afterwards you may enjoy whatever pleasures my casino provides."

Kusler paused at the door. "You know the penalty for failure to deliver on your portion of the bargain."

Craig returned his steely gaze. "I receive a personal visit from the surviving residue of the Gestapo?"

"Your glib tongue and talent for disguise will not help you. I'm like the wolf stalking the swift antelope. Eventually I have my feast."

Craig flashed a smile. "Don't stand upwind of me. Your odor is very distinctive."

Kusler glowered at him, seemed on the verge of a retort, but turned and disappeared through the doorway.

Craig shifted his attention back to Brauder. "There must be a full moon out tonight. Kusler is drooling at the mouth again."

That brought a harsh laugh from Brauder. "You have lost none of your American wit. Gerhard enjoys the taste of blood. You and I are professionals who know the value of trust in a business deal. I have a marvelous dinner waiting and an old friend who is anxious to see you."

He led the way through a side door into an adjacent room. A table lavishly apportioned with fine china, silver, and flickering candelabra filled the room.

But the tall woman beside the table claimed Craig's attention. Her short blonde hair outlined a face filled with fleshy lips, large cheekbones, and smoldering blue eyes. Large breasts protruded against the plunging V-neck blouse. Folds of satin in the cocktail dress magnified a figure that exuded voluptuous femininity. Her thick legs spread apart like a German nightclub entertainer promenading on stage before leering patrons.

Memories of what had been, and what might have been, flooded into Craig's mind. Four years ago, while negotiating a deal with Brauder, he met Groda Voight at the gaming tables. She was one of Brauder's casino hustlers, seducing heavy gamblers back to the table, urging them to higher bets, and dangling the lure of a night liaison after they finished off one more stack of chips. In that role, Groda had no equal.

Craig had glanced up from his poker game that evening to see her standing in the same pose as tonight, her fierce eyes consuming him, seemingly penetrating into his body and mind to search for his soul. Without a word, not even a nod of recognition, she had walked away.

When he had returned to his suite two hours later, she was waiting. That night had been like no other he had ever experienced. Her undulating body and ravenous mouth were irresistible and insatiable. He had returned to Lubeck Bay a half dozen times after that. A few times he dealt with Brauder, sometimes he gambled, but mostly he came to see Groda. The fervor of their relationship escalated with each visit.

After eight months, he abruptly quit coming. He hadn't been back to Lubeck Bay since that time, choosing instead to conduct his business deals with Kusler in Hamburg. He hadn't seen or spoken to Groda in three years.

Brauder's voice interrupted the trance. "Groda directs all of the casino's activities now. As my most trusted confidante, she's involved in every phase of the business."

Craig reached out to clasp her outstretched hand and kissed her on the cheek. "Congratulations. I'm certain you're a valuable asset."

Her hand gripped his tightly, her fingers stroking his palm. "I've missed you. It's good to have you back at Lubeck Bay again." She handed him a glass of wine and lifted hers. "Let's toast to success in all your endeavors."

Craig sampled the wine. "You remembered that I like full-bodied Bordeaux."

Her smile deepened. "I remember everything about you." She seated herself directly across from him.

For the next two hours, they dined, starting with thin slices of herring seasoned with apple and onion bits, proceeding through three other appetizers to the heartier fare of wine-basted venison and potato croquettes, and finishing with apfelstrudel, paper-thin layers of pastry filled with apple slices, raisins, and nuts. Conversation ranged through Brauder's recent purchase of several extensive wine collections, the continuing escalation in prices of fine art, and the substitution of the Eurodollar for European currencies.

"The Euro is an insult to the dominance of Germany and its Mark in the European economy," Brauder had groused. Brauder had also probed numerous times for a hint of what merchandise would be stolen.

Craig spoke vaguely of "breathtaking jewelry pieces out of circulation for many years", tossed in the subterfuge of an array of uncut and polished diamonds, and described the oil paintings as "a cross-section of European masters, which insurance companies would gladly redeem".

Dinner with Brauder always included the finest German wines, mouth-pleasing cuisine that settled heavy on the stomach, and civilized conversation. All of it aimed at graciously masking the undertone of manipulation and threatened dire consequences of not delivering as promised.

Every time Craig looked at Groda, her eyes were locked on his face, studying each feature, probing every reaction. How many times during their eight month liaison had he awakened to find her lying beside him, staring into his face with those penetrating eyes? Tonight, each facial expression and every inflection of her voice rekindled a memory. Not for a moment had he doubted that she would survive well without him and soon attract Brauder's personal attention. Brauder used the hustlers at the Casino as his personal sexual harem. But none of them had ever attained a position in his business. Groda Voight had become both his mistress and his casino partner.

They concluded the evening with drinks on the balcony overlooking Lubeck Bay.

"Kusler has made arrangements for the money to be transferred to your account," Brauder said. "After we've completed the business transactions, a stack of chips will be available to you, compliments of the casino. You'll find Tanya Schumann to be a very attentive hostess."

"She's younger than your traditional hostesses," Craig commented.

"Karl won her at the gaming tables," Groda said. "She's the daughter of a wealthy banker who became too enamored with our women and strong drink.

His debts pushed him to the brink of bankruptcy. Rather than see her father endure Kusler's collection methods and the humiliation of bankruptcy, Tanya agreed to work for us until the debt is repaid." Her tone shifted sarcastic. "It seemed a pity to waste her talents in the kitchen."

Brauder motioned toward the door. "Come to my office. Kusler has the paperwork ready for completing our business transaction."

Craig reached out to clasp Groda's hand. "It was good to see you again. I'll come say goodbye tomorrow before leaving."

Her fingernails dug into his palm. "I'll look forward to that."

Brauder watched her step through the doorway and stride down the corridor. "Groda's great grandmother was the half sister of Hitler's mistress Eva Braun. She possesses the same magnificent Germanic spirit and the sexual prowess of a Nordic goddess. A very remarkable woman, as you're well aware. It was fortunate that you chose to leave her when you did. It saved me the trouble of having you killed. Groda would have remained your mistress as long as you were alive." Brauder opened the door to the office. "But you didn't come here for casual conversation. Let's conduct business."

Craig followed him into the office. "Why don't you let Tanya Schumann go? With Groda, you don't need another mistress and you have seductive women standing in line to be casino hostesses."

The corners of Brauder's lips turned up in a semi-smile. "I'm not the one that's keeping Tanya Schumann here. She belongs to Groda."

Two hours later, Craig stepped into his suite and closed the door behind him. He had gambled without fervor or success, glad to see the chips disappear. Tanya Schumann had apparently decided to wait in the suite to serve his late night needs. Brauder's words replayed in his mind. "She belongs to Groda."

His ears picked up the sound in the bathroom of splashing water. He tossed his coat onto the chair. The vision of Tanya's lithe body stretched out in the bathtub beneath semi-transparent bubbles appealed to him. She still retained a sensual innocence, a pleasant contrast to the hardened lust of Brauder's usual casino hostesses.

He eased through the bathroom doorway.

A woman with succulent red nipples protruding from her breasts and a gloating smile on her fleshy lips lolled in the spacious marble tub.

Craig folded his arms. "Where's Tanya?"

Groda slithered up from the water, hands on hips, and legs spread apart in her patented pose. "Do you really care?"

Craig's eyes scanned her fleshy body. Lustrous blonde pelvic hair matted against her tanned skin. He grasped a towel and tossed it to her. "You'll catch a cold standing in a wet bathtub." He turned to leave the bathroom.

"Don't you dare walk away from me again!" Groda yelled.

He leaned against the doorframe and watched her dry herself and ooze into an almost transparent mini-robe. "I didn't walk away. I ran for my life."

Her husky voice conveyed a mixture of anger and strained emotion. "I waited for you to return. I waited a week, a month, almost a year. Every time footsteps paused outside the door, my heart jumped into my throat, hoping you had come back. At the least, you could have said good-bye."

"An alcoholic doesn't go back to the tavern to say good-bye and have a final drink to celebrate the decision on abstinence. You're an intoxicating narcotic that requires more each time to satisfy the need. The only relationship you understand is master and slave." He turned away into the bedroom.

She caught up with him and reached up to massage his arms and shoulders. Her lips lingered inches from his as she spoke. "It will be different this time. You can have everything you want from me and still control your own life."

"Brauder would be less than pleased by that arrangement."

"You and I could own Brauder's empire. I know all the details and all the contacts. You can control his men." She opened the mini-robe and pressed her body against him. Her hips gyrated as her mouth massaged his neck and cheek. "You and me," she purred. "Together we can have it all."

Craig shifted his eyes toward the bed and saw disheveled covers. "You horny bitch." He pushed her away. "Still as versatile as ever, aren't you? You came in here and ravaged Tanya as an appetizer and threw her out to make room for the main course. You're right about it being different this time. Four years ago, you were a young woman with an insatiable sexual appetite and a desire to be with powerful men. Now you're the shark devouring everything you touch. Power isn't enough. You lust for the taste of flesh."

She leaned back against the table, her breasts pushed out and her legs spread open. "Someday you'll have to deal personally with me. On that day, you'll crawl on your hands and knees to beg me for another chance. But there won't be another chance. Either feast with me now or be devoured when judgement day comes."

"I've never liked the taste of raw flesh." Craig walked over to the liquor cabinet and pulled out a bottle of red wine. "Close the door on your way out."

Groda grabbed her dress and yanked it on. "For now, I'll sate my appetite on Karl Brauder and anyone else who comes into my ocean. I especially enjoy tasty morsels like Tanya Schumann." She played her tongue over her lips. "I like the sheer euphoria of tasting young succulent flesh while they struggle to escape. Their weakening whimpers and the smell of their desperation arouse me."

She paused at the door. "You arouse me in an entirely different way. I never wanted to devour or hurt you. I only wanted to wrap my body around you and never let you go. If you should decide to swim with the shark, I'm in the room on the left down the hall. The door will be unlocked and slightly ajar. But this is your last chance to join me as a partner. If you walk out on me again, you're throwing blood in the water. When there is blood in the water, the shark comes to feast."

Groda stalked out into the hallway.

Craig paced onto the balcony and stared down at the beach. A solitary couple strolled in the darkness beside the water. They were either lovers or people too broke to gamble any more. The noise and lights of the casino filled the night air. The salty aroma of Lubeck Bay filled his nostrils.

For the tenth time, he debated his decision to do an exclusive deal with Brauder. Kusler will begin sniffing around, trying to ferret out his target. Groda will lurk in the wings, relishing the opportunity to help Brauder double-cross him. In a confrontation, Brauder will compromise in order to get the treasures. But Kusler and Groda want both his treasures and his blood.

But regardless of the increased risk, dealing with Brauder allows him to keep his promise to Joan. Take Joan home and give her a chance to be happy. He would not renege on that commitment.

But what about the other woman that was important to him? His mind flashed back to Darlena's gymnastics on the stone fence. He visualized her eyes glistening and her perfectly formed body virtually floating in air. He mused about her contagious, childlike enthusiasm at Villa d'Este. Darlena possessed more than beauty. She exploded with vitality, audacity, and warmth. She freely gave all she had without reservation. Yet, she retained an unrelenting independence and an unconquerable spirit. Would Darlena consider coming with him to the United States?

Craig shook away the fantasy. Duping Thad into helping him rob the Vatican would be unforgivable. Darlena represented the magnificent, sparkling crown jewel that he could never hope to hold.

CHAPTER 23

▼

Craig tossed his travel bag on the tapestry-like spread of the canopied bed. The spacious room contained an ornately carved mahogany dresser, a rose-colored settee, two upholstered chairs, and a mahogany writing desk with elaborate scrollwork. Louis the Fifteenth would feel right at home. He walked to the draped window and scanned the backside of the resort. Twilight silhouetted trees stretching away toward gently sloping hills. Below him, a wooden deck spanned a small stream and dropped down to a grassed pathway meandering through landscaped gardens and ending at lighted clay tennis courts. People playing doubles occupied three of the four courts.

He punched in a number on his cell phone and heard Romano's gruff voice answer.

"Brauder's men," Craig said, "followed my taxi here in a black BMW, using the transmitter signal Brauder inserted inside the lining of my bag at Lubeck."

"I saw the car come in," Romano replied. "It's backed in among parked cars in an unlighted section. There are two men. One is a short, balding man in a brown business suit. The other is a large blond-haired German wearing a short-sleeve brown and blue stripped turtleneck. The big German is sitting in the driver's seat. The short man has intermingled with people at the outside bar next to the entry fountain."

"I'll distract the short guy," Craig said. "You take care of the man at the BMW and disable their car. Don't make a mess. We don't want police speculating about a couple dead bodies."

"I'll give him a headache he won't forget," Romano replied.

Craig clicked off the phone. It was time to disappear. The fifteen million Euros deposited in Paris had already siphoned through a variety of accounts, making it impossible even for a man of Brauder's connections to trace. With the exception of two million Euros, the money would vanish in the labyrinths of the European banking system. Brauder's tracking system would detect the two million resurfacing in a series of transactions at a small Paris bank. Kusler would quickly narrow the list down to three possible robbery targets in France.

Craig dialed the front desk.

A few minutes later, a young uniformed bellhop appeared at the door. Craig handed him the travel bag and some Euros. "Take this down to the tennis courts and set it beside the net on the unused court."

The short bespectacled man attired in a brown business suit heard the beep on his cell phone and clicked it on.

"Reynolds is on the move with his bag," the man hunched in the driver's seat of the BMW said. "He's going out the backside. This may be the rendezvous with his accomplice."

"I'll see what he's doing," the glasses-wearing man replied. "You watch the front." He hustled through the manicured front gardens and along the shadowy pathway circling toward the rear of the resort.

He heard the faint plonk, plonk of rackets pounding tennis balls.

He never heard the footsteps behind him.

The big man in the BMW lit a cigarette and settled back, scanning the parking area and periphery of the hotel through night vision binoculars.

A figure emerged from a side entrance and hurried toward the parking area.

The German climbed from the BMW, crushed his cigarette into the ground, and adjusted the zoom on his night vision goggles. The tall figure disappeared and then re-emerged among a row of cars. It was definitely Reynolds.

But why did the transmitter still show Reynolds behind the resort? The German clasped his cell phone and raised it toward his mouth to alert his partner.

A steel blade plunged into his back and pierced his kidney. A huge leathery hand smothered the scream in his throat. The momentum of the thrust drove the German against the door of an adjacent car. Paralyzed by pain and pinned by the powerful man behind him, his lifeblood ran down his buckling legs.

Romano spoke into his cell phone. "My man is immobilized."

The headlights of an Audi blinked twice and then sped away into the night.

Romano hoisted the husky man onto his shoulder and carried the limp body into the nearby forest. He would dump the burly German into a ravine where the body would never be found. But Brauder would quickly surmise what had happened to his man. Craig Reynolds was a clever jewel thief, but he lacked the brutality necessary for dealing with men like Brauder. Killing the henchman would send a clear signal. Anyone who tries to double-cross us will die.

As Romano lifted the body onto the rocky ledge, his flashlight beam momentarily illuminated the arm. He stared at the Swastika emblazoned on the muscular arm. Romano's grandfather had been captured, tortured, and disemboweled by SS troopers near the end of the war.

The large blade in Romano's hand hacked into the flesh of the German's arm. Romano would send Brauder a gift appropriate for a man who still admired those Nazi bastards.

CHAPTER 24

▼

Craig met Thad at the Arch of the Bells gate and followed him onto the Square of the First Roman Martyrs. A group of African nuns milled ahead of them, listening to a priest chattering in a strange language. Craig guided Thad along the wall of the German College and Cemetery and paused beneath the 'Teutones in Pace' inscription over the entry. Sprawling cypress trees, their skin darkened and their limbs creaking from old age, shaded the gravesites.

He took Thad's hefty shoulder bag and glanced inside to assure himself that Thad had transferred all the needed equipment from the suitcase Thad had carried in an hour earlier. Vatican guards never search suitcases of Vatican priests. Now he had all the necessary electronics and gear for reconnoitering the catacombs and cracking the vault.

"Where are the rest of Sergio's drawings?" he asked.

Thad shook his head. "I haven't been back to the Archives to retrieve them. The only drawings you don't have are the museum buildings and underground garage. I don't understand why you want those."

"We need an alternate location in case something prevents us from using the summer house. You said the basement section beneath the museums is used only for storage. Bring me everything Sergio had. The more we know about the building layouts and unused passageways, the better our chance of keeping the Pope hidden from Lastavis."

"I'll go into the Archives tomorrow morning and get the rest," Thad replied. He wiped perspiration from his forehead with the palm of his hand. "We need to tell Baccalete what's happening, so he can begin assembling physicians and support people."

"Soon, but not yet," Craig reiterated. "We can't risk someone tipping off Lastavis. Leave a message at the hotel when you have the drawings."

Craig walked away before Thad could reply. He cut between St. Stephen's Abyssinian church and the back of the basilica. As soon as Thad disappeared into the San Carlo Palace, he reversed his direction and headed for the railroad station. Two priests strolled past him, going toward the gardens. Four men worked on unloading a freight car pushed back into the hollowed-out hill behind the railroad station.

He scrambled on hands and knees beneath the wooden loading platform beside the tracks, rolled onto his back, assembled the battery-powered drill, and wrapped it in a soundproofing blanket. Flattened out on his stomach, he began drilling a hole through the hard soil, stopping to add new sections to the bit as the hole deepened.

Down and down the bit went. It finally broke through into empty space. Craig extracted the drill bits and fed a long flexible antenna from a spool into the hole. Then he attached a global positioning signal to the antenna, activated it, and buried the transmitter in the dirt. Romano could track the signal to find the exact location to dig up from the catacombs.

Next he anchored one end of heavy nylon fishing line into the bottom of the railroad platform and spooled the weighted line down the hole. It would hold the weight of a heavy man like Romano.

His eyes scanned the area. The men remained preoccupied with the railroad car contents. He crawled from beneath the platform, brushed dirt from his clothes, and strolled away from the railroad area. Task number one had been completed. He crossed behind the basilica, intermingled with a group of Papal workers, and walked to the post office in Vatican Village.

A big man in work clothes, carrying a carpenter's toolbox, ambled up beside him.

Craig handed Romano an electronic pack that looked like a handheld computer. "The global positioning signal is buried at the tracks. This will pick up the signal. The computer is programmed with Sergio's sketches of the catacombs. Use it to guide you through the catacombs to the signal. Before we go to the carriage garage, let me show you a unique fountain."

They walked down Via della Posta to the far end, circled around a building, and emerged onto a small plaza. A fountain resembling a seventeenth-century galleon squirted water from sixteen cannons. Water gushed from some of the sails.

Romano frowned. "Why are we looking at this fountain?"

Craig pointed as though discussing the fountain. "Behind you to your left are the Vatican's fuel storage tanks. Fire is the Vatican's greatest nightmare. If the robbery comes unhinged and we need to fight our way out, lighting off those tanks will create a hell of a diversion. I've stashed firepower in the incoming freight cars, including armor-piercing bullets and incendiary grenade attachments for the AK-47 assault rifles. The tanks could also be lit off from a museum window. Orient yourself before you leave so you know how to hit these tanks from various locations."

They walked past the fuel tanks, through the Belvedere Court, and alongside the museums to the Giardino Quadrato plaza. One huge wooden door leading into the carriage garage was open.

"Let's hope they're not washing carriages," Craig muttered.

When they reached the vaulted corridor containing the carriages, Craig heard voices at the other end of the garage. A quick glance told him three men were working beside a fancy carriage. Two had their backs turned. The third crouched, facing them, as he pounded with a hammer.

They pressed back against the wall, watched, and waited.

The man turned away and scrounged in a large wooden box. Craig and Romano hustled across the open passageway into the wash section. Craig yanked up the grating. Romano clambered into the drain and reached up for his toolbox and Craig's shoulder bag.

"Use the cell phone to let me know when you're finished in the catacombs," Craig said.

Romano disappeared through the opening. Craig replaced the grating and left the garage. With the electronic signal and Sergio's drawings that they already had, Romano should have no problem tracing the catacomb routes to the railroad station and Papal Palace.

One more day of reconnoitering and his knowledge would be complete. But Craig needed Sergio's drawings of the museums to determine the most secure route for moving treasures to the carriage garage and catacombs. If they became trapped during the robbery, one option would be to duck into the catacombs, emerge into the Papal Palace, and escape down the Pope's Royal Staircase to the Bronze Door. Wound the Swiss Guards at the door and vanish into the crowd in St. Peter's Square. The more options they had, the better the odds of living through a no-quarter-asked-none-given confrontation.

But barring an unforeseen problem, there would be no confrontation. The Vatican would be left with an empty vault, stripped museums, and an angry, humiliated Cardinal Lastavis. With his papal ambitions destroyed, Lastavis would have no reason to continue drugging or to kill the Pope. Candalio would not return to the Vatican. So the Pope and Thad would be safe.

Craig figured that Darlena still would never forgive him for using Thad to help in the robbery, but perhaps she would not hate him. That would not be much consolation, but it was all he could hope for.

CHAPTER 25

▼

Karl Brauder glared at the crude sickle carved into the flesh, oblivious to the reek of putrefying flesh on the mutilated arm. The sickle point slashed into the heart of the Swastika. "Strasser's grandfather directed an espionage office during the war. No family has remained more loyal to the memory of the Third Reich." Brauder slammed his fist on the desk. "Mutilating his body is a deliberate insult."

Kusler stalked to the door and threw it open to lessen the stench. "I'll carve a Swastika in Reynold's heart after this is over."

Groda Voight reclined in an upholstered chair, her leather mini-skirt spread open at the top of her thighs to expose her silk thong. "I told you it was a waste of time to trail Craig. But this wasn't his work. He kills only when there's no other choice and he never advertises the fact. The sickle carved in Strasser's arm is the work of a Communist fanatic. Bring Brom Eidler in here. He knows more about the old regional Communist groups than anyone else."

The baldheaded, stooped man, his flushed face filled with sagging wrinkles, tossed the arm back into the box. "The sickle superimposed over a Swastika on captured Germans was done by Communists in Italy near the end of the war. It was especially popular among Communists in the Rome area."

Brauder scowled. "That means Reynolds is using an Italian Communist as a cohort in his robbery scheme. He would do that only if the heist location is in Italy. We've been looking in the wrong country."

"If we find that man, Craig will be nearby," Groda said. "Send people to canvas the major Italian cities, especially Rome. They can identify possible robbery targets and hunt for our Communist savage. Craig always picks working class accomplices who have strong knowledge of the area. They are adroit criminals in their own arena but unknown outside their locale."

Brauder leaned back in his leather chair. "Find that Communist bastard, but don't kill him until after the robbery."

His eyes focused on Groda Voight. "Then we'll deal with Craig Reynolds. This will be his last heist."

CHAPTER 26

▼

Darlena trudged up the stairs toward her fourth floor apartment. Five days of gymnastics tournaments in Romania and Bulgaria had exhausted her usually boundless energy. The return airplane flight had been cancelled by fog, forcing her to sit in the airport for twelve hours. She should have arrived yesterday evening instead of late forenoon of a dreary day following a sleepless night.

The realization that Italians were noncompetitive with Eastern European women gymnasts contributed to her weariness. Romanian women had swept all the awards. Watching tapes of the eighty-five pound, five-foot, fourteen-year-old Romanian Nadia Comaneci winning three gold medals with perfect scores at the 1976 Olympics had inspired Darlena to become an ardent gymnast. In gymnastics, small and lithe is good.

Perhaps this trip would inspire her again. She would carry a powerful message back to the Turin school. Rome is not the competition. To be the best in Italy is not enough. The standard for measuring performance is Eastern Europe, Russia, and the United States. Italian women could be that good. Someday they would be. One good night's sleep would transform her exhaustion and despair into determination and a direction for her new life.

Darlena unlocked the door to her apartment, lugged the cumbersome travel bag into the bedroom, dumped it on the floor, and stripped off her backpack. Nothing needed to be unpacked now. She plodded back to the front room, closed and bolted the door, pulled a bottle of carbonated water from the tiny refrigerator, and sagged down into the raggedy upholstered chair that represented one-fourth of the room's furniture.

The zesty carbonation tasted like vintage wine. She tossed her belt purse over the top of the wooden kitchen chair and watched with satisfaction as it ker-plunked expertly onto the cluttered three-legged table that served as dining table, work desk, and accumulator of anything that belonged elsewhere but wasn't worth the effort at the time.

With equal adroitness, she flipped her cell phone into the trash can. Papa had good intentions when he bought the cell phone for her, but his lack of knowledge had left her with a cell phone that was largely useless in Romania and had died completely during the layover at the airport. Tomorrow she would buy a new one that had more capability and a decent battery.

A small stack of mail sat on the lamp stool beside her upholstered chair. The landlady had collected her mail and put it in the room. She gulped more carbon-ated water as she browsed through the letters. She hoped for a particular letter. A voice deep inside kept warning her that Craig would not write or ever see her again. She refused to believe the voice. He would write and he would come to see her.

The first two letters were advertisements. She tossed the envelopes into the wastepaper basket without opening them. A small brochure showed sexy night-gowns and lacy undergarments. She glanced at the first several pages and dis-carded it. The landlady had said a woman needed sensuous nightwear to properly arouse her husband. Darlena figured at this time she didn't need sexy nightwear. She didn't have a husband. She didn't have any man to arouse.

The address on the fourth envelope had been printed by hand. She eagerly tore it open. Words scrawled across the page in almost illegible Italian. A Bulgar-ian coach hoped to visit Rome next month and wanted her to join him for din-ner. Let him know her schedule and he would plan accordingly. She tossed it into the wastepaper basket. He was forty years old, married, and possessed a roving hand that lingered on the wrong places during instruction. The last letter was a bill. She flipped it back on the table and finished her drink.

Was she somehow cursed? First she fell in love with a man who became a priest. Then she let a jewel thief beguile her. Fate, plus her immaturity and unre-alistic expectations for love, had doomed her to hopeless romantic fantasies. She would die a bitter, unfulfilled old woman.

Maybe Craig had chosen to call her instead of writing. That would be more like him. She hustled into the bedroom. Her apartment phone had an answering machine.

Aha! The phone showed three messages. Craig had tried more than once. The vision of doddering, lonely old age vanished, replaced by a vision of the brochure containing sexy nightwear. She perched on the bed and pushed the message button.

"Hi, Darlena. Uh, this is Carlos, wondering if you would like to go to the Verdi opera with me next weekend. We could have dinner before. Let me know when you get back from the trip." The telephone voice came on in its monotone. "Thursday, three sixteen p.m."

Darlena smiled. Carlos was a gymnast four years her senior. She liked him, but only as a friend. She would have to make that clear to him. Then they could have some good times together. She punched the message button again.

"This is Thad. I saw Candalio waiting outside the Vatican gate. Some cardinals are putting pressure on Lastavis to move the Pope to a hospital. Lastavis can't let that happen. So Candalio is probably going to kill the Holy Father this time. I tried to reach Craig, but he must be gone on a business trip. I have the rest of the drawings showing the museum passageways and entries into the catacombs in my room. You need to deliver them to Craig. I've signed approval for you to enter at the Porta Sant'Anna gate. I'll meet you there or in my room."

Silence, followed by the telephone voice monotone. "Friday, eleven forty-one a.m."

Darlena stared at the phone. A shudder ran the length of her body. Thad can't fight a man like Candalio. And why is he trying to contact Craig? What was the stuff about catacombs and drawings? She replayed the message and glanced at the clock as it finished. He had called at 11:41 this morning. It was now 12:30.

She dumped the contents from her backpack onto the floor. If she had to bring out his papers, she needed something to put them in where they wouldn't be conspicuous. But why would he want to give Craig the drawings of the buildings and catacombs?

She grabbed her purse, hustled toward the door, and then remembered that there were three telephone messages. She shook her head, trying to settle herself down and think rationally as she hit the message button.

Thad's voice again. "It is twelve twenty now. I can't wait any longer. I'm going through the old passageway and carry the Holy Father to a safe hiding place. For now that'll have to be the catacombs. I've marked on the drawings where I plan to hide him. Craig knows the details. He unlocked the doors so I could reach the Papal Palace. I've told Father Guiseppe, who you know, about the conspiracy, but not about our plans to hide the Holy Father in the catacombs. I haven't mentioned Craig's role in this. Father Guiseppe is in his room waiting for you. He'll call Bishop Baccalete and tell him everything. Don't talk to anyone else, because Lastavis probably has spies everywhere. I'm leaving now to hide the Holy Father. Pray for me. Pray for all of us."

Darlena sagged down on the edge of the bed. Her brain swirled in hopeless disarray. All questions, no answers, and no time to think about what to do.

She erased the messages, ran out the door, raced down the stairway to the street, and searched for a taxi.

CHAPTER 27

▼

Darlena shuffled her feet and pushed hair away from her face as she waited at the Porta Sant'Anna gate. The Gendarme checked her identification and slowly scanned a list. Why was the Gerdarme taking so long? Did Lastavis already suspect something? Perspiration dotted her forehead.

He smiled, handed back her identification, and motioned for her to enter.

Darlena hurried along the Via di Belvedere roadway, forcing herself not to run. She dodged and pushed her way through people plodding in all directions, most of them workers and residents of Vatican Village, and finally reached the less crowded Belvedere Court. She ran across the plaza and turned down the narrow corridor toward the Piazza della Zecca. From there, she could circle behind the basilica and reach Thad's room in San Carlo Palace.

Her ears heard shouting and a scream, coming from her left. People ran toward her from the archway leading into the Borgia Courtyard. A nun staggered through the passageway and made the sign of the cross as she collapsed onto a bench. Three Papal Gendarmes rushed into the archway. Other Gendarmes, priests, and Swiss Guards swept past her.

The Borgia Courtyard led to the Courtyard of St. Damascus, where Thad had watched Perrin and Candalio enter the doorway leading to the Papal living quarters. Darlena plunged through the passageway and onto the small plaza.

People milled at the entrance to the Courtyard of St. Damascus. Her ears picked up snatches of words.

"… fell from the window."

"A priest …"

"… from the Holy Father's living…."

A shiver convulsed her body. She fought through the crowd and saw a group of Gendarmes, priests, and Swiss Guards huddled in a circle around something on the courtyard, next to the Papal Palace wall. A Gendarme leaned out of a shattered window in the Papal Palace, shouting to the soldiers below. The man in the window was Perrin, the Papal Gendarme who escorted Candalio through the heavy wooden door into the Papal Palace.

Darlena pushed up closer, straining to see the figure sprawled on the stone plaza.

The figure wore the garb of a priest. Her legs turned rubbery and her mind blurred. She squeezed between two priests. The body lay in a pool of blood. A Gendarme blocked her view of the face.

She pushed closer. The Gendarme turned and held out his arm to block her approach.

She saw the priest's face. His mouth gaped open, a final scream obliterated by the collision with the stone plaza. His eyes gazed unblinking at the Gendarme in the window of the Papal Palace.

Darlena stared in stunned disbelief.

The dead priest was Thad.

CHAPTER 28

▼

Perrin killed Thad! The words screaming in Darlena's mind jolted her back to life. She wanted to reach Thad and cradle his head in her arms. That would be a mistake. The Gendarmes would not allow her to reach him. If she did, they would hold her here and question her.

What would she tell them? That Perrin threw Thad out the window when he tried to rescue the Holy Father from Candalio? That Lastavis planned to kill the Holy Father and usurp the Papacy? No one would believe her. Lastavis would force information from her and kill her, just as Perrin had killed Thad.

She had to reach Thad's room before the Gendarmes. Gather up the papers and drawings and tell Father Guiseppe what happened. Then they would contact Baccalete. Baccalete would believe them. She jostled back through the growing crowd and ran toward Thad's dormitory.

Darlena slammed through the building doorway. A priest started to tell her that women were not allowed here. She brushed past him, careened up the stairs, stumbled, staggered the final dozen steps, and pushed open the door of Thad's room. Once inside, she shoved the door closed, locked it, and gasped in breaths as she scanned the room.

Where were the drawings? Thad wouldn't hide them if he expected her to pick them up.

Two large manila envelopes lay beneath his Bible on one corner of the study table. She pulled out the contents. Yellowed drawings plus a dozen pages of Thad's notes were tucked inside plastic folders. A scribbled message lay on top. "Here are the drawings and other information that Craig needs. Below is the phone number and name he's using as a contact source at the hotel. Leave him a message there, telling him where you are. He also has a friend helping him. A big man with huge tattooed arms. I saw them together in the village area. I don't know the other man's name or how to contact him."

Darlena reread the message. The big man had to be Romano Pantel. No one else would fit that description. For some reason, Craig and Romano Pantel were helping Thad. Craig must have returned to Rome. If she could contact him, he would know what to do.

She saw Father Guiseppi's name and room number on a pad on Thad's desk. A quick search of Thad's room satisfied her there were no other significant papers. She stuffed the manila envelopes against her stomach inside her blouse and jeans. The guards at the gate would not search her body.

Darlena hurried out the door, ran down the stairs, and pounded on Father Guiseppi's door.

No answer. Guiseppi must have left, attracted by the commotion in the Courtyard of St. Damascus. She turned the doorknob. Not locked. Darlena scurried to his desk, tore a sheet of paper from the notepad, and scribbled a message.

"I have Thad's notes. Call me at my apartment as soon as possible. The phone number is on the bottom of this note. I will leave tonight for Luguri and have Papa take me to see Bishop Baccalete. Lastavis murdered Thad. I'll see him burn in Hell. Darlena Aldonzo."

She reread the note and realized she had summoned her fiery temper to drive out the numbing knowledge of Thad's death. Rage had replaced fear and grieving in her mind. She debated whether to rip up the note and rewrite it without the final two sentences.

Seeing those two sentences strengthened her resolve. She would avenge Thad's murder! The note would upset Father Guiseppe, but he needed to be upset. He needed to understand the deadly conspiracy fomenting inside the Vatican.

Darlena hustled down the stairway, out the front door, and into the busy courtyard. Priests milled everywhere, talking and gesturing. She slowed to a brisk walk. Don't run. Don't attract attention. She walked past the priests, making no eye contact.

Concentrate, she told herself. Leave the Vatican, return to her apartment, and wait for Father Guiseppi to call. His call might be on her answering machine by the time she arrived.

First, go by Craig's hotel. Oh God, please let Craig be there. If Craig is gone, leave him a message, go to the apartment, and call Papa. Tell him that Lastavis has killed Thad and that she is coming home.

At the gate, Darlena waited nervously behind four others. What if they decided to retain her? Why would they do that? No one knew her connection to Thad.

The Gendarme finished checking the others and glanced at her. It was the same Gendarme that approved her entry earlier. He lingered over her papers and made a cursory search of her backpack. Did he suspect something?

He smiled and handed back her papers. The smile suggested a man appraising an attractive woman and connecting the name to the face, in case he wanted to contact her later. She forced the semblance of a smile.

Once through the gate, she ran into the street and flagged down an approaching taxi, stealing it from a well-dressed couple standing on the curb.

Ten minutes later, Darlena jumped back in the taxi. Craig was not at the hotel. She had left a message, trying to word it so that the desk clerk would not connect it to Thad's death. "The physician has dealt with our naïve soccer player. I'm going to my apartment and then taking the train home. Your friend from Villa d'Este."

In the taxi, Darlena debated going now to the railroad station and call Papa from there. Get out of Rome before there was any chance of Lastavis connecting her to Thad.

She rejected the idea. She needed to replenish her supply of money, depleted during the delayed return trip. These clothes had been on her for two days. The blouse reeked with perspiration generated during the frantic past hour. Dirt from trekking across muddy streets at the Romanian airport had soiled her jeans. Her shoes felt soggy.

A change of clothes would refresh and make her more alert. She needed to stay alert, despite almost no sleep last night. It would be easier to make phone calls from the apartment. So make the calls, pick up money that she kept stashed behind the small refrigerator, change clothes, and head for the train station. Hopefully, Father Guiseppe would call before she left. Concentrating on what to do blocked the numbing grief of Thad's death.

At the apartment, Darlena stripped off the backpack and clicked on the small black and white television, hoping to see news of what happened at the Vatican. The screen showed only the usual drivel. She dialed Papa. Hearing his voice would mean so much. But don't talk long. Keep the phone clear for Father Guiseppi's call. What if Guiseppi didn't call? She would leave for Luguri and call him from the railroad station.

Maria, the housekeeper, answered the phone.

Without a word of greeting, Darlena asked for Papa.

"Your papa is in Milan at a regional agriculture council meeting today," Maria replied. "I expect him back late this evening. Perhaps as late as ten o'clock."

Darlena blew out an audible groan. She wanted to hear Papa's firm, confident voice reassure and counsel her. "Tell Papa that Thad Raphano is dead," she blurted out. "Murdered. I'm coming home on the train. I know who killed him."

She heard Maria begin sobbing out a question, but hung up. She didn't have time to deal with Maria's emotions. Next she dialed Father Guiseppi's room.

Two rings. Three rings. Four rings. She hung up. That was it on phone calls. She would call Craig's hotel again from the railroad station. She glared at the discarded cell phone in the waste paper basket. This was the worst possible time to not have a working cell phone with her.

Darlena grappled the refrigerator away from the wall, retrieved her stash of Euros, stuffed the wad in her belt purse, tossed the purse on the table, and hurried into the bedroom to change clothes.

The shift of sound on the television caught her attention. The program was being interrupted for a news bulletin. A reporter's voice filled the small room. "A priest plunged to his death today from the Papal Palace. A Vatican spokesman confirmed the story, but refused to discuss any details. Unnamed sources said the priest broke into the living quarters of the Pope and attempted to attack the Pope. Quick action by a Papal Gendarme prevented any harm to His Holiness. The priest leaped from the window in an attempt to escape, and died on the Courtyard of St. Damascus. The same source speculated that the priest is a member of a radical dissident group opposing current policies of the Catholic Church. We'll bring you more details as they become available. Again, to repeat …"

Darlena stormed into the bedroom. They're making Thad the villain. It's easy to figure who was the unnamed source. Lastavis will twist this to his advantage. The news media will crucify Thad before any of the truth can be told. She yanked out clothes, tossed them on the bed, scooped up a few bathroom items, and threw them into her backpack.

Her apprehension surged. The nightmare was mushrooming out of control. Lastavis was saying that Thad tried to kill the Pope. What can Bishop Baccalete do now? Lastavis murdered Thad and nobody can do anything about it. Her shoulders drooped as she sagged onto the bed. Energy drained from her.

Like a thunderbolt, anger cascaded through her body. "I will expose Lastavis!" she yelled.

The words blasted away Darlena's inertia and fear. She yanked out a pair of fresh shoes, tossed them on the bed, and began unbuttoning her blouse so she could remove the manila folder still stuffed against her stomach.

Her ears picked up another bulletin being announced on the television. She stepped back into the other room to listen.

"A Vatican source has now confirmed that two priests died this afternoon. The second apparently committed suicide in his room after learning of the first priest's death. According to a priest at the scene, the second priest has been identified as Father Guiseppi, a veteran priest from northern Italy, who has been working the past four years at the Vatican. It is not known whether Guiseppi is a member of the dissident group."

Darlena staggered against the table to keep from collapsing. Why would Father Guiseppi kill himself? He was the only priest who knew the truth.

Her mind swept back through the events of the afternoon. Father Guiseppi's name and room number were on a pad in Thad's room. As soon as Lastavis saw that, he had him killed.

Her name was on the note that she left in Father Guiseppi's room! Cold fear swept the length of her body.

Darlena heard a shuffling sound outside the apartment door. She saw the doorknob rotate and heard a clicking sound like a key being inserted. The door inched open and stopped as the door chain caught.

Her body turned to clay, her feet frozen to the floor, her eyes riveted on the door.

Fingers squirmed through the narrow opening and grasped at the chain latch, but couldn't get a grip. The fingers slid away.

The door shuddered. Another heavy thud cracked the wooden doorframe around the chain latch.

Darlena's mind screamed at her. Run!

But where could she run? She lunged into the bedroom, grabbed the phone, and began dialing the police.

Her ears heard the door splintering. She dropped the phone, slammed the bedroom door closed, and shoved the wooden chest against it.

She was trapped in the bedroom! Darlena pounced to the window. A narrow ledge protruded beneath the window. She kicked out the screen, scrambled through the window, lowered herself onto the ledge, and shuffled along it with her stomach against the brick wall. Four floors below her, piles of trash littered the brick alleyway. The alleyway dead ended against the building walls. A closed gate sealed the exit to the street.

A head shoved through the window frame, glanced the other way, and then spotted her.

Candalio's cruel eyes stared at her.

"Come back," he called out. "We only need to ask you some questions, Miss Aldonzo. Then you're free to leave."

Darlena glanced ahead and spotted a concrete drainpipe for the roof gutters protruding downward past the ledge. She closed her eyes for a moment to get her brain focused. The ledge was slightly wider than a balance beam. She moved quickly along it toward the drainpipe.

A sideward glance told her Candalio continued to watch her from the window. His smug leer indicated he expected at any moment to see her plunge downward from the precarious position. He didn't know she was a gymnast. Maybe she could buy some time.

"I'm scared to come back to the window," Darlena shouted. "The ledge is so narrow. I can't climb back inside."

He stretched his hand toward her. "Move back this way slowly and grab my hand. I'll help you."

A husky man in coveralls appeared at the alleyway entry gate. He stood there, watching her like a wolf singling out a limping deer in a fleeing herd, waiting for it to fall behind before moving in for the kill. Sliding down the drainpipe to the alley would trap her.

Climbing to the roof offered the only escape route. She grasped as far up on the drainpipe as she could and clawed for a handhold on the cast concrete. One slip and she was dead. But she would die if she stayed here.

Darlena flexed her knees and lifted herself upward. Her legs clamped onto the pipe. She shifted her hands higher and shinnied toward the roof. Sweat formed on her face and hands, making her grip on the smooth pipe more tenuous. She concentrated on the climb, not distracting herself by glancing toward Candalio or his henchman at the alley entry.

Her hand grasped the overhanging gutter. She swung her legs free and dangled in space. The gutter twisted downward from her weight. Metal sheeting bit into her clinging fingers.

Her arm muscles strained to pull her upward. Her breasts cleared the gutter edge. An upward lunge carried her body over the gutter and against the sloping roof.

Darlena clambered to the top of the roof and down the other side toward the fire escape. The fire escape platform jutted out six feet below her. She jumped and landed on the rusty metal grating, letting herself tumble forward to lessen the impact on her legs. She fled down the fire escape and jumped the final five feet to the ground.

The husky man in coveralls and another man emerged from the adjacent crossover street and ran toward her.

Darlena became a gazelle in wild flight from killer dogs. She dodged people and whirled into side streets, trying to vanish among the crowd. Finding a policeman would momentarily protect her, but Lastavis would pry her from their hands, claiming she knew the assassin priest. Then he would orchestrate her suicide.

The assailants bulled past slow moving pedestrians, closing the gap to twenty feet.

Darlena bounded up concrete steps leading toward a terraced park.

The assailants began to lag, unable to maintain her frenetic pace on the steps.

Her lungs heaved against her ribs. Muscular legs, honed by years of gymnastics regimen, dug into the deepest reserves to continue beyond exhaustion. She reached the park, sprinted across it, and onto a crowded sidewalk.

Darlena ran. And ran, weaving into crowds along busy streets, turning down narrow curving alleys to reach other streets. She ran with no pattern and no logic. She simply ran.

She finally staggered into heavy shrubbery inside a small park and collapsed onto the ground among shadows of early evening. Her legs had become concrete pillars. Her lungs convulsed with pain.

How many hours had she been running? Where was she? She had no idea.

She squirmed deeper into the shrubbery. Oncoming darkness and the isolation of the park would hide her from Candalio while she rested to rebuild her strength. The muscles of her legs contorted in oxygen-deprived agony. Her chest pumped fresh air into depleted lungs. Grime streaked with perspiration covered her face and soaked her clothes.

Her mind began functioning again. What should she do? Her purse lay on the table at the apartment. She had no money and no credit cards. Candalio would quickly learn everything about her.

Anywhere she went for help, they would be lurking in the shadows, faceless hunters waiting to kill her.

The smell of impending death filled the air around her.

CHAPTER 29

▼

Darlena trudged over to a fountain with a statue spraying water from its mouth. The first rays of morning sunlight sparkled dew clinging on shrubs and trees. She splashed water over her face. Driblets trickled down her neck onto her grimy blouse. The cool water increased her shivering. She had spent the night in short stints of restless sleep, awakened by every sound, terrified that Candalio would be leering down at her.

A numbing ache permeated her entire body, a combination of physical exhaustion, no food since yesterday morning, and a sense of hopeless desperation. Thad was dead, branded as a radical dissident who tried to kill the Holy Father. She was running for her life.

Darlena slouched down on the concrete rim of the fountain basin and closed her eyes to lessen the throbbing in her head and neck. What could she do? Candalio certainly has men watching her apartment and the gymnastics center. Going to the police won't help. Lastavis will brand her as a co-conspirator and have her killed.

She needed to locate a shopkeeper who will let her telephone Papa. Papa would arrange for someone to protect her and then drive to Rome to pick her up. Papa will know how to deal with these evil men.

For the next hour Darlena walked. Shops began opening. She studied several and selected one that sold casual clothes. A woman with graying hair and a neat but not expensive dress eyed her as she hesitated and then paced into the shop. Her disheveled appearance and dirty clothes marked her as an undesirable patron.

"I need your help," Darlena said, trying to keep her carefully crafted comments from sounding rehearsed. "I'm a visitor to Rome. Last night men attacked and robbed me. I barely escaped with my life. I need to call my Papa. He lives in northern Italy in Luguri. If you'll let me use your phone, I'll have the call charged to him. All I ask is that you let me use your phone."

The woman's eyebrows flexed downward, deepening the creases in the skin around the corners of her eyes. "If they robbed you, why do you have an expensive ring on your finger?"

Darlena glanced down at her hand and remembered she still wore the opal ring that Papa had given her as a graduation gift. Her mind struggled to generate a reply. "The men were more intent on me than on the valuables I had. I lost my purse while escaping."

The woman's features softened. Perhaps the tremor in Darlena's voice convinced the woman of her predicament. Perhaps the woman wanted to dispense with this tramp as quickly as possible.

The woman picked up the phone from the counter, dialed, and held out the receiver. Darlena gave the operator the number. Her fingers drummed on the counter as the phone rang once, twice, three times.

Surely Papa was home. Maria had to be there.

A voice answered. It was a man's voice, but not Papa. Darlena couldn't place which of the farm laborers it was. Why didn't Maria answer?

The operator's voice came on the line. "I have a collect call for Dominic Aldonzo from Darlena Aldonzo in Rome. Will you accept the charges?"

"Just a minute," the man's voice replied.

Darlena heard the muffled sound of voices in the background. "I need to talk to Papa now!" she shouted into the phone.

"Wait until the collect call is approved," the operator admonished.

Another man's voice came on the line. "I'll accept the charges. Darlena, where are you?"

Another familiar voice but she couldn't place it. "Who is this? I need to talk to Papa."

"This is Officer Lorenzo."

There was an ominous pause. Nausea bubbled up into her throat. "What's wrong? Where's Papa?"

"I'm sorry, Darlena. Your Papa is dead."

The words destroyed every thread of strength remaining in her. Her hand began shaking and her legs turned limp. Her other hand grasped the edge of the counter to keep her from collapsing.

Officer Lorenzo's voice continued. "Your Papa and Maria were murdered sometime during the night by robbers. Tell me where you are. I'll arrange for the Rome police to pick you up and bring you home."

Darlena lowered the phone back into the cradle. "They murdered Papa," she murmured. "They've killed all the others and they'll surely kill me next."

CHAPTER 30

▼

Darlena paused beneath bright neon lights piercing the darkness on a narrow brick street. She had wandered through the Dipanico District for the past four hours, searching for the Paesada Casino mentioned by Romano Pantel at the train incident. The drab building hunkered between a closed bread shop and a decaying three-story apartment building with shades and curtains drawn over most of its darkened windows. The sound of a woman laughing spilled from one window. Peeling green paint covered the bricks of the casino. Light glistened from the open door and one large window.

When she stepped through the doorway, the stench of cheap beer and cigarette smoke choked her nostrils. Men in sleeveless shirts and stubby beards talked and laughed, almost obliterating the harangue of music. Her worst expectations hadn't prepared her for this scene. She debated turning around and leaving. But where would she go?

Darlena edged toward the bar, maneuvering to avoid rubbing against men in her path. Heads turned to ogle her. Burly voices rose above the din. Most offered her a drink. One man vulgarly propositioned her. The urge to turn and run increased. But she had to find Romano Pantel. He was her only link to Craig.

The bartender, a short man with sprawling black hair and chapped lips beneath a mustache in need of trimming, leered as she approached. The cracked mirror behind him and the tattered bar reinforced her apprehension.

She sucked in a deep breath, slid onto a barstool, and gagged from the smell of the sweaty, beer-soused man beside her. "I'm trying to find someone," she said. "Romano Pantel." Despite her best effort, her voice quivered.

The bartender's reddened eyes embraced her breasts pressed against her damp blouse. "He's not here. But one of them would know where you can find him." He pointed toward a table where four men played cards. The one facing her wore an undershirt and clenched the stub of a cigar between yellowed teeth.

No way would Darlena trust those men to take her anywhere. "Will Romano come back here tonight?" she asked the bartender.

He raised his shoulders almost to his ears and opened his palms in a shrug that said "don't know, don't care." He motioned with his head toward a table where three men talked boisterously with a woman. "Rita would know. But she's conducting business right now. You'll have to wait. What can I fix you to drink?"

"Nothing right now."

"I'll give you the first drink free."

She had heard that women's drinks were often drugged at places like this. "Maybe later." She turned away from him and studied the woman bending over the table. Rita laughed as she poured beer into glasses. Her gaudy blouse hung open, exposing the upper flesh of breasts bigger than Darlena had ever seen. Rita moved around the table, her body swaying in a seductive rhythm. Men shifted position for a better look. One reached out to caress her buttocks. She shifted her body away with the finesse of a fisherman enticing a trout to latch onto bait.

Darlena watched mesmerized, seeing for the first time a prostitute at work. Rita exuded sensuality. Wonder if Craig had slept with her? The thought bothered her. How could she compete for Craig's attentions against someone like Rita? No wonder he called her a naïve girl. Craig had probably slept all over Europe with women like Rita.

"Buy you a drink."

The voice and a hand caressing her arm startled her. A husky man with the heavy smell of alcohol on his breath ran his fingers along her arm and against her breast.

"No thank you." She worked her way to the far end of the bar, slipping past men who deliberately blocked her path, forcing her to press against them as she wriggled through.

Nearby, a woman stood in front of a seated man, her legs spread brazenly apart to accommodate his hand probing inside her skirt. All the women were procuring lovers. A dozen men eyed her. They probably pegged her as an inexperienced prostitute. Why else would she be in a place like this? The urge to flee engulfed her. Rita remained engrossed with the men at the table. Maybe she should interrupt her and tell her what she needed.

One of the men stood up and snugged his arm around Rita's waist. They maneuvered through the clutter of chairs and tables toward a dark hallway at the rear of the bar.

Darlena plunged through the melee of men and caught up with Rita near the doorway. "Rita. Wait."

The woman turned and gave her a puzzled glare.

"I have to talk to Romano Pantel," Darlena blurted out. "I have to talk to him as soon as possible. Please tell me how to find him."

The woman's face displayed no sign of recognizing the name. She sullenly studied Darlena's bedraggled clothes and face.

"Please," Darlena begged. "You're the only hope I have of finding him. I have to find either Romano Pantel or Craig Reynolds."

Surprise flashed across Rita's face. Then she shrugged. "We'll talk later. Wait here in the casino."

"Is there some place else I can wait?"

"Later," Rita reiterated. She turned away and rejoined the man. They disappeared into the shadows of the hallway.

Darlena's shoulders sagged. She couldn't wait alone in this bawdy casino until Rita finished her love tryst.

"You're new here, aren't you?" A pair of hands slipped around her waist from behind.

Darlena twisted around and stepped back.

A handsome, muscular man crowded up close to her. The odor of sweat intermingled with the smell of tobacco and a hint of alcohol on his breath. But his casual shirt and khakis, reasonably neat hair, and no beard stubble elevated his appearance above other patrons.

"Let's find a table and talk," he said. "I'll buy you a drink."

He didn't resist as she pushed his hands away from her body. "I'm waiting for a friend to return," she alibied. "It'll only be a few minutes."

"I'll wait with you."

Darlena tried to size him up. He didn't appear to be drunk and he behaved much less brazen than the others. Perhaps the best strategy would be sit with him. Maybe the other men would leave her alone. "Just until my friend returns," she replied.

He led her to a small table in a dark corner. Darlena declined a drink, although her parched throat rasped. Any alcohol would have a strong impact on her weary body. A drugged drink would leave her hopelessly vulnerable. She had to stay alert.

They talked. She answered questions vaguely, some with partial truths, some with outright lies. His smile indicated he knew that. She tried to divert the conversation to him.

Twenty minutes passed. He told her that he had grown up in the Dipanico District and now worked for a construction company as a welder. That was a skilled job that paid well. His conversation suggested a reasonable education level. He was definitely a cut above the other patrons.

Another twenty minutes dragged by, with no sign of Rita. Darlena fought mounting fatigue and continued to parry his constant questions and veiled propositions. Stay alert, she repeated over and over to herself.

His voice came through her foggy thoughts. "Your friend obviously isn't showing. Let's you and me go somewhere nicer than this. Would you like something to eat?"

The thought of food tempted her. But she had to wait here for Romano. "My friend is Rita," she replied. "I have to talk with her tonight."

He laughed. "Rita has men waiting in line. She won't be back in here tonight."

Darlena slumped in her chair. Her voice had deteriorated to barely a whisper. "I'll wait here all night if I have to."

"You're going to fall asleep in that chair. Rita has an extra room right behind the casino. Let me take you back there. You can lock the door and sleep. I'll tell Rita where you are."

Was he luring her into a trap or offering help? Darlena peered into his eyes. They were friendly eyes. "I'm in desperate trouble and Rita is the only one that can help me," she blurted out. "I'm not a prostitute. Please believe that."

"Then you picked a hell of a place to wait for Rita. Look around. When I walk away from this table, these men will swoop down on you like vultures. They'll spread you out and rape you right here on the table."

Her bleary eyes surveyed the room. He was right. All of the other women were gone.

He stood up and reached out his hand. "I'll escort you out of here before someone stakes a claim. I don't relish a fight in this place."

What choice did she have? Darlena took his hand.

He clasped it gently and guided her past the tables and through the doorway leading into the narrow hallway.

Her legs plodded like feet sinking into concrete.

He pushed open the back door. They stepped outside into a patio surrounded on three sides by the solid walls of buildings. A glimmer of light reflecting from the street left the patio in deep shadows. A dingy door opened into the building directly ahead of them. To her right, a bricked fence containing a narrow closed gate blocked entry to the street.

The breeze refreshed her face. For the first time in hours, her lungs sucked in air free of choking cigarette smoke. But the smell of garbage and vomit tainted the air.

He led her across the patio toward the gate.

Darlena stopped and turned to face him. "You said Rita's room was behind the casino."

His arms clamped around her, pinning her arms to her sides. His lips smothered her mouth, gagging her with the smell of his beer breath.

She kicked at his legs and struggled to break free.

He dumped her onto the rough brick ground and straddled her, his body weight crushing her stomach. One hand locked on her throat. "You yell or struggle and I'll choke the life out of you."

His fingers gouged into her windpipe and then eased enough to allow her to gasp in a shallow breath. "Lay still and I won't hurt you. I know how to make a woman beg for more."

His other hand began unbuttoning her blouse.

Darlena clawed at his fingers gripping her throat.

His free hand lashed across her cheek, stunning her. His fingers dug into her windpipe again. "I said, don't struggle," he growled.

She would die rather than submit to rape. She clawed at his hand again. Her feet pounded upward against his back.

He spewed out profanity, yanked her upward, and slammed her back down against the ground.

Darlena cocked her head up to keep it from banging the hard bricks. The last wisp of air jolted from her lungs.

His fingers clamped around her throat again.

Darlena struggled to pull his hand away. His grip tightened. Oxygen vanished from her lungs. She felt her blouse and bra being torn away.

His weight suddenly came off of her. His hand yanked away from her throat.

Through blurred eyes, she saw a massive figure lift the man into the air and slam him against the wall. A hoarse, angry voice filled the patio. "That's my woman."

"I didn't know," the young man gasped. "I swear I didn't know."

"If you ever come here again, I'll turn you into a squeaky soprano."

The young man let out a howl of terrible pain and staggered through the doorway.

The huge figure stooped down and cradled her in his massive arms. "That piss-headed Casanova tries to screw every woman that walks into the casino."

It was Romano Pantel's voice. Darlena drooped her head against his shoulder and gasped in air. The reek of his perspiration and tobacco didn't bother her. Relief overwhelmed all her other senses.

Romano carried her across the patio, up the stairs into a dark hallway, pushed open a door, and flipped on a light.

A single bulb hanging from the ceiling illuminated a room containing a metal frame bed and a battered nightstand. Romano laid her on the bed and sat down heavily beside her. He stroked her hair like a father comforting a daughter. "Rita told me you were here. One of my men was supposed to be watching out for you, but he fell asleep. He's gonna pay big time."

Darlena struggled to a sitting position and pushed her back against the metal frame of the bed. She saw his eyes ogling her. Her blouse spread open and her ripped bra hung loosely, exposing her breasts. She fumbled to refasten the bra, gave it up as hopeless, and closed her blouse using the two remaining buttons. The tattered blouse sagged open enough to leave her breasts visible to the edge of her nipples.

"Are you still unplucked?" Romano asked.

Darlena frowned at the question. Then she remembered the discussion at the train riot. Despite his lecherous eyes and criminal bent, she knew Romano Pantel would not hurt her. In his own boisterous, bullying way, he would be gracious and protective of her.

She choked out the words. "Thad Raphano is dead. Lastavis and Candalio killed him."

Scowl wrinkles creased Romano's forehead and his eyes narrowed. "The priest is dead?"

"Thad is dead. And Candalio came to my apartment and tried to kill me. After I escaped, Candalio went to Luguri hunting for me. He killed Papa. And he won't stop until he's killed me." The final words blurred and she fought back tears.

Romano hit his fist in his hand. "Damn. That blows everything apart."

The door opened and Rita stuck her head in. "Bring her to my apartment. It'll be more comfortable."

Romano wrapped his arm around her waist to steady her. "We'll talk more about this when Craig arrives."

"Craig's coming?" The thought of seeing Craig ignited a surge of energy in Darlena. He could help her escape from Lastavis.

"Craig's been contacted." Romano guided her down the hallway to another door.

The lavish furnishings in Rita's apartment surprised her. Some of Rita's clientele must be wealthy. Again, the thought flashed through her mind. Was Craig one of those generous clients? She spotted a ceramic bathtub on legs sitting in one corner of the bedroom. Bathtubs weren't supposed to be in bedrooms. The bathtub probably served as a source of entertainment.

"A hot bath will refresh you," Rita said. "I have everything you need. Soak as long as you want."

Romano started to follow them into the bedroom. Rita closed the door in his face.

Darlena stripped off her soiled clothes. The ferocity of Rita's gaze made her uncomfortable. Only once before had a woman been so intent on her undressed body. At a gymnastics tournament when she was twelve, a woman offered to sponsor her gymnastics training if she came and stayed with her in Milan. Darlena had been flattered until others warned her about the woman's reputation for procuring young gymnasts for sexual pleasure. But Rita wouldn't be interested in sex with a woman. Or would she? Craig's comment during their first encounter flashed through her mind. "Don't be naïve." She had resented the comment then. Now she realized how much truth his words conveyed.

Darlena climbed into the tub and slid down into the caressing heat of hot water.

Rita poured a slow stream of luxuriant bath oil into the water. "You could be one of the richest young women in Rome. Wealthy men would give everything they have to make you their woman. For sure, as a mistress, and maybe as a wife."

Darlena scooped up floating bath oil and rubbed it on her face and arms. The delightful aroma soothed her irritated nostrils. "I'll never sleep with a man I don't love."

"Then you're a fool," Rita retorted. "I had no education and no money. I exploited my talent to excite and please men. Love has nothing to do with it. Men want to own women, especially beautiful women. So make them pay for displaying and fondling the trophy."

Rita poured the rest of the bath oil into the water and walked toward the door.

Darlena called after her. "I don't understand this kind of world. I'm scared."

Rita looked back at her. "You should be scared. This is the jungle. You're either a predator or a feast. There are no other choices and no second chances.

With your beauty and social graces, you can have it all. I can teach you what you need to know and introduce you to the right men. Those men pay big money to screw me but they wouldn't be seen in public with somebody like me. They'll wrap you in furs and parade you in front of their friends. Once you have your hooks in them, you can trade up from one man to the next until you find what you want."

She sauntered into the other room, leaving the door open.

Darlena serpentined deeper into the tub, burying herself in soothing water and fragrant, bubbly froth. She shampooed her hair. For the first time since leaving on the gymnastics trip, her body felt luxuriously clean. The pain of bruises and strained muscles subsided.

Romano lumbered into the bedroom and set a wine bottle and a plate holding a sandwich overflowing with meat and cheese on the marble stand beside the tub. He lingered to survey her body only partially concealed by soapy bubbles.

"Make the rich bastards pay to pluck you." He clomped out of the room.

Darlena devoured the sandwich and half the bottle of wine. The hot bath and food rejuvenated her. Like pieces of information being pulled up by a computer, events of the past two days swarmed back into her mind.

Tears filled her eyes. She shoved her fist into her mouth and bit down on it to keep from sobbing out loud. Papa was dead. Thad was dead. The two men she loved with all her heart and soul were dead. Nothing would ever be the same again.

She forced the tears to stop, climbed from the tub, wrapped the huge red towel around her body, sat down in front of the mirror, and robotically combed tangles from her hair.

Darlena paused and studied the face staring back at her from the mirror. Was she a predator or the next meal?

"I am a predator," she said out loud. Her hands brushed her hair more vigorously, the pace and force intensifying as she repeated the words. "I am a predator. I will make Lastavis and Candalio pay for what they've done."

She snuggled into Rita's silk velvet robe, sagged into the chair, and closed her eyes.

"I am a predator," she mumbled over and over.

CHAPTER 31

▼

Craig opened the door to Rita's apartment and stepped inside. Although the Vatican had not officially announced the name of the dead priest who supposedly tried to kill the Pope, he had worried that it might be Thad. Romano's late night message confirmed his fears. Darlena's involvement and the death of her father complicated an already rapidly deteriorating plan.

Romano sat at the table, drinking coffee. Without speaking a word, Rita poured another cup of coffee, refilled Romano's cup, and went into the bedroom, closing the door behind her.

Romano rubbed his brawny hand on the table. "Can we still rob the Vatican without the priest's help?"

Craig slid into the chair opposite him. "Thad's death complicates the task. Priests can go anywhere in the Vatican, day or night, without arousing suspicion. He was going to bring me the rest of the layouts of buildings and catacombs. I can probably create another way to have freedom of movement inside the Vatican grounds. But moving treasures out of the museums will be more difficult and riskier without knowledge of all the passageways beneath the buildings."

The bedroom door opened and Darlena stepped into the room. She was wearing one of Rita's plush robes. The disarray of her hair indicated it had been combed without much concentration.

Craig rose from the chair and came toward her, intending to embrace her.

She held up her hand to stop him. Her eyes blazed. "Helping Thad protect the Pope was a ruse, wasn't it? You were planning to rob the Vatican."

Craig chose to not reply.

"You deceived Thad into giving you detailed drawings of the Vatican and all the old passageways and catacombs that Cardinal Sergio explored." Darlena's voice escalated. "You were going to make Thad an accomplice to robbery. You betrayed his trust. You betrayed my trust."

"I showed Thad a way to protect the Pope," Craig replied. "I figured that entitled me to a reasonable reward. I warned him not to try anything foolish around Candalio."

"You gave him access to the Pope's living quarters!" Darlena yelled. "Because of you, Thad is dead. Because Thad is dead, Papa is dead."

The accusation angered him. "Thad became a dead man the day he spotted Candalio going into the Papal Palace and decided to try stopping him from killing your beloved senile Pope. I kept Thad alive. He would still be alive if he had listened to me."

"That's right," she retorted. "Thad would still be feeding you information you need to rob the Vatican. He would still be giving you access to everything there. Still trusting you until you robbed the place. Still trusting you right up to the time that you killed him. You did plan to kill him, didn't you? You would have to kill him, because he would know too much."

"I didn't need to kill Thad. He was a decent, likable person. I kept you isolated from what was happening to protect you. I did intend to rob the Vatican. But Cardinal Lastavis and Candalio killed Thad and your father."

The fire remained in her eyes, but tears dribbled down her cheeks. "I can't even attend Papa's funeral. I'm running for my life."

Craig wrapped his arms around her and pulled her close. "I'm so sorry."

Darlena clung to him, buried her face against his shoulder, and sobbed.

After a few minutes, she eased free and gazed into his face. "Are you still going to rob the Vatican?"

"It will be much more difficult. I needed all of Sergio's drawings and Thad made it possible for me to enter and leave without attracting attention. But I had a backup plan for getting inside. Robbing the Vatican will discredit Lastavis and destroy any chance of him being elected Pope. So you'll get a small measure of revenge. Even more important, once Lastavis is discredited, he has no incentive to kill the Pope and no reason to send Candalio to kill you."

Darlena stared at the floor as she rubbed her hands together. When she looked back up at him, the fire had returned to her eyes. "The rest of Cardinal Sergio's drawings and Thad's notes are in the large envelopes in Rita's bedroom. I grabbed them before Candalio came after me."

Romano clenched his fists triumphantly and hurried into the bedroom. He returned quickly and dumped the drawings and notes on the table.

Craig perused the information. "Some of our plans will have to change," he said to Romano. "But we're back in business."

"I want to expose Lastavis's conspiracy, regardless of the consequences for me," Darlena said. "Otherwise, the murder of Thad and Papa will go unpunished."

Craig paced around the room, mulling the possibilities. Finally, he turned back to face Darlena. "I need your help on getting back inside the Vatican. You help me and I'll position you to expose Lastavis's conspiracy."

Her eyes narrowed. "You want me to help you rob the Vatican?"

"Robbing the Vatican is the only way to stop Lastavis from killing the Pope, claiming the papacy, and walking away unpunished for killing Thad and your father. Until Lastavis is discredited, Candalio will keep hunting for you. Sometimes a greater wrong can only be stopped by another wrong."

Darlena stood gazing at him.

Craig sensed that she was debating his offer. But her face and eyes gave no hint of what Darlena would choose to do.

CHAPTER 32

▼

Craig and Darlena lounged at a sidewalk cafe table a few blocks from the Vatican. Craig's silvery gray hair, slightly stooped shoulders, neatly trimmed mustache, and tailored dark suit suggested a middle-aged banker or successful businessman. Contact lens gave his eyes a hazel color. His accent marked him as a member of an upper class family from the Tuscany area north of Rome.

Darlena wore a white turtleneck sweater and charcoal flannel pants that snugged against the important curves of her body. A pale purple sleeveless vest converted the outfit into the attire of a perky professional or perhaps a model. Her groomed raven hair glistened in the sunlight.

"The tall Swiss Guard sitting on the left is the one we're interested in," Craig said. "His name is John Montayne. He's a sergeant and has been here four years. He is unmarried, enjoys drinking strong beer with his comrades, and enthusiastically attends soccer games and operas. He tolerates Italian food, but prefers traditional Swiss cuisine. Unlike many fellow Swiss Guards, he speaks reasonable Italian, although with a distinct Schwyzerdutsch accent. He's my height and my build, making him perfect except for that damn Schwyzerdutsch. It's a difficult dialect to master."

"How do you know all that?" Darlena asked.

"I make my living by knowing the right information. Sergeant Montayne also enjoys the company of attractive women."

Darlena glanced toward Montayne. "I've never tried to seduce a man. Why me instead of Rita? She knows all the tricks."

"Rita is a whore. A Swiss Guard like Montayne dreams of a beautiful young woman that he can take home with pride to the Swiss Alps. His fantasy is a virgin with a burning passion that will succumb to his Swiss uniform and masculinity."

"I'm not going to sleep with him," she asserted.

"You don't have to," he replied. "You can remain unplucked."

Her irritated frown told him that she disliked that word.

"So how do I meet him?" she asked.

"He's already noticed you. So first, look at him while we talk. Every time he glances toward you, you'll be watching him. Shortly we'll walk over and you'll ask him if he would let your father take pictures of you with a Swiss Guard. After a half dozen pictures, I'll have to hurry off for my afternoon meeting. Then you rope him in with the scenario I gave you. Whatever it takes, get him to the apartment on Friday evening. We carry out the robbery Saturday night. Make certain your Swiss Guard visits you Friday evening in uniform and that he's off duty on Saturday."

"What if his schedule doesn't allow that?" she asked.

"Trust me. John Montayne will change his schedule to accommodate you."

Darlena shook her head. "I can't participate in helping you kill an innocent person."

"Montayne will suffer a significant blow to his ego, but he'll be very much alive."

"Promise me that you won't kill him."

"I won't kill him." Craig reached over to pick up the camera. "It is time to take pictures."

Darlena blew out a deep breath and strolled over to the Swiss Guards' table.

All three men watched her approach.

She walked directly to John Montayne. "Could I ask a favor of you?"

He scrambled to his feet. "Certainly, signorina."

She gave him a nervous smile. "I know you must get tired of being asked all the time. But would you let my Papa take a picture of us together?"

"I would be pleased to do that," Montayne replied.

"Sit with us," the older Swiss Guard said in stumbling Italian. "You can tell your friends you knew three Swiss Guards and two of them were not married." He chuckled.

Darlena looked into John Montayne's dark eyes. "I'd rather it was only you."

The older guardsman made a comment in Schwyserdutsch. The other guardsman laughed.

Montayne pointed toward the patio wall adjacent to the cafe. "Perhaps there. The bougainvillea would be a perfect background."

She snuggled her hand inside his arm and let him lead her to the wall. "You're very tall, like Papa. And you speak such good Italian. How long have you been in Rome?"

"I'm beginning my fifth year." Montayne stepped back against the wall and turned to face the camera.

She pressed her hip against his. "A friend told me that Swiss Guards dislike speaking Italian. But you've obviously worked very hard to master the language. I admire a man who cares about the country he visits."

Craig snapped a picture. "How about one that's a little less formal?"

Darlena shifted partly in front of Montayne and snuggled her head against his shoulder. Montayne seemed uncertain where to put his hand. She clasped it and pressed it against her stomach, just below her breasts. "I'm going to be the envy of every girl at the university," she purred.

Craig snapped pictures, some with the zoom to give him a close-up of Montayne's face. He glanced at his watch. "I need to return to the conference. I'll drop you off at the apartment."

Darlena shook her head. "I want to go back to St. Peter's Basilica and climb up to Michelangelo's dome. I can take a taxi to the apartment."

Craig frowned. "You're not familiar with Rome. I would rather you came back with me. Perhaps we can return this weekend after the conference is finished."

"Please," she sighed.

John Montayne stepped toward Craig. "I have two hours before going back on duty. I would enjoy touring your daughter through the basilica and seeing her safely back to the apartment." He glanced at her. "With your approval, of course."

"I would love that," she gushed.

Montayne extended his hand. "I am Sergeant John Montayne. I can assure you, your daughter will be safe with me."

Craig shook his hand. "I don't doubt that." Craig kissed Darlena on the cheek. "The dinner meeting will probably last until ten tonight. So I'll see you in the morning for breakfast. Have a good time."

Darlena clasped Montayne's hand. "My name is Maria Delmara. Papa is so busy with his meetings and presentations. He expects me to tromp around with conference delegates' middle-aged wives. I'm coming back next month to begin study at the university. I hope you and I can be good friends."

Craig nodded approvingly to Montayne, hurried out to the street, and flagged a taxi. This part had gone exactly as planned. John Montayne's smile suggested a man sailing into paradise. Darlena was a siren perched on rocks, spreading out her arms and singing to lure the unsuspecting traveler. Montayne's boat would wreck on the rocks.

CHAPTER 33

▼

Darlena uncorked a bottle of Burgundy and poured some into a crystal wine glass. Sergeant John Montayne lounged on the sofa, his eyes transfixed on her. Hopefully he would interpret her nervousness as the uncertainty of a giddy young woman enthralled in her first adult romance. They had spent every hour of Montayne's free time together over the past two days, sightseeing around Rome and cuddling together during a boat ride on the Tiber. As Craig had predicted, Montayne rearranged his duty schedule to be with her this evening and tomorrow on her final weekend before she returned to Florence.

She sidled up close to him on the sofa and handed him the glass. "I purchased this wine especially for you. Tell me if I did okay."

He swirled the glass, sniffed it, sipped some, and nodded. "This is the most superb red wine I've ever tasted."

"Papa says the first glass of a vintage wine cleanses a man's palate. The second glass soothes the soul and warms the heart. So a man drinks the first glass with gusto. The woman joins him on the second glass. That glass is sipped to pledge friendship and strengthen affection."

"An interesting tradition I had not heard before." Montayne lifted the glass in a salute to her. "To a pure diamond that sparkles brighter than the whitest snow on the highest peak of the Alps."

The words sounded rehearsed to her. Montayne was not agile with flowery phrases. He had probably spent hours agonizing through ways to romantically compliment her. She sensed that he had no intention of seducing her tonight. He had elevated her to virgin goddess status and would not stain her innocence. Deceiving a man who treated her with such sincerity and respect bothered her.

Montayne would bear forever the shame of being duped into aiding the robbers of the Vatican. But it was too late now to back away.

Darlena watched him down the wine as he savored the beautiful young woman beside him. He probably thought life could not become any better than this.

Montayne set the glass aside on the lamp table, reached out to caress her hand, and started to say something. The words garbled in his mouth. His tongue flopped, suddenly thick and unresponsive. His eyes glazed over.

She caught him as he slumped forward and eased him down onto the sofa.

Craig entered from the bedroom.

Darlena watched in silence while Craig stripped off the uniform and injected a drug into the muscular arm of the unconscious guardsman. He dragged him into the bedroom, handcuffed his hands to a metal ring embedded in the floor, and tied his legs. Then he blindfolded him and put tape over his mouth. Now, as events unfolded, apprehension and guilt roiled her body. Perspiration dotted her forehead. Maybe all these events were part of a long, continuous nightmare that would end when she awoke. Her mind knew better. Papa was dead, Thad was dead, and she had become an active participant in robbing the Vatican.

An hour later, Craig paused in front of the mirror. "What do you think?"

Darlena shook her head. "It's unbelievable. I think you're John Montayne."

He clasped her arms firmly but without pain. "Listen carefully to me. If Montayne escapes, I'm a dead man. So if he should revive before you leave, don't remove the blindfold or the tape on his mouth. Don't loosen any ropes and don't talk to him. He'll have to endure the misery until we're finished at the Vatican. Sanitize this place like I showed you. As soon as you finish, go to my apartment and stay there. I'll call you sometime Sunday to let you know I'm safely out of the Vatican. Whenever you leave the apartment, cover your head, put on dark glasses, wear the raincoat, and plod. A lot of men would remember a woman with your hair and eyes and figure. I should be back within a week."

Craig opened a small satchel and handed her a revolver. "Do you know how to shoot one of these?"

She took it in her hand and studied it. "Papa taught me the basics of guns. He believed a woman must be prepared to defend herself. This one is very light."

"It's a thirty-eight, with a short barrel. Holds five bullets and has a release here to swing the cylinder open for reloading. The hammer is shrouded to keep it from snagging as you pull it from your purse." He took the gun from her and loaded the cylinder. "If you run into Lastavis's men, I don't want you defenseless.

These bullets pack more punch than a normal thirty-eight. One bullet will stop a man. Aim for the center of the chest and don't hesitate. Hesitating or trying to wound rather than kill is a sure way to die." He held up a thin gold-plated metal pack. "This looks like a cigarette case. It contains ten bullets. Practice loading the cylinder until you have the procedure down pat. If you have to shoot, count your shots. If possible, reload before you're empty."

He put the gun and cigarette case in her purse, reached into the satchel again, and held up what looked like a fountain pen. "This is a miniature phosphorus flare. Clasp it in the palm of your hand, put your thumb in the middle like this, and bend it until you feel it break. Count to three, toss it toward your assailant, and close your eyes. It will momentarily blind anyone within ten feet. That can save you in a tenuous situation."

Craig handed the purse to her and kissed her softly on the lips. "The key is to stay inconspicuous, which means spending most of your time in my apartment. If you run into trouble, go to Rita. She'll hide you until I return. I will come back for you. Remember, leave Montayne bound and gagged."

Before Darlena could say anything, he slipped out the door, closing it behind him. She bolted the door and watched from the window until he disappeared at the far end of the street. Nausea burned her stomach. Despite the cool breeze coming through the window, perspiration dotted her face. The farm in Luguri, the security of home, and the smell of gymnastics training rooms had become remote memories from another life. Lastavis had wiped away her past. Only the present and the future existed.

What about the future? What happens after the robbery? She didn't know and refused to speculate. For now, concentrate on surviving. Darlena sagged onto the sofa. Lastavis would continue searching for her, thinking a naïve frightened young woman remained the only danger to his conspiracy. That thought brought a weak smile to her face. She wasn't the danger. Craig Reynolds, the master jewel thief, was stalking the beast of the Vatican. Craig could be as cunning and ruthless as Lastavis.

Darlena sensed that she had no future. But shortly, neither would Lastavis. That belief comforted her.

CHAPTER 34

▼

Craig paused in the shadows and scanned St. Peter's Square silhouetted in evening moonlight. People mingled at the fountains. Some strolled among colonnade pillars. Others lounged on the basilica steps. None paid particular attention as he crossed the square with the confident stride characteristic of a Swiss Guard.

At Porta Sant'Anna gate, he spoke a greeting in coarse Italian to the Gendarme, who nodded and let him pass without checking his identification papers. Craig stepped inside the Vatican walls. Every nerve, every muscle, every brain cell clicked into overdrive. Over the next thirty-six hours, he would rob the Vatican and walk back out through this gate.

To his left were the Swiss Guard barracks. He could not afford to be trapped into spending time there. The Pope's Village angled off to the right. On the other side of the village sat the fuel storage tanks. Ahead to the left were the walls of the Apostolic Palace, containing administrative offices and the Pope's apartment. Four priests passed by without taking note of him. Two Gendarmes traversed his path and disappeared into the darkness of an archway leading into the Belvedere Court. No one pays attention to a Swiss Guard walking around the Vatican grounds. Once he entered the buildings, the rules would change. Gendarmes have responsibility for patrolling the buildings. But Cardinal Sergio's drawings made him more knowledgeable about hidden passageways, unused building entries, and remote corners of Vatican buildings.

Craig walked along the outer wall of the Sistine Chapel, stepped through a vaulted door, and emerged inside St. Peter's Basilica. The basilica appeared more massive in the deserted semi-darkness than he remembered from his daytime visits. Each footstep echoed along the nave. He paused at a side alcove containing a bronze tabernacle ornately decorated with colored marble and flanked on each side by two life-size bronze angels. A priest bowed at the altar in silent prayer. His catlike night vision surveyed the vast interior, matching up dark images with his mental visualization of the basilica layout and his daylight observations. The door on the left side led to the Royal Staircase, used by the Pope for entering the basilica on occasions when a ceremonial entry through the front doors was not preferred.

Craig softened his footsteps, noting that the echo of the heavy Swiss Guard boots diminished but did not disappear. Ahead of him, the central altar loomed. Massive bronze pillars spiraled upward a hundred feet, supporting the magnificent Baldacchino canopy over the papal altar and tomb of St. Peter. Some called it the most awesome work of indoor structural art in the entire world. The Michelangelo Dome stretched far above him. He couldn't steal the Baldacchino or Michelangelo Dome, but the basilica would be an ideal place to make a stand if trapped. The Vatican would hesitate to risk damaging these priceless relics by attacking. Even more potent, threatening to destroy the Baldacchino would force the Papacy to bargain.

He lingered, relishing the exhilaration of being an infinitesimal speck invading the most opulent spiritual empire in the world. Like a virus, the speck would wreak havoc on this gargantuan religious organism and destroy Lastavis's conspiracy.

Craig stepped out into the evening light, paced across the Santa Marta Square, and swung past St. Carlo Palace. Two priests knelt in solitary meditation under the branches of an oak tree. Priests wandering around the grounds at night or cloistered in prayer in a remote corner presented a potential risk of being seen moving treasures. He would need to reconnoiter the route immediately before hauling loot to the carriage garage.

The freight car containing marble for Granople was parked against the hollowed-out hill behind the railroad station, almost out of view. He scanned the vicinity and saw no one. His hands unlocked the huge sliding door on the freight car and shoved it open enough to allow squeezing inside. He quickly located the appropriate crate. Pressure with his palm on a painted label swung one side open on concealed hinges. He reached in, pulled a metal handle off an inside wall of the crate, and inserted the handle into a notch in the freight car floor. Rotating the handle disengaged the trap door from its locked position, making it accessible for Romano's entry.

Craig pulled the Sig Sauer nine millimeter automatic off the crate wall and inserted it out of view into the back of his belt. After closing the crate, he climbed from the freight car and put the padlock back on the sliding door.

At exactly 10:07, Craig paused on the deserted Via Pio X in the Pope's Village, clicked on a cigarette lighter, extinguished it, and re-lit it.

Romano emerged from the shadows, carrying a wooden toolbox. Craig loaded electronic gear taken from the freight cars into the box. They walked up the narrow boulevard toward the Vatican Library building.

Two figures emerged through an archway on the opposite end of the courtyard bordering the Vatican Museum.

Craig muttered in a low whisper to Romano. "They're Papal Gendarmes making a random round. Maybe they'll ignore us since I'm dressed as a Swiss Guardsman."

The Gendarmes cut across their path as one called out. "Identify yourselves."

Craig saw Romano's free hand slide into his jacket and clutch a knife handle. "It's too early to have bodies begin disappearing," Craig whispered. "The Vatican will suspect something. Let's talk our way past."

He paused and waited for the approaching Gendarmes. "I'm Sergeant Montayne, escorting the craftsman to a repair job at the library."

The older Gendarme frowned. "Such a job at this hour requires permission from the Duty Officer of the Papal Gendarmes."

Craig replied politely but firmly. "When Cardinal Cumara personally requests service, we do not hesitate to render the service."

The Gendarme glanced at Romano slouching like a bored laborer irritated at being roused out late in the evening. "This is not proper procedure," the Gendarme admonished.

"The circumstances make prompt action necessary."

The Gendarme's frown deepened. "What circumstances?"

"The cardinal ..." Craig hesitated, and finally continued. "Cardinal Cumara has a rather embarrassing personal need."

The Gendarmes looked at each other. The younger man gave the traditional exaggerated Italian shrug, bringing his shoulders up close to his ears. "Perhaps it is better that we don't know the details," he said.

The other Gendarme frowned again at Craig. "It is not the proper procedure."

"I realize the violation and apologize."

The Gendarme's frown diminished. An apology from a Swiss Guardsman obviously pleased him. Gendarmes and Swiss Guards defended their assigned procedural responsibilities, clashing on trivial issues, always with polite but resolute firmness. Apologies were rarely offered. The Gendarme motioned to his partner. They continued on across the courtyard.

Romano watched them disappear into the archway. "You have nerves of steel and the mind of a sly fox."

"Protocol is a way of life here," Craig said. "The protocol is meticulously carried out with a polite, firm, and inviolate tedium. It can work to our advantage. They'll brag about the apology to other Gendarmes, but they won't make a formal report of the incident."

They crossed the garden to the corridor of the underground garage. Craig unlocked the heavy wooden doors, then closed and re-locked them after they entered. He led the way through the darkness to the washing alcove and used a small light to illuminate the drain grating. Romano stooped down, lifted off the grating, climbed down into the pit, and pushed away blocks sealing the entryway into the catacombs.

Craig lowered the toolbox to Romano. "Leave the electronic gear just inside the catacombs. I'll need it for aborting the security systems on the vault and museums. When you climb from the catacombs to the railroad platform, you'll be ten meters from the freight car. It's parked back against the hill and has a distinctive white star on the sliding door. The bottom trap door to the car is unlocked. I'll see you back here at seven fifteen tomorrow night. Bring appropriate weapons from the freight car. We can hide them in a carriage in the garage, in case we need them quickly."

Craig replaced the grating, smoothed away all marks on the floor, and checked his uniform to remove clinging dirt.

As he reentered the carriage garage, he heard the ominous clatter of keys. A Gendarme and fireman were making a nightly round fifteen minutes early. Thad Raphano had told him they never deviated from their schedule. Craig knew from experience that Italians abhor the regimen of the clock. He ducked behind a carriage as their flashlights pierced the darkness. They wouldn't demand an explanation if they saw him here, but they would remember his presence after the robbery. He didn't want any attention focused on the carriage garage.

The two men plodded along the corridor, stopping often to peer into alcoves, chatting to each other in Italian. The Gendarme continued down the long aisle to the end of the building and sauntered back, motioning to the fireman to follow him as he walked toward the exit door.

The heavy door slammed shut behind them.

Craig crept out into the corridor running between rows of carriages. Vatican night patrols were always on the prowl, but the clanging keys dangling from the fireman's belt would alert him to their approach. Thad had explained the procedure. A Papal Gendarme and fireman begin their nightly round at the Governor's Palace. Over a five-hour period, they walk through every tunnel, corridor, dark passageway, and dimly lit garden area, tromping up and down hundreds of steps. They check every building, virtually every room, searching for signs of fire or water leakage. The nightly ritual is never neglected and never shortened. The fireman carries a heavy ring of keys that open fifty different locked doors. They stop to sign their names on revolving paper drum timers at numerous locations, verifying that they've been there and saw no fire and no leaking water pipes. Two hours after the first team begins, a second team starts on the same route, tracing each footstep taken by the first two men. Their main concern is fire. Fire is considered a much deadlier enemy than any intruder. So the schedules are rigidly the same, with the men readily detected by the clatter of keys.

Craig hustled across the huge chamber, unlocked the massive wooden door, slipped through, relocked it, and stepped into the vast gardens. Disciplined military training reflected in every movement as he repeated the words to himself. "All right, Guardsman John Montayne, it is time to think like a Swiss Guard, talk like a Swiss Guard, breathe like a Swiss Guard."

He smiled thinly. "And rob the Vatican while you're doing it."

CHAPTER 35

▼

At his Rotterdam house in the Netherlands, Inspector Martin Von Meier set aside the book on Greek history that he had been reading, pulled the pipe from his mouth, and picked up the ringing telephone.

"Von Meier here," he said into the receiver.

"This is Lieutenant Palermo of the Rome Investigative Division," a voice said. "I have some information that may be of interest to you."

Von Meier flipped through his notepad to an empty page. "Go ahead."

"You alerted us that Karl Brauder's people have made several trips to Milan, Florence, and Rome. One of my men doing drug surveillance at the Rome airport noted the arrival of Gerhard Kusler, accompanied by a baldheaded older man. They were met by two men, one apparently German and the other Italian. Our man made no effort to follow them."

Von Meier puffed on his pipe. "The older man would be Brom Eidler. It's unusual for him to travel that distance. Kusler travels only to close deals, coordinate collecting merchandise already stolen, or kill someone."

"We have no recent robbery large enough to attract someone of Kusler's importance," Palermo said.

"Then I suspect a major robbery is imminent," Von Meier replied. "I'll be there as soon as possible."

"Let me know your flight schedule and I'll meet you at the airport," Palermo said.

"Thank you." Von Meier started to hang up and then spoke again. "Bring the list of significant potential targets in Italy that use the Bratius security system."

Von Meier replaced the receiver, leaned back in his chair, and puffed on his pipe.

Maybe the American jewel thief was doing business with Karl Brauder. If so, the magnitude of the heist would be large. Very large.

CHAPTER 36

▼

The forenoon sun warmed the air as Craig strode down the Via di Belvedere roadway adjacent to the Pope's Village. Workers in coveralls intermingled with drably dressed women plodding toward the Porta Sant'Anna gate for a shopping trip to the markets. The smell of baked bread enlivened the light breeze. Except for a few hours sleep huddled in a storeroom of the mosaic workshop, he had spent the night reconnoitering the sprawling museums, confirming that they contained no new hidden door alarms and no complex locks. Archaic electronic eyes positioned in entry corridors and alarms for detecting removal of individual paintings had been easy to disable.

Craig crossed the Belvedere Court and turned toward the entry to the underground vault. To the left, the luxurious gardens of the popes glistened in the sunlight. The sprawling green lawns of the Giardino Quadrato Garden, with its massive fountain in the middle, covered the area ahead. Beneath the green lawn, the vault and its treasures awaited him.

He stepped into the concrete passageway leading down into the cool underground and walked confidently to two Papal workers sitting at a desk. "What's the problem with the alarm system?" he said in Italian harshened by Schwyzerdutsch and assumed an authoritative stance.

The two men looked at each other and shrugged. "Nothing is wrong."

Craig stalked through the heavy wooden doors leading into the vault area. "We've received an alarm twice today in the barracks security room. It's an irritating nuisance."

One man followed him. "Monsignor Pompa is not here right now. I'm certain he's already made arrangements to have it corrected."

Craig surveyed the surroundings. The locked metal panel housing the alarm mechanism for the doors and vault looked typical of Bratius protection systems. His boots thudded on the tile floor, but softer shoes could move silently down the concrete-walled tunnel. The massive wooden doors came within an inch of the floor. Stuffing blankets against the cracks would seal off any detection of light from the other side of the doors while they opened the vault. Further ahead, a massive vault door protruded from the wall facing him.

With his back to the two men, Craig eased out a digital camera and took three pictures of the vault door. Later he would study the pictures to determine the exact model number and details of the locking mechanism. He shifted his attention to the man. "Has the vault been opened today?"

The man spread his hands, palms up. "The vault is opened only twice a week and almost never on the weekend. It was not opened this morning." Subtle irritation surfaced in the man's voice.

Craig stroked his chin, feigning deep thought. "Then the vault would not likely be the problem." He stepped up to the locked metal cabinet. With his back to the man, he pulled out a set of wire keys and inserted them into the padlock. Standing behind him, the man would assume he was opening the lock with a key from Vatican Security.

The padlock clicked open. Craig swung the metal door aside and studied the interior, matching the maze of wiring with his knowledge of the Bratius security system. Jumbled bundles of wires indicated they had not removed old wiring from the box during modifications. That would complicate the job. He began tracing key wires.

The sound of voices at the desk caught his ear. The second man was talking with someone. From the comments, it must be Monsignor Pompa. He had hoped that Pompa would not come here on Saturday forenoon. His eyes sped along the wiring, searching for the wooden doors alarm terminal.

He spotted it, imbedded behind a bundle of wires. His fingers squirmed past impeding wires, removed the input wire, and inserted onto the terminal a miniature electronic device. He reconnected the input wire to a clip in the electronic device, neutralizing the alarm system on the wooden doors. But Pompa's arrival had kept him from verifying the location and path of key connections to the vault alarm.

"Sergeant, what seems to be the problem?" Pompa demanded. "I know of no inadvertent alarms."

Craig partially closed the panel door and turned to face Pompa. The monsignor was heavyset, with a few remaining wisps of hair around his ears. He breathed like a man perpetually out of breath, through a wide flat nose that flared open with each exhalation.

"Surely they notified you, Monsignor," Craig said. Appearing upset, he picked up the phone and, with his back partially blocking Pompa's view, dialed a number. After a short conversation, he hung up. "My deepest apologies, Monsignor Pompa. The alarm originated from the Governor's Palace, not your vault area." His face flushed. "I am sorry for such a foolish mistake and inconvenience to you."

Craig hurried back to the panel, locked it, and shuffled uncomfortably as he again faced Pompa. "I sincerely apologize. Someone communicated the wrong location."

Pompa raised a stubby finger. "Procedures require contacting my office first whenever the security system malfunctions. Remind your on-duty officer of that." He shifted to the demeanor of a priest offering solace to a chastened confessor. "Your promptness was commendable. Good day, Sergeant."

Craig mumbled another apology as he backed through the wooden doors. Pompa began talking with the two workers, admonishing them to polish the vault door today. Craig clenched his fist in triumph as he hurried up the passageway and into the sunlight. Papal officials relish giving pious reprimands to staff members for mistakes, but no one questions the integrity of Vatican personnel. The Vatican was truly a unique world. Beneath the protocol, politeness, and spiritual passion, fierce territorial battles and political intrigue roiled the holy waters. That made it a perfect target.

He glanced at his watch. In less than ten hours, he and Romano would begin stripping the Vatican. In twenty-four hours, he would be outside the Vatican walls or in a deadly confrontation with Vatican security people. Every nerve and muscle in his body pulsed. Fear of failure disappeared. Confidence and concentration, but no cockiness, would dominate every action from this moment forward.

Craig had never been so certain of his destiny. He would stamp his name indelibly into the lore of those who dare to do the impossible.

CHAPTER 37

▼

Two men, one a tall Swiss Guardsman and the other a broad shouldered priest, walked silently up to the massive wooden doors barring entryway to the vault. Craig glanced at his watch. 7:34 p.m. "There shouldn't be any rounds in this area for at least thirty minutes." He knelt and inserted slotted metal probes into the door lock. His fingers moved with the assurance of a skilled surgeon, immune to the slightest flicker of nervousness. Despite the warmth of the corridor, no perspiration dotted his forehead.

Romano paced back and forth in the passageway, listening and watching for unexpected intruders.

The heavy bolt clicked back, unlocking the door. Craig pushed a massive door open and slipped through. Romano came in behind him, re-locked the door, and began stuffing blankets along the bottom to seal off all light.

By the time Romano finished, Craig had unlocked the metal cabinet beside the vault and laid out electronic gear in a pattern rehearsed a dozen times. He positioned a small light to study the maze of wires in the interior of the cabinet and illuminated drawings spread in front of him with another light.

His eyes darted back and forth between the drawings and the alarm cabinet. A mild frown grew progressively more intense.

"Something is wrong?" Romano asked.

"The part that I need to reach is buried behind a jumble of wires. Over the years they've made changes and left old wires dangling. Disarming the vault alarm will be more difficult than I had expected."

Romano gazed over his shoulder. "What can I do to help?"

Craig's eyes remained focused on the cabinet wiring. "Go sit beside the doors and listen for the return of the guards. Your panting breath and pacing distract me."

Ten minutes passed.

Another ten minutes passed. Still not a drop of sweat formed on Craig's face. His fingers plied wires and positioned new connectors without the slightest tremble. He picked up another small bag and set out tools one by one, placing each in a precise position. "Now I can use your help," he called out to Romano.

Craig talked slowly, pointing with his fingers. "The vault alarm circuit is located behind these four wires. You spread the wires apart with the wooden prong so I can reach through. The wood can't conduct electricity, but jarring any of this stuff might activate an alarm. So we'll do everything with the patience of a brain surgeon."

Romano grasped the wooden prong with his thick, callused hands, blew out a long breath, and slid the prong in among the wires.

Craig meticulously disconnected and repositioned wires, silent except for an occasional instruction to Romano. For the first time, beads of sweat formed on his forehead, drawn out by the musty warmth of the tunnel. He paused and dried his hands with a towel, maneuvered a small plastic screwdriver through the maze of wiring, loosened an electrical terminal, inserted his own wire, and repeated the procedure on the adjacent terminal. After connecting his leads to an electronic instrument, he switched it on.

The needle on the dial jumped. "We're now tied in parallel with the signal going from the locking mechanism of the vault to the alarm," Craig said. "This instrument will maintain an input signal, aborting the vault burglar alarm."

His hand slid small pliers between wires and locked onto the plug. "If I touch a connecting wire as I bring this out, or if something exists that I haven't recognized, the alarm may activate. If it does, we need to leave in a hurry."

He began extracting the pronged plug from its socket, his hands moving with the unwavering precision of a slow motion mechanical robot.

The plug eased outward and cleared the wires. Craig smiled. "The operation is a success. Our patient has been anesthetized."

He hurried to the vault and spread instruments on the floor around him. A glance at his watch showed 8:15. A little behind schedule. Romano worked as the nurse assisting the surgeon, handing tools to Craig in an operation rehearsed at Romano's apartment. Heavy insulation muted the high pitched whine of the tiny diamond drill bit penetrating into the tumbler mechanism. While Craig drilled, Romano kept pacing back to the huge wooden doors to listen.

The drill was almost to the correct depth now. The drilling had gone faster than Craig had allotted in his plan. They were back on schedule.

Romano ran back from the wooden door to Craig and tapped him on the shoulder. "I hear the sound of keys coming into the corridor on the outside of the door."

Craig turned off the drill and lights. They knelt in the blackened silence.

The sound of clanging keys came closer. Footsteps paused at the wooden doors. Muted voices conversed.

Craig's heartbeat quickened. Why had the guards stopped at the door? Was it part of the routine or had they seen something suspicious?

The clatter of keys moved away from the door and slowly faded into the distance. Craig heard the shish of Romano's knife sliding back into its sheath.

Romano switched on the lights. Craig began drilling again.

Five minutes later, he inserted a thread-sized probe and attached the lead wire to a hand held computer. His eyes studied the computer screen as his fingers meticulously worked with the vault dials.

Finally Craig stopped and wiped his face with the towel. Not even his robotic concentration could block a quiver of apprehension. "We're at the moment of truth. A false combination automatically locks the tumblers for one hour. A second mistake locks the vault for eight hours."

He grasped the heavy metal handle and pulled the lever down to its lowest position.

No sound. Romano scowled.

Craig clenched his fist. "We've got it. I felt the tumblers drop."

Romano jubilantly grasped the heavy door and swung it open.

Craig stepped inside and switched on the light. "This is a cavern, not a vault. It's much bigger than I visualized." He studied the lock on a large metal cabinet. "These are simple locks. I'll open them and you check the contents."

They moved methodically along the wall, Craig unlocking cabinets faster than Romano could search them.

"Mother of Jesus, look at these," Romano exclaimed.

Craig glanced back where Romano had unwrapped a satin cloth, revealing a glittering array of huge uncut diamonds. "Package them up and admire them later."

Craig had opened ten cabinets when Romano waved some sheets of paper in front of his face. "These look like a list of what's in each cabinet."

Craig perused them. "We hit the jackpot. These will save us a lot of time. Some of the listing has handwritten changes scribbled in. We'll carry the list with us. I suspect whatever lists they have elsewhere are not up to date."

He smiled as he began unlocking specific cabinets. "These guys are arrogantly confident. The greatest collection of art, jewelry, and wealth in the world is stored here. Yet, they guard it with an archaic alarm system and a vault that is simple to crack with the latest technology. Then they put lists inside to make it easy."

"Only the master thief could have reached the vault," Romano replied.

Craig moved throughout the vault, unlocking selected cabinets. Romano piled the contents into bags, often letting out breaths of delight.

"This cabinet contains cash," Craig said. "It must be reserve currency that the Vatican keeps for emergencies. There must be over ten million dollars of Euros, U.S. currency, Japanese Yen, and others. They've all been previously circulated, which makes them untraceable. This just gets better and better."

An hour later, Craig stopped unlocking cabinets and gazed at a back corner where heavy velvet fabric covered something large beneath it. "The Vatican does everything first class. No covering stuff with a cheap tarp. Let's see what lies underneath."

Craig flung the cover back.

Romano gasped at the glittering display. "Is that gold bullion?"

"It must be the bullion the Vatican bought from the United States in the nineteen thirties." He did a quick count of the rows and stacks, ran the math through his head, and blew out a breath. "We're staring at fifty million Euros worth of gold that we don't have to move through a dealer. I know a smelter who will melt it down, recast it, and fence it for a reasonable fee."

Romano grasped four bars in his arms. "These will be heavy to carry out of here."

Craig checked his watch. "You start hauling gold bars to the catacombs while I open and empty the most valuable cabinets. We can't risk being spotted crossing the open plaza. Take the route through the garden edge that we discussed. We have about thirty minutes before the next round by the patrol. But priests or Gendarmes can be in the garden anytime. Scout the route before you carry any gold bars out."

With the inventory list, Craig concentrated on the important five percent of the remaining cabinets. He unlocked them with the speed of a person using a key, dumping contents into cloth bags. One large cabinet contained richly jeweled crowns, probably confiscated from deposed kings. Another contained magnificent jeweled gold figurines brought back from pillaged Aztec and Inca cities by Spanish conquerors. Diamond necklaces and bracelets crammed other drawers. Compilations of Vatican wealth had vastly underestimated the enormity of jewelry accumulated by contribution and confiscation over the centuries. Equally important, he suspected many of the items had never been photographed or described in detail, making it difficult to issue a meaningful list of stolen items. He stifled a rising euphoria and concentrated on the task.

Romano hustled into the vault, pushing a wheelbarrow. "I can haul much more on each trip with this."

Craig shook his head. "The wheelbarrow will leave tracks. They'll be able to follow your path directly to the garage."

Romano grimaced. "I didn't think of that."

"It's still a good idea. Use the wheelbarrow to haul gold and bags to a hiding place in the garden near the garage entry. We'll lug them from there into the garage. Make several trips with the loaded wheelbarrow all the way to the north wall. They'll think we somehow took the gold over the wall. Trying to figure how we could do that without setting off the wall alarms will distract them from searching for other ways to haul out the loot."

Romano gazed around the vault. "I still can't believe we're in here. The greatest treasure in the world and we're hauling it off."

Craig continued rifling cabinets. "Don't get cocky. We still have to get it to the catacombs and then move the freight car to Granople."

A distant bell tower tolled one in the morning as Craig and Romano moved the wheelbarrow along a narrow path in the garden. Sweat drenched them. They had carried jewelry and treasures to the catacombs and hauled a significant quantity of gold bars to a remote fountain. From there, the gold had been hand carried through the garage to the catacombs. Craig's muscles ached with fatigue. Romano's massive arms seemed impervious to the burden of heavy bars.

Two figures emerged ahead of them on an adjacent path. Gendarmes were making an unscheduled round of the gardens. Romano twisted the wheelbarrow off the pathway, dumping the contents into shrubbery. They crouched down as the two soldiers came their way.

Craig motioned to Romano. They crawled along the edge of a flowerbed and slipped among statues adorning the corner of the plaza. A three-quarter-moon gliding luminously between scant clouds bathed the area in golden twilight.

The Gendarmes paced slowly toward them, their boots clinking on the rocks of the walkway, their flashlight beams sweeping the area.

A Gendarme called out. "Is anyone here? Identify yourself."

"It's probably those accursed cats," the shorter man complained. "They're overrunning the gardens this year. There won't be any birds left if they don't start trapping the cats. The cardinal says cats keep rats under control. I would rather deal with the rats. Let's swing past the basilica and stop at the Hospice. Sister Greta always leaves a pot of coffee brewing and some of her spiced cookies in the lobby." He clicked off his flashlight.

The other Gendarme continued along the walkway, illuminating shrubbery with his light. "Bishop Maurice complained that some villagers use the gardens for a late night rendezvous. He found condoms stuffed into the base of a saint's statue. The captain said the bishop virtually foamed at the mouth." He raised his voice. "Anyone caught defiling the sanctity of the gardens will be banished from the village."

He made one more pass with the flashlight, turned to leave, and then swung back around to re-examine one section of shrubbery. His light illuminated the tip of the wheelbarrow handle among leafy bush branches. He stepped into the shrubbery. "Some clumsy workman left a mess here. Or perhaps he is hiding something that he plans to steal later tonight."

Craig whispered to Romano. "We can't allow them to see what's in the bag."

Romano unsheathed his knife. "I'll slip around behind and kill them before they have a chance to sound a warning."

"Give me your priest's robe," Craig replied. "Maybe I can distract them. If not, you take the burly one with the mustache. I'll handle the other one."

Romano scowled as he yanked off his robe. "We better kill them now."

The Gendarme played his flashlight onto the large, lumpy sack and edged further into the brush, careful not to snag his uniform on branches.

Craig moved a dozen yards away, stepped onto the walkway, and hurried toward them.

Both Gendarmes turned at the sound of his footsteps.

"I'm glad I found you," Craig said as he panted for breath. "The wheelbarrow tipped over and I was unable to lift the contents back on by myself."

The Gendarme's mustache rolled up along the edges of his nose and his forehead furrowed. "What are you doing with a wheelbarrow in the gardens this time of night?"

"They are consecrating cornerstones for three new churches tomorrow. We must label the cornerstones properly for the ceremony." Craig wiped perspiration from his forehead. "Frankly, I cannot imagine why they could not wait a few more days. I have spent the night hauling these heavy bricks to His Eminence for certification." He bent over the sack and prepared to lift it back onto the wheelbarrow.

One Gendarme assisted him while the other steadied the wheelbarrow.

With the wheelbarrow back in the pathway, Craig grasped the handles. "Thank you. I had despaired of finding anyone to help at such a late hour. God seems to take compassion on overworked, under-appreciated priests."

He started pushing the wheelbarrow.

The older, burly Gendarme held out a hand to stop him. "Procedures require an escort for anyone moving materials late at night. His Eminence should have notified the Duty Officer."

Craig's mind spun through several possibilities and rejected them. No way to avoid a confrontation. The backside of the Pope's Summer Cottage was hidden from view, plus the splashing noise of a nearby fountain would mask sounds of struggle. "I do what I'm told to do," Craig said in a loud voice to assure Romano hearing his words. "His Eminence is working in the Pope's Summer Cottage. You can discuss this with him."

The other Gendarme flashed a sympathetic smile and helped steady the wheelbarrow as Craig shoved it along the path. The more arrogant one followed behind them, commenting again about violation of procedures.

Craig maneuvered the wheelbarrow past the front side of the cottage and onto the pathway leading to the rear entrance. His eyes spotted a light shining in the window of the cottage. Who would be working in the cottage this time of night? They would have to kill the two Gendarmes first and then deal with whoever is in the cottage.

The rear door of the cottage swung open. Even in the dim light, the red of a cardinal's garb stood out. Despite the slouched shoulders and bent back, the figure conveyed bulky mass as he called out gruffly. "Where have you been? I need you to identify which cornerstones go to St. Vincent's."

Craig lowered the wheelbarrow handle and turned to face the two Gendarmes, blocking their pathway toward the cottage door and obscuring their view of the red-garbed cardinal. "This is not a good time to explain protocol. His Eminence is already irritable and we still have several hours of work." Then his face brightened. "We could use your assistance on stacking cornerstones in position for labeling."

"Labeling cornerstones are your problem, not ours," the older Gendarme replied. He motioned to the other Gendarme. "Sister Greta's cookies will be gone if we linger here. Let's finish our round." He turned back to Craig. "I will write this up in the nightly report. It is important that procedures be properly followed, even by His Eminence."

The other Gendarme stared toward the hulking figure with hands clamped on hips, made a sympathetic comment to Craig in a low voice, and followed the older Gendarme toward the front of the cottage.

Craig watched them disappear and then wrapped his arms around the oversize cardinal wearing garb that barely reached below his knees. "How did you get into the cottage?"

Romano laughed. "I also have some expertise at entering locked buildings. The presence of a discarded cardinal's robe was pure luck."

Craig glanced at his watch. "It'll be daylight in five hours. We don't have time to haul any more gold from the vault. You begin moving what we have stashed at the fountain to the catacombs. I'll go back and lock the vault. With the inventory sheets gone, they'll have a difficult time determining what we heisted. Any delay gives us more time to fence merchandise. As soon as we finish here, we'll start on the museums. The museums will be riskier. In the vault we could work behind closed doors. The guards check the museums regularly for fires."

Then he smiled. "But what is available in the museums is worth the risk."

CHAPTER 38

▼

Craig and Romano pressed back against a narrow doorway in the museum building wall, watching two Gendarmes talking a mere twenty feet away. The moon glistened above the walls of the Vatican, bathing the Belvedere Court with shimmering, shadowy patches of light. One guard turned and started toward the archway on the other side. The second followed him.

Craig and Romano eased from the doorway and ran along the wall to the far side of the plaza. It took Craig less than a minute to unlock the wooden door. Once inside, they climbed the narrow stairs to another locked door, which yielded quickly to his keys.

They gazed into the semi-darkness of the Vatican Library. Row after row after row of shelves crammed with books and manuscripts spread away in both directions. Vaulted ceilings decorated with magnificent frescoes reinforced the enormity of the cavernous room. Their black soft-soled shoes made a faint shuffling sound on the marble flooring as Craig led the way to a large cabinet.

"This cabinet contains the Vatican Codex, a Fourth Century Old Testament written in Greek. The Roman Catholic Church ordained it as the Biblical authority for scripture. The Codex and the first printed Gutenberg Bible are the most revered manuscripts in the Vatican. We'll take them with us to use as hostages if we're trapped. The Vatican will accept almost any terms to prevent destruction of these books."

Craig unlocked the cabinet, sealed the Bible in a ziptop plastic bag, slipped it into Romano's knapsack, and placed a similar looking book in the cabinet.

Two locked doors later, they entered the vast Pinacoteca Museum, a semi-maze of corridors and rooms with walls bedecked with paintings. Craig oriented himself in the dim lighting. "We have eight paintings to collect in here. There are no dark alcoves to hide in. If the guards show up on their rounds, we need to hide in another section. So keep your ears tuned."

Romano took the long cylindrical bag from his shoulder, spread it on the floor, and helped Craig lift a gold-encrusted frame from the wall. Craig slit the supporting backing away from the frame, enclosed the picture within thin protective cloth, and slid it into the cylinder. While he did that, Romano taped the replica into the frame and repositioned the picture on the wall.

They moved from picture to picture, doing a job they had rehearsed until the exact technique for each picture had been perfected. An hour later, eight paintings were securely encased inside the cylinder.

Craig glanced at his watch. "We can expect the guards in twenty minutes. Let's make a quick pass through the Etruscan and Pio-Clementino Museums."

With the same precision, they grabbed exquisite vases, a unique jade statue, and intricately jeweled figurines.

As Craig closed a cabinet, his ears picked up a distant jangling. Romano's raised eyebrows indicated he also heard it.

They hustled back inside the Vatican Library. Craig guided Romano to the far end of a narrow aisle and into a tiny alcove containing a writing table. They climbed atop the table and squeezed into the narrow space between the end of the bookshelf and the wall.

The thunk of the heavy lock disengaging and the wooden doors swinging open echoed in the emptiness. The doors closed again. The clank of the key locking the door reverberated off the vaulted ceilings.

The jangle of keys, intermingled with the sound of voices and dull footsteps, approached. The clanging keys told Craig the fireman walked in front, followed by the sharp staccato of Gendarme boots striking the marble floor. He squeezed deeper into the narrow space as a light beam played across the front edge of the aisle. The fireman would stare down the long, dark shelves, his eyes searching for the flickering glow of a beginning fire, his nose sniffing for the slightest scent of smoldering embers. Intently looking, but looking for the glimmer of fire, not figures shoved back into the shadows.

The glow of the flashlight disappeared. The jangling keys and footsteps faded away.

They climbed down from the table and trailed the dull, distant sound of clanging keys. The Gendarme and fireman entered the Metal and Coin Cabinets Museum, perused every corner, exited through a distant door, and locked it.

Craig removed selected ancient coins and rare Papal coins from the cases, replacing them with a group of coins intended only to prevent guards making rounds from noticing empty display cases. Then he shifted his attention to the locked metal cabinets along the wall.

Despite tension and growing fatigue, he smiled as he gazed around the huge vaulted room. "What the Vatican extorted from people over the centuries and promenaded in their Medalgliere has now been returned to the common man."

Romano hoisted the bags onto his shoulders. "My days as a common man have ended. Are we done?"

Craig led the way toward closed wooden doors. "One small insult remains. A short visit to the Pope's gift room to snatch a few prizes and we can say farewell to the Vatican Museums."

The first faint streaks of sunrise lightened the night sky when they entered the Belvedere Court, lugging bulging knapsacks. The vault and museums had been gutted of five hundred million dollars worth of gold, cash, jewelry, exquisite artifacts, coins, and paintings.

Craig glanced at his watch. They were fifteen minutes ahead of schedule.

At the edge of the archway, Romano stopped. "Someone is coming along the walkway on the outside of the courtyard," he whispered.

They listened as footsteps approached, reached the archway, and turned toward them.

Romano grimaced. "He's coming this way. The sound says it's a Gendarme."

Craig set down the bag, pulled off his backpack and shoved them beside a shadowy bench. "Act casual."

They stood in front of the bench, shielding it from view, apparently in quiet conversation.

The Gendarme came through the archway and stopped to look at them. "Identify your self," he said in a protocol-sounding, non-accusatory voice.

Romano spoke in a low voice. "I am Father Quasalvi, the marble tile monk."

The Gendarme's forehead wrinkled and his eyes narrowed as he stared at Craig's feet.

Craig realized the Gendarme's flashlight had illuminated the dark tennis shoes on both men's feet. Unusual wear for a priest and absolutely out of place for a Swiss Guardsman.

Craig's fingers clamped onto the Gendarme's windpipe, trapping challenging words in his throat.

The Gendarme grasped for his gun. Romano pinned his arms and drove him backward against the archway.

Jammed against the brick wall, with his breath throttled, the Gendarme struggled helplessly.

Craig heard the rustle of Romano's knife clearing its sheath.

"No knife," Craig growled.

He slammed the Gendarme's head against the wall. The guard slumped to the ground.

"Dead men don't talk," Romano replied, still grasping the knife.

"Bloodstains do. Check the other courtyard."

Romano ran to the opposite side of the archway, scanned the area, and returned. "There is nobody else around."

Craig gagged the unconscious Gendarme and began tying his hands. "When the Gendarme fails to report back, they'll start searching for him. All the irregularities of tonight will surface. They'll pinpoint a priest and Swiss Guard as suspects. So we need to move fast."

Romano scowled. "Why not strangle this guy? He can identify us."

"John Montayne might be greedy enough to help rob the Vatican, but he would never kill a Gendarme. I want them to believe Montayne personally participated in the robbery. We'll dump the Gendarme in the workroom behind the Pope's Summer Cottage. When they find him, he'll only verify what they already suspect."

At the workroom, Romano stuffed the trussed Gendarme into a closet and shoved heavy furniture against the door.

They hurried across the gardens, slipped through the heavy wooden doors into the Pope's Garage, climbed through the drain into the catacombs, and dumped the knapsacks onto the floor beside gold bars and other treasures from the vault.

Romano raised his clenched fists above his head. "We did it! The Vatican treasure house belongs to us."

Craig plopped down and leaned back against a tomb. Concentrating on alarms and locks, hauling loot, and outmaneuvering wandering guards had exhausted him. No previous robbery had been so complex, so lengthy, or so perilous. He felt no exhilaration yet. "Wait until we have the treasures out of the Vatican before you celebrate. You'll be busy the rest of the day moving bullion and treasures through the catacombs to the tunnel beneath the railroad platform. My disguise won't hold up very long once they discover the robbery. They'll seal all exits and search everywhere. The electronic detectors in the freight car will send a signal to your radio when they search the railroad car and relock it. Then you can load everything on the freight cars. I'll close the deal with Brauder and throw some confusion into the path of Vatican security people."

Romano clasped his massive hands onto Craig's shoulders. "No one else could have done this. No one else would even attempt such a brazen robbery. Leave quickly or you may be trapped."

Craig sensed the feeling of camaraderie. "If for some reason, you can't hide the treasures in the freight car and ride out of the Vatican, I'll figure a way to bring you out. With us holding the treasures, our bargaining position has improved dramatically."

He climbed up into the washing alcove of the Papal Garage, shed the priest's robe he had donned while climbing into the drain, and tossed it down to Romano. He replaced the grating, smoothed out all traces of footprints, put on the Swiss Guardsman boots, and checked the uniform to be certain it was clean and proper.

It was time to get out of the Vatican. Craig walked in military pace across the Giardino Quadrato to the Belvedere Court, resisting the impulse to hurry.

A cluster of Gendarmes rushed past him toward the Vatican gardens. Ahead, he saw three Swiss Guardsmen hurriedly exiting the courtyard, apparently headed for the barracks.

That wasn't normal activity. He needed to leave quickly, but exiting through the Porta Sant'Anna gate meant going directly past the Swiss Guards barracks.

"Sergeant Montayne!" a voice called out from behind him.

Craig glanced back and saw a Guardsman running toward him. This could be big trouble.

The man caught up with him and talked as he fell into stride. "Colonel Borgan has summoned all Guardsmen not manning a vital post to come immediately to the barracks. Something serious has happened. I've never seen him so distraught."

Craig stared straight ahead. "I already know about the problem. Colonel Borgan sent me to gather up Guardsmen in the Pope's Village. I'll meet you at the barracks."

"Yes sir." The man ran on ahead.

Craig veered toward the left. He circled the newspaper shop and came back down the Via Del Pellegrino roadway toward the gate. Priests and workers milled in front of Gendarmes blocking the gate. Craig pushed through the crowd and didn't slow when he reached the Gendarmes. "I'm going after Guardsmen at the cafe. Tell others that arrive to go immediately to the barracks."

One Gendarme started to say something.

Craig brushed past the guards and hurried onto the street. He walked a block and then veered away from the Vatican wall and onto a crossing street. A turn into an alleyway brought him to the cluttered back door of a clothing shop. He knelt beside a heavy metal dumpster and pulled out a plastic garbage bag stuffed behind it. He put on the ankle-length, dingy cloth coat and positioned a skull cover of a partially bald, gray-haired man over his head. Next he pulled off his boots, slipped on scuffed shoes, and shoved the boots into the bag.

He exited the alleyway as a plodding, stooped laborer carrying a lunchbox and a bag.

Craig entered the apartment and pushed open the door to the bedroom, satisfying himself that John Montayne remained securely tied and blindfolded.

He stripped off his Swiss Guard uniform. Next came the plastic face mask and colored contact lens, followed by a hot shower to rinse sweat and dirt from his body and remove dye from his hair. The pounding beads of hot water relaxed his muscles and cleared the lethargy of sleepless nights from his mind. It felt good to be normal again. No more wearing that uncomfortable uniform. No more Schwyzerdutsch to irritate his throat.

Craig went into the bedroom and cut the ropes binding the Guardsman's legs, leaving the arms handcuffed to the metal ring. "You're entitled to a certain amount of dignity." He put the trousers of the uniform back on the man.

Montayne kicked blindly at him.

Craig circled behind him, wrapped a rope around the Swiss Guardsman's throat, and strangled him into unconsciousness. He went to the refrigerator, pulled out a beer, and slowly drank it. The cold liquid soothed his raspy throat and lessened the emerging throb of a headache.

He walked back into the bedroom, picked up the telephone, dialed a number, and spoke into the phone. "The treasures have been removed as planned. The boat leaves tonight. I'll meet you in Barcelona tomorrow. Be prepared to transfer the rest of the money to my account. I carried out additional prizes. The price has increased fifteen million Euros."

Craig left the apartment, walked for six blocks, and hailed a taxi. Up to now, every step had been executed flawlessly. Exhilaration bubbled through his body, tempered by the knowledge that two critical tasks remained.

Remove the treasures from the Vatican and make the transfer to Brauder without being double-crossed.

CHAPTER 39

▼

Inspector Martin Von Meier sat in the velvet upholstered chair, one hand holding his pipe a few inches from his mouth, his eyes studying the face of Cardinal Lastavis. The Cardinal's clenched fists pressed down against the wooden top of his massive, carved desk.

"Assuming that our thieves completed their robbery of your museums early Sunday morning," Von Meier said, "they've been gone from the scene almost forty-eight hours. It would have helped if you had notified the Rome Police immediately, rather than waiting until Monday night."

Lastavis's furrowed forehead and narrowing eyes heightened his already brooding face, indicating that he resented being reprimanded or having his decisions questioned. "The robbery appeared initially to be much less extensive," Lastavis retorted. "We knew the robbers were trapped within the confines of the Vatican walls. I can assure you they have not left the Vatican since we imposed total control of the gates early Sunday morning. No one has entered or left since that time."

"I understand that you allowed freight cars and selected vehicles to enter and leave the Vatican yesterday," Von Meier continued.

Colonel Guista started to speak but Lastavis interrupted. "All freight cars inside the Vatican were searched Sunday. Every container, the undersides of the cars, everything. In addition, nobody could carry treasures from the museums to the freight cars without being observed. Only a dozen vehicles have been allowed to leave and all of those were thoroughly searched. The treasures are still within the Vatican walls."

Von Meier turned his attention to a rotund man sitting uncomfortably in a chair next to Colonel Guista. "Have you documented the extent of the robbery?"

Monsignor Andrietti, Curator of the Museums, shuffled through a stack of papers, his heavy breathing filling the momentary silence. Sweat beads drenched his bald head, forcing him to periodically wipe his thick glasses. "They stole the most valuable coins from glass display cases and locked metal cabinets. We have now confirmed that they removed eight of the most important paintings and replaced them with replicas."

He hesitated, and then continued in a voice on the verge of cracking. "The Codex and Gutenberg Bible were taken. They selectively carried off gifts given to previous Pontiffs by kings and national leaders and jewelry from both the glass counters and locked cabinets. Somehow, the thieves knew which jewelry items and paintings were imitations for display and which ones were real. Alarms on the pictures and all of the motion detectors had been aborted."

Von Meier puffed on his pipe. "Everything suggests the work of our elusive American jewel thief. His trademarks are intricate planning, knowledge of the most valuable items, and the ability to abort every detection system. The thief's ability to move within the Vatican without being seen displays expertise belonging solely to one man. Catching him before he sells the treasures may be impossible, since you have given him a two day head start."

Colonel Guista scowled. "He was seen. Corporal Calmes intercepted the thieves as they were leaving the museums. They overpowered him before he could sound the alarm and left him bound and gagged in the workroom behind the Summer Villa. The corporal's itinerary gives us an excellent fix on the time the thieves exited the museums. Our study of all traffic leaving the gates after that time absolutely assures us that the thieves could not have carried the stolen treasures from the Vatican. This thief, who has always eluded you, has not eluded us. He is still trapped inside. We will find him."

"What about the wheelbarrow incident and their obvious trip to the north wall?" The question came from a mustached man with intense dark eyes, sitting next to Von Meier.

Guista's attention shifted to Lieutenant Palermo of the Rome Investigative Division. "My Gendarmes encountered a priest who purported to be carrying cornerstones being prepared for consecration. The story by the priest was a ruse, but the alert actions of my soldiers aborted their plan for escaping over the wall." Guista gazed at Von Meier. "I'm surprised that your ingenious thief planned to climb the wall. Attempting an escape over the wall would have triggered alarms. Those alarms were not designed or installed by Bratius. They cannot be aborted.

We maintain multiple systems of sophisticated alarms on the walls to protect His Holiness and Vatican personnel from attack by terrorists."

Lieutenant Palermo snorted. "None of your other alarm systems presented any problem for the jewel thief. He probably temporarily disarmed the wall alarms. I think he hauled everything over your impregnable wall."

"The alarm system was, and still is, intact," Lastavis retorted. "The thieves and the treasures are trapped inside the Vatican walls. There is no need to expand the search beyond the Vatican or involve any police agencies at this time."

"You can't continue to hide this from the news media," Lieutenant Palermo replied. "They know something serious has happened. Why else would you shut down the museums and all access to the Vatican?"

"The thieves and the treasures are still here," Lastavis reiterated.

"You've searched every corner of this place and found nothing," Palermo responded. "If you had notified me immediately after discovering the robbery, we could have sealed off the area and perhaps trapped the thieves. My men were doing a surveillance of the airport for a suspected drug dealer last week. They noted the arrival of Gerhard Kusler, who closes deals for the most notorious stolen property dealer in Europe. Kusler was probably coming in to take delivery after the robbery Saturday night. I suspect your precious treasures are already gone from Rome. They are probably gone from Italy."

Von Meier sensed growing hostility between Palermo and the Vatican officials. Palermo had a history of brash interactions and abrasive investigative methods. It would be best to divert them from this debate. "What was so heavy that the thieves needed a wheelbarrow?" Von Meier asked.

Monsignor Andrietti wiped profuse sweat from his forehead with a linen cloth. "There was no item of exceptional weight. But altogether, they weighed over two hundred kilograms."

"Two thieves could carry that out in a few trips," Von Meier replied. "It would be foolish to use something as conspicuous as a wheelbarrow. Nothing you listed as stolen matches the heavy contents in the wheelbarrow."

Von Meier studied the layout map of the Vatican spread across the desk. "The time and location of the wheelbarrow encounter seem wrong. The location would be more appropriate if they were carrying hefty treasures from a place other than the museums."

Small puffs of smoke curled out around the edges of his mouth. His finger moved from place to place on the map and stopped at the location of the Giardino Quadrato Garden. "Perhaps they were moving items from the vault. Have you checked the vault?"

Guista growled. "That would be impossible. No one could enter the vault."

"The American jewel thief stole the Bratius drawings of your vault security system," Von Meier replied. "Did you change your protection system after our discussion?"

Lastavis glowered at Monsignor Andrietti. "Have Pompa check the vault. Do it immediately!"

Andrietti lurched up from his chair and hurried from the room.

Von Meier leaned back and sucked slowly on his pipe as he mulled the clues. The American jewel thief most certainly carried out this robbery, which means the treasures are somehow already gone. But how did he circumvent the security system on the walls? Why did he use a wheelbarrow? Why did the wheelbarrow tracks lead to the wall? Were these important clues or subterfuges? The jewel thief always spreads a web of misleading clues.

"Review again for me all of the unusual encounters Saturday night," he said to Guista. "Give me the times and the locations."

Guista thumped his stubby fingers on the Vatican layout drawings and began talking. His tone and demeanor suggested that he considered this an exercise in futility. His time would be better used coordinating the search for the trapped thieves.

An ashen Pompa steadied himself against the doorway of Lastavis's office. "We are still checking cabinets. But we know that jewelry, currency, and many bars of gold bullion are gone. At least three paintings were stolen from the vault."

Pompa's knees wobbled. He struggled to continue speaking through quivering lips. "The thieves apparently stole all the valuable jewels and took the inventory lists from the vault. We have a copy in the Papal Palace, but that copy is twenty years old. Much of it is still correct but there have been significant additions and changes. It will require many hours, perhaps several days, to determine exactly what the thieves stole."

Complete silence engulfed the room, broken only by the tick-tock of the fifteenth century jeweled mantle clock sitting on the cadenza behind Lastavis. Guista's shoulders slumped. Even Lastavis's haughty face sagged.

Palermo glared at Guista. "The thieves hauled gold bullion over your wall while your play soldiers strolled around signing inspection sheets. They even helped the fake priest push a wheelbarrow filled with stolen gold."

Guista glared back but remained silent.

Von Meier turned to Colonel Borgan, who had stood without speaking throughout the morning. "Tell me more about the missing Swiss Guardsman

John Montayne. We know he was ardently pursuing a beautiful young woman. We know he escorted a husky worker through the gardens on Friday night, in violation of procedures. We know he left the Vatican through the Porta Sant'Anna gate on Sunday morning, shortly after the robbery of the museums was discovered."

Borgan's posture remained erect, as unmoving as a statue. "It is inconceivable that Sergeant Montayne aided the thieves."

"It is inconceivable to think anything but that Montayne was an accomplice to the thieves!" Lastavis's voice exploded in anger. "He provided them with the knowledge, provided them with the access, and helped steal the treasures."

Borgan made a half-hearted rebuttal.

A knock on the door interrupted them. A middle-aged priest peered into the room and motioned to Inspector Von Meier. "There is an urgent telephone message for you."

Von Meier followed him to a small office down the corridor, closed the door as the man left, and picked up the receiver.

He listened for a few minutes, puffing slowly on his pipe, and then set the pipe on the desk. "You have my word. Where shall I meet you?"

He listened again and nodded. "I'll be there in fifteen minutes."

Von Meier stepped from the office and motioned to the priest. "Tell Cardinal Lastavis that I have an important matter that I must attend to. It may have a direct bearing on our investigation. I'll return later this morning."

Von Meier descended the Scala Regia Staircase, exited through the Bronze Door, walked half a mile to a small park, and paused beside the fountain. He had checked behind him to assure himself that no one from the Vatican followed him. He didn't know why that concerned him, but his instincts warned him to be cautious.

He scanned faces of people milling around the plaza. There were no tourists here. Older men sat on the rim of the fountain and on stone benches. Two husky men in coveralls munched on cheese and olive sandwiches. Another man, surrounded by empty wine bottles, slouched against a tree. Water gurgled from a cracked statue and spilled onto the algae-smeared marble base. Sparrows nibbled on bread crumbs. A late-morning breeze rustled leaves of overhanging tree branches.

A petite woman stepped from the heavy shrubbery on the opposite side of the fountain and walked hesitantly toward him, as if debating whether to continue or flee. The ankle-length raincoat, heavy scarf wrapped around her head, and dark glasses made it impossible for him to judge her age.

She stopped ten feet away and removed her glasses.

Even with the scarf concealing her hair, Von Meier recognized the beautiful, expressive eyes of Darlena Aldonzo.

CHAPTER 40

▼

Darlena led Inspector Von Meier to a secluded stone bench beneath a huge elm with sprawling limbs burdened down by summer growth. Despite the humid warmth of the day, she kept the scarf and raincoat on. It left her face dominated by the mesmerizing green emerald specks within her hazel eyes. Nervousness made her eyes flitter like a foraging squirrel watching for potential predators.

They talked for an hour. Sometimes her voice broke off into barely a whisper. Her hands clasped at each other, rubbed against her raincoat, gestured to emphasize a comment, clenched and unclenched, unable to remain still for more than a fraction of a minute.

Von Meier listened, occasionally asking a question, but mostly puffing slowly on his pipe.

Darlena told him everything. How she met the jewel thief on the train and their first visit to the Vatican together. That Thad saw the Gendarme Perrin escort Candalio to the Pope's living quarters and suspected Lastavis was drugging the Pope in his bid for the papacy. How Craig conned Thad into giving him Cardinal Sergio's drawings of the Vatican buildings. The murder of Thad, the suspicious death of Father Guiseppe, the attempt on her life by Candalio, the murder of her Papa, and finally, her decision to help Craig entrap John Montayne. She included her deep emotional feelings for Craig and her determination to expose the conspiracy of Cardinal Lastavis. She chose not to tell him Romano's name or Craig's name.

After she finished, Von Meier shifted position to look directly into her face. "When we go to the apartment to free the Swiss Guardsman, we'll find him dead. That will make you an accomplice to murder."

"Craig promised me he wouldn't kill Montayne," she blurted out.

"Unfortunately," Von Meier continued, "your jewel thief never leaves loose ends lying around to stumble over. John Montayne could identify you and possibly the jewel thief."

Darlena glanced at the ground, then back up at Von Meier. "You and I were dangerous loose ends and we're still alive. He is a jewel thief. He is not a murderer."

Von Meier nodded. "That's true. He has wounded people when necessary to escape, but up to now, he has never killed anyone."

Darlena struggled to her feet. Her legs felt rubbery. Perhaps telling Von Meier what she knew had been a mistake. But who else could she trust with the truth about Lastavis and Candalio's threat to the Pope? "I've given you all the information that I have," she said. "Now you must carry out your part of the agreement."

"You haven't told me how the treasures were removed from the Vatican."

She shook her head. "I don't know. I truly do not know. He didn't tell me any details of what he planned to steal, how he would do it, or how he would escape with the treasures."

Von Meier limped momentarily as they started back toward the fountain. "I believe you. So how do you intend to accuse Lastavis?"

Darlena whirled to face him. Anger suppressed by discussion of the robbery stormed back to the surface. She spit words out between clenched teeth. "I want to walk into the Vatican and confront Lastavis in your presence and the presence of two of the most powerful cardinals. Cardinal Sangore, because he's a trusted confidante of the Pontiff; and Cardinal Muller, because he's not Italian and is a close friend of Bishop Baccalete. You can make that happen. I want Lastavis to know that my information has already been sent to Bishop Baccalete. I'll stand trial for my participation in the robbery, but the trial will focus on Lastavis. I can't prove anything, but I can destroy his reputation. Lastavis took away everything that was important to me. I will do the same to him."

Von Meier smiled, something he rarely did, especially during such an intense discussion. "The first time I talked with you, I wondered why the jewel thief let you live. But when I look into your eyes, I see so much life and so much fiery spirit. He saw that and could not kill you. Before we go to the Vatican, may I see your purse?"

Darlena hesitated, and then handed it to him.

He reached into it, pulled out the revolver, put it into his coat pocket, and handed the purse back to her. "Do you still want to confront Cardinal Lastavis?"

"I'm going there to destroy him, not kill him. I want to kill him, but his reputation will suffer more if he stays alive to face my accusations in public. He killed Papa and Thad. I will make him pay for their deaths."

"Confronting Lastavis," Von Meier replied, "means you'll face the consequences of what you've done. Helping the jewel thief rob the Vatican is a crime, compounded if anyone is killed in the aftermath. Lastavis will discredit you and probably try to kill you before you can testify in public. Many people won't believe your story."

He placed his hands on her shoulders. "You should say that protecting the Pope rather than gaining revenge motivated you. Then the Pope may intercede on your behalf and the courts may be more lenient. But you face spending years in prison, damned by your Church and condemned as a criminal by most people. Is punishing Lastavis worth that? I promised that you could walk away. I will honor that promise and reveal nothing about our conversation if you so choose."

"I don't have a choice," Darlena averred. "I love Thad and Papa too much to allow their murderers to go unpunished. I can't allow Lastavis to kill His Holiness. Helping rob the Vatican was wrong. But sometimes, justice can only be served by using a wrong to destroy a greater wrong. If that makes me a criminal, then I will face the consequences."

Von Meier clasped her hands.

Darlena saw his normally stolid facial features soften. They gazed silently at each other.

Finally he spoke. "You can walk away now and disappear. I'll tell your story to the cardinals. The newspapers will print your accusations. Even if most people don't believe the accusations, the adverse publicity for the Church will wreck Lastavis's bid for the Papacy. And the Pope will be safe."

The concern on his face and in his voice surprised her. In their earlier meeting, she judged Von Meier to be an uncompromising enforcer of the law and a predatory pursuer of his quarry. Yet, he was encouraging her to leave.

"Why do you want me to walk away?" she asked.

"My wife Helga died five years ago," Von Meier said. "Like you, she possessed boundless energy and a contagious zest for life. She died from colon cancer. I sat beside her bed during those terrible months and watched the cancer drain life from her body and heard her pray to die. I helped her die. I loved her too much to allow her to continue suffering. Like you said, sometimes only another wrong can prevent a greater wrong. Prison will drain your vitality and leave you an empty shell. You are not a criminal. Like Helga, you deserve a chance to live."

Darlena pondered running from this nightmare.

But where would she run to? Her life hangs by a thin thread, with no safe haven. Even more than the fear, her anger would not allow her to run. Papa is dead. Thad is dead. Blood drips from Lastavis's hands and he walks free.

Darlena eased her hands away from Von Meier's grasp. "I have to confront Lastavis. I want the world to know the truth from my lips, regardless of the consequences."

CHAPTER 41

▼

Von Meier led Darlena down the corridor of the Papal Palace and opened the door to a small office containing filing cabinets, a wooden desk, and three straight-backed chairs.

One of Lieutenant Palermo's police officers hurried toward him. "Inspector, they want you in Cardinal Lastavis's office immediately. The Swiss Guardsman John Montayne escaped from the thieves and knows where the stolen treasures are hidden."

Von Meier glanced at Darlena. No words were necessary. Craig had kept his promise to Darlena. He had not killed Montayne.

Von Meier guided Darlena into the office and turned to the policeman. "Sergeant Moreno, stay here with Miss Aldonzo. Close the door and do not let anyone except me into this office. Do not tell anyone that she is here. I'll be back as quickly as possible."

He paused at the door to look back at Darlena. "You will have your opportunity. I promise you that. But first, I must deal with this change of events in the robbery."

Von Meier stepped into the room, interrupting an intense discussion between Lastavis, Guista, and Borgan. "I understand that the Guardsman John Montayne has returned safely."

Colonel Borgan's face beamed. His chest swelled beneath his erect, stiff shoulders. "The robbers held him prisoner and assumed his identity to gain access to the Vatican. They returned to the apartment after the robbery and strangled him, leaving him for dead. But God ordained that he should not die at the hands of those devils. Sergeant Montayne survived the strangulation and feigned death until they left. By kicking on the floor, he managed to eventually bother a tenant enough that they complained to the landlord. The landlord found and freed him an hour ago."

"Sergeant Montayne overheard the thieves discussing their destination," Lastavis said. "They have traveled to Barcelona, to meet a freighter bringing the stolen treasures. The freighter is due to dock in Barcelona this evening. Lieutenant Palermo has already talked with Interpol and taken a taskforce to meet the freighter. We'll catch your elusive American jewel thief and the dealer when they pick up their prize. Your clever thief will rue his blasphemous attack on the Holy Church."

Lastavis's intent gaze indicated he expected a congratulatory reply from Von Meier.

The Inspector stroked his chin and remained silent.

Lastavis continued. "You don't seem pleased by this fortunate turn of events."

"The American jewel thief does not make mistakes," Von Meier replied.

Lastavis's eyes narrowed. "God intervened. Not even this jewel thief, who you so admire and find impossible to apprehend, can escape the terrible retribution when he robs God."

Von Meier met his steely stare. "Yes, there is retribution far beyond what any man can conceive when he plays God. I also have important new information concerning the robbery. The information is especially significant to the leadership of the Church. Since the appropriate actions relative to recovering the stolen treasures are underway, I insist on discussing that matter now."

Lastavis frowned. "What are you implying?"

"I am not implying. I am telling you that someone highly trusted in the Vatican is responsible for the robbery. I know who that person is and I have the evidence to prove it."

Colonel Borgan stepped forward to speak but Lastavis silenced him with his hand.

"Because of the extreme seriousness of the accusations," Von Meier continued, "I insist that three cardinals be present. You, plus Cardinal Sangore and Cardinal Muller."

Lastavis stood up and braced his hands on the desk. "That won't be necessary. With His Holiness incapacitated, I represent the ruling authority in the Church and will assume responsibility for dealing with this problem. You and I will discuss this matter in private."

"Although not involved in the robbery plot, I believe Cardinal Muller will be able to provide additional insight after hearing what I have learned." Von Meier's teeth clamped down on the stem of his pipe. "I insist on you three cardinals being present. Otherwise, I'll handle this through regular police channels and the information will quickly become public."

Lastavis glowered at him. The deepening lines on his face indicated anger at having his unilateral authority questioned. He gestured toward the two colonels. "Locate and bring Cardinal Sangore and Cardinal Muller here. Say nothing of this conversation to them or anyone else. Only that an urgent matter related to the robbery must be discussed now."

Borgan and Guista hustled from the office, closing the heavy wooden door as they left.

Lastavis settled back into his chair behind the desk and motioned toward an ornate upholstered armchair. He refilled his silver goblet from a crystal decanter and reached for another goblet. "Would you like some wine? It has been a difficult day for all of us."

Von Meier remained standing. He suspected Lastavis intended to feign friendliness while probing for more information. "No, thank you. I'll wait in the office that Lieutenant Palermo was using." He turned away toward the door.

"How did you learn this new information?" Lastavis called after him.

Von Meier paused in the doorway. "As with the fortuitous escape of your Sergeant Montayne, perhaps God himself has intervened to expose the traitor who made the attack on the Church possible. Call me when you are ready."

Von Meier pondered the situation as he walked down the vaulted corridor. The gauntlet had been thrown down. Darlena Aldonzo would face the Vatican's most powerful cardinal, a Machiavellian conspirator willing to kill his own Pope. How could Darlena hope to convince Sangore and Muller of Lastavis's guilt? How could she avoid going to prison for helping the jewel thief rob the Vatican?

His mind visualized Darlena sitting in the park, pouring out the story to him, her emerald eyes glistening with tears one moment and blazing with anger the next. She could have and should have walked away. It would be wrong to imprison her for trying to stop Lastavis from killing the Pope. She was not a criminal. But she had participated in a crime that might have precipitated the murder of John Montayne and others if it had gone awry.

Von Meier's mind clicked back to the conversation with Lastavis. If the jewel thief intended to kill Montayne, not even God could have stopped him. What if he deliberately let Montayne live? What if the information about the treasures being on a freighter bound for Barcelona was a ruse to detract them from the real location of the treasures? The timing of Montayne's rescue seemed too perfect. The more he mulled the series of events, the more he suspected that the jewel thief had orchestrated it.

He saw the door to the small office partially open. He had given specific instructions to Sergeant Moreno to keep the door closed and locked.

The young officer jumped to his feet as Von Meier entered the room. "She left," he blurted out. "I tried to catch her, but lost her in the maze of corridors." He swallowed nervously. "She was looking out the window and suddenly gasped and ran to the door. She said to tell you that Candalio is back in the Vatican. She repeated it twice."

Von Meier charged down the corridor, pushing his way past priests and workers.

CHAPTER 42

▼

Three hundred miles to the north, Craig paused from loading boxes into the back of the truck. "I'm going to check the perimeter again."

Romano hoisted a heavy wooden carton into the truck and slid it past the AK-47 assault rifle leaning against another box. "That nosy priest wants to come in and admire the marble for the fountain. I think we should kill him."

Craig reached inside his jacket, pulled the Sig Sauer 9mm automatic from his belt, shoved the noise suppressor over the barrel, and slid his hand and the gun into his jacket pocket. "The police would link the murder of the priest with the shipment of marble from the Vatican. We want them to spend the next few days watching the freighter after it docks at Barcelona tonight. When they finally realize we smuggled the treasures out with the marble for Granople, we'll be long gone. The priest will describe me as a middle-aged Frenchman with thick gray hair. He's only had a glance at you from behind."

He unbolted the door and stepped from the dilapidated wooden storage garage. Afternoon sunlight filtering through sparse clouds reflected off the railroad siding tracks and cast shadows from the freight car. The honk of an impatient motorist intermingled with intermittent traffic on the street adjacent to the church. He eased along the wall to the corner of the garage.

Beyond the manicured shrubbery and flowerbeds, the church posed majestically, its buttressed stone walls, twin belfry towers, and stained glass windows soaring above the small tiled-roof houses and squat brick buildings of Granople. In the center of the plaza fronting the church, Bernini's crumbling circles of marble, elevated water spouts, and angelic statues languished in disarray. Water dribbled from the broken mouth of a fish, splattered into the fountain basin, and gurgled onto the plaza stones through a gouge in the marble.

Craig circled the storage garage and stopped beside the freight car to survey the area again. There were no signs of anyone and yet every nerve in his body tingled. Was it normal apprehension or premonition? He slithered partway underneath the freight car and scanned the pond on the opposite side. Three ducks bobbed on the water at the shallow end. A frog on a lily pad slurped a water bug dancing along the shimmering surface. Pine and elm trees bordering the pond could provide concealment for someone spying on them.

He kept the gun in his jacket pocket but slid his finger around the trigger. Scooping up a handful of gravel from the track, he walked around the backside of the freight car and sauntered along the edge of the pond, flipping pebbles into the water and watching circles broadcast outward. A longer toss sent the frog splashing into the water.

Only four trees had trunks massive enough to hide someone. He swung a few yards deep into the sparsely treed area and satisfied himself that no one lurked behind the first two trees.

His ears detected the miniscule rustle of feet shifting stealthily. He eased the Sig Sauer from his pocket and lined the barrel up with the thick trunk of an elm ahead to the left.

One eye, half a face, and a hand grasping a Heckler & Koch automatic appeared from behind the tree. Craig's two bullets, muffled to a thud by the suppressor, ripped through the man's eye and forehead. The assailant collapsed backwards without firing a shot.

Craig picked up the fallen Heckler & Koch and searched the man's pockets. As expected, he found no identification. But short blond hair, black turtleneck pullover, and German-made gun left no doubt in his mind. He hoisted the body over his shoulder and staggered back over the railroad tracks and into the garage.

"We have trouble!" he shouted to Romano.

Romano jumped from the back of the truck, the AK-47 assault rifle grasped in one hand. "Police?"

"No. Somehow Brauder tracked us here." Craig dumped the body into an empty wooden box. "Did you tell Rita we were coming to Granople?"

Romano's face flushed. He grabbed the cellular phone from the makeshift tabletop and dialed a number. He listened, angrily punched off the phone, and dialed another number. "This is Romano," he growled into the phone. "Find Rita."

His face paled and then flushed livid red. He clicked off the phone. "They tortured and killed her. She was found this morning tied to her bed. The bastards carved a Swastika into each breast."

Craig bolted the door shut. "Brauder won't attack us here. Gunfire would bring police. But he probably has a dozen men headed this way, planning to ambush us when we leave. We have everything loaded except part of the gold bullion. Leave the rest. Stack the crates of fruit and produce into the truck to conceal the other boxes. We'll make a run for it and try to lose them after we cross into France. I have a place to stash the stuff in the foothills on the French side."

"We can't outrun them in the truck," Romano replied. "They'll follow us and wait for the right place to attack."

"They can follow us," Craig replied, "but we'll pick the time and place for the fight."

CHAPTER 43

▼

The truck lumbered from the storage garage and turned onto the narrow streets of Granople. When it reached the main highway, it headed west. Craig glanced in the rearview mirror. A black Mercedes sedan with four men inside trailed him at a distance. He saw no sign of a second car, but figured men in another car would check out the abandoned storage garage and then join the Mercedes in pursuit.

His route would soon tell them where he planned to cross the border. The second car would pass him and pick a location for the ambush. They would try to spare the truck and use it to finish transporting the merchandise. A hill with embankments on both sides would be the danger zone, allowing them to come up alongside and kill him, betting that the lumbering truck would survive the impact into the embankment. When crunch time came, they would learn this was not a typical produce hauling truck. The supercharged engine and special design transmission enabled the truck to outrun many cars. But it would be no match for their Mercedes.

Craig opened the glove compartment, placed the Heckler & Koch automatic into a metal slot beneath the dashboard where he could quickly grab it, and shoved the spare fifteen round magazine into his jacket pocket. On the passenger side seat, the dead German sat propped upward, wearing Romano's coat and hat. Hopefully, Brauder's men thought Romano had come with him.

A black Opel sedan pulled up beside the freight car at the Granople church. An unruly-haired stocky man clutching a Luger climbed out of the front passenger side door and prowled over to the storage garage door. The driver, wearing a jacket to conceal his holstered automatic, walked to the edge of the garage and scanned the plaza and church. The priest was coming toward them.

The man in the jacket pointed toward the railroad car. When the priest looked that way, the man stepped up behind him, wrapped a cord around his throat, and strangled him. He hoisted the body into a garbage dumpster and nodded to his accomplice.

The stocky blond-haired man pushed open the garage door and scanned the clutter of crates. "They left gold bars in their rush to get away," he called back to the driver. "Call the pursuit car and tell them we're loading the gold into the trunk. We can still catch up to the truck before it reaches the foothills."

He walked over, shoved back the canvas, and ogled the glistening stack. Eight bars of pure gold. He laid his gun on the stack and hoisted up a bar to admire it.

Romano lunged out from among the crates, driving the man backward against the wooden workbench. His knife flashed forward into the German's stomach just below the chest. The blade gouged upward, severing arteries.

The man pounded at Romano's head with his fists. The blows didn't register through the seething anger consuming Romano's mind. The man's knees buckled.

Romano yanked out the knife and slashed the man's face, carving ribbons of crimson flesh.

The sound of the Opel backing up to the garage door penetrated the rage in his mind. Romano lifted the body over his head, hurled it behind the crates, and picked up the man's Luger.

The door opened and the jacketed man stepped into the doorway.

Romano emptied the Luger into his chest, knocking him against the open trunk. He dragged the body inside, threw it behind crates, and spread canvas over the gold bars.

The lure of money no longer drove Romano. He would avenge Rita's death by killing every one of the Nazi bastards. No matter how long it took, he would hunt down Brauder and Kusler and personally kill them. Only then could he enjoy his new wealth.

But now he had to catch the Mercedes before Brauder's men killed Craig and seized the treasures. He clambered into the Opel and sped toward the highway.

CHAPTER 44

▼

Darlena paused beside the heavy wooden door emblazoned with a large gold-leaf medallion and waited while a priest and two clerical workers walked past. This had to be the door that Craig unlocked for Thad. What if someone had locked it again? Her hand grasped the doorknob and turned it. She pushed on the door. It creaked open a few inches. She pressed her shoulder against it to widen the opening, slipped through into a vaulted corridor, and closed the door.

A high, dust-covered window provided enough light for her to discern a long passageway cluttered with furniture. Her mind visualized Thad's drawings showing the route to the Pope's living quarters. The door to the closet beneath the Pope's apartment would be on the right.

Darlena ran down the corridor, raking her fingers along the wall to find a door as darkness swallowed her. Cobwebs tangled into her hair and face. Dust and musty mildew odor overpowered her nose and rasped her throat. She stumbled over high-backed chairs, their once luxurious fabric now rotting clumps hanging from ornately carved wood. Increasing darkness made it difficult to see.

Her hand felt a door. She turned the heavy brass knob and strained to pull the door open. It was locked. Her heartbeat jumped. Maybe this wasn't the right door. She continued along the wall, her already tenuous confidence sagging.

Her fingers found another door. She grasped the doorknob.

The door swung open. Darlena entered a room dimly lit by a small solitary window near the ceiling. Old furniture laden with dust sat in stacks. Her eyes spotted crude wooden stair steps. These must be the stairs leading to the trap door opening into the closet adjacent to the Pope's living quarters. Sweat drenched her face and blouse and irritated her eyes. Her breath came in gasps.

How could she carry an incapacitated old man down these stairs and through the corridor? Candalio and Perrin may already be here.

Darlena scrambled up the wooden stairs, braced her legs on the steps, and strained to raise the trapdoor. The door moved upward. She grappled to push aside the rug on the floor above, scrambled through, and swung the trap door fully open. Best to leave it open in case she needed to flee back through it.

A narrow band of light outlined the bottom of a door in the opposite wall. That must be the entry into the Pope's apartment. She tiptoed across the floor, counting her steps so she could find the trapdoor in the darkness, and pressed her ear to the door. She heard no sound of voices or movement on the other side.

Her trembling fingers rotated the doorknob and eased the door open a crack. Light momentarily blinded her. She blinked to clear her vision.

A stoop-shouldered, wrinkle-faced man in a white robe sat in an upholstered chair, reading a document. A wine goblet and a plate with the remnants of lunch sat on the marble table beside him.

Darlena pulled the door open and stepped into the room. "Your Holiness."

He turned toward her, his face mirroring surprise at the voice and puzzlement by her sudden appearance. But he showed no alarm. "Yes, my child."

She hurried over and knelt down to look up into his face. "There are men coming here to kill you. We have to leave now, go into the corridor beneath the closet, and seek refuge in another section of the Palace. Please trust me. They're coming to kill you."

He gazed into her eyes with a probing intensity that made her blink. "I know you believe what you're saying," he said in a calm voice. "I will summon the guards."

"You can't. A guard is one of the conspirators." She grasped his arm and tried to pull him from the chair. "They've been drugging you. That's why you're incapacitated. We have to go now. Please trust me."

His eyes searched her face. "I believe you, my child."

His words electrified her. The spiritual leader of the Holy Church believed a sweaty, dust-covered young woman. She would save the Pope, both for his own sake and because it would stop Lastavis's drive for power.

With her help, the Pope struggled to his feet and put an arm around her shoulder. They shuffled across the room toward the closet. Darlena sensed his frailty. How would she get him down the wooden stair steps to the corridor?

They were almost to the closet door now.

Darlena heard the sound of a door opening and glanced behind her.

The Gendarme Perrin stood in the doorway, staring open-mouthed at them. Candalio shoved in behind him and closed the door.

Perrin lunged toward them.

The Pope held up his hand. "It's all right. I am in no danger from her."

Perrin stopped. His lips and eyes twitched with nervous uncertainty.

Candalio stepped up behind and to the side of Perrin. His narrow eyes studied her. "She is the priest's friend," he snarled.

Darlena continued to steady the Pope and glared at Candalio. "And you are Dr. Candalio, the Devil's physician. Candalio has been drugging you, Your Holiness. He plans to inject you with a lethal drug when Cardinal Lastavis feels he's consolidated enough power to be your successor. The young priest Thad Raphano was trying to warn you when they killed him."

Candalio stepped over to the marble table and picked up the sharp meat knife. "None of that will be necessary now. The public will believe you came here seeking revenge for the death of the priest who was your lover. Perrin killed you, but not before you plunged the knife into the Pope's heart."

He held the knife out to the Gendarme. "Kill him first with the knife and then shoot her. Make certain that both of them die."

The aged Pontiff gazed into Perrin's face. "Do not put this terrible deed on your soul. What you have done can be forgiven."

Perrin yanked his hand away from the proffered knife as if he had touched a hot ember. "I won't be part of killing His Holiness." His lips trembled as he faced the Pope. "That was never my intention."

Perrin's mouth gaped open. A gasping scream froze in his throat. His hand flailed downward and tried to yank the gun from his holster.

Candalio blocked the hand. Perrin fell forward onto the floor, a massive red blot spreading outward on the back of his uniform.

Candalio stepped around the fallen Gendarme, one hand holding the meat knife, the other holding the bloodied cane sword. A thin smile curled around the corners of his mouth. "Sometimes it is best to do the job yourself. Then you know it will be done correctly."

Darlena kept her eyes fixed on the long thin blade of the cane sword and held her clenched hand out toward the approaching Candalio.

He was ten feet away.

Now six feet. Darlena squeezed her fist and felt the pop of the small cylinder in her palm. She counted to three, tossed it into the air toward him, and squeezed her eyes closed as she twisted her head away.

Even with her eyes closed, the brilliant flash of phosphorus light partially blinded her.

Candalio staggered and let out a snarling groan. He threw his arm across his eyes and lunged toward them.

She pushed the Pontiff to the side, dodged the probing sword blade, and grabbed the fallen Pontiff.

Candalio whirled toward her, his head cocked to decipher her movements from the sounds.

Darlena half dragged, half shoved the Pontiff toward his chair and then pounced in the opposite direction, making no effort to conceal the noise of her steps. She represented the immediate danger. Candalio would come after her first and then deal with the Pope.

Candalio shuffled backward to block her path to the apartment doorway, slashing at the air around him with the cane knife.

She bounced back and forth to keep his attention focused on her. Anger overrode her fear. This is the man that killed Thad and Papa. Every muscle and every nerve in her body pulsed.

Candalio blinked his eyes and squinted. "I can see enough of you," he growled and stalked after her.

She retreated between a heavy chair and a marble table. The wall behind her blocked further retreat. She wanted Candalio to think she was trapped.

Candalio lunged at her.

Darlena somersaulted across the marble table, using it like a pommel horse, landed on her feet, knocked the table into his path, and scrambled toward the fallen Gendarme.

Candalio stumbled around the table in pursuit.

Darlena dove to the floor and yanked the gun from Perrin's holster.

Candalio grasped the cane sword like a spear and plunged it downward toward her. She rolled sideways. The blade sliced the upper sleeve of her blouse but missed her arm.

Darlena catapulted to her feet, jumped away from his next thrust, swung the gun upward, and fired. The roar of the gun deafened her.

The bullet slammed into Candalio's chest, staggering him. The second bullet drove him backward against the wall.

"That was for Thad!" she screamed. "This is for Papa!" Darlena emptied the gun into his slumping body.

Candalio tumbled sideways to the floor. His coat and shirt turned the crimson of a cardinal's robe. He struggled onto his elbows, still grasping the cane knife.

His mouth twisted in a grotesque effort to spew out words. Blood gurgled between the paling lips. His body convulsed and he slumped onto the floor. His unmoving hand remained gripped around the cane sword.

Darlena's hand sagged, dangling the gun barrel toward the floor. "Like you said," she mumbled, "if you want a job done right, you have to do it yourself."

The door burst open and three Gendarmes rushed into the room.

"Do not hurt her," the Pontiff called out.

Two Gendarmes seized Darlena and stripped the gun from her hand. The third rushed to assist the Pontiff into a chair. The two Gendarmes slammed her onto the floor and pinned her face down. Her compressed lungs gasped but couldn't pull in any air.

"Let her go." The Pontiff's frail voice filled the room. "She saved my life."

They yanked Darlena to her feet. One Gendarme checked the fallen men. The other continued to grasp her arm.

Colonel Guista and Von Meier stormed through the doorway and stared at the carnage.

"The two men are dead, sir," a Gendarme said.

Guista motioned to the Gendarmes. "Take His Holiness to the sitting room."

The Pontiff stretched his hand out toward Darlena. "Come with me. We must talk."

The Gendarme released his grip on her arm. Darlena staggered over and grasped the Pope's extended hand. "I want Colonel Guista and Inspector Von Meier with us, but no one else," she mumbled.

The Pontiff nodded. Aided by the Gendarmes, he shuffled toward the adjacent room.

Lastavis entered through the doorway from the corridor. The arrogance on his face shattered as he surveyed the scene.

Darlena whirled and pointed a finger at him. "You'll burn in Hell with Candalio, you murderer! If I still had a gun, I'd kill you."

Von Meier placed his arm around her waist and forced her into the sitting room. The Gendarmes assisted the Pope to a chair, poured a glass of wine for him, and closed the door as they left.

Darlena sagged onto a velvet sofa opposite the Pope. Her throat burned. Her energy had drained away. She asked for water.

Guista frowned but poured bottled water into a wine goblet and handed it to her. Von Meier sat down beside her. Guista remained standing.

The Pope's body appeared collapsed into the fabric of the chair, but his eyes told her that his mind remained alert. Darlena pondered whether to speak or wait for him to open the conversation.

Von Meier broke the silence. "Miss Aldonzo learned about a conspiracy within the Vatican to elevate Cardinal Lastavis to the Papacy. The conspiracy included keeping you drugged and killing you at the appropriate time."

The Pope clasped his hands together in his lap. His eyes closed.

Darlena wondered whether he was praying for God's guidance or too weary to deal with such devastating information.

"Tell me what you know," the Pope said in a barely audible voice.

Darlena began with Thad spotting Candalio being accompanied to the Papal Palace by Perrin, described her participation with the jewel thief in seducing the Swiss Guardsman Montayne, included her meeting with Von Meier in the park, and concluded by saying she saw Candalio come back into the Vatican.

Guista occasionally interrupted to justify actions by his Gendarmes. The Pope asked her numerous questions. As the discussion progressed, he seemed to become more alert.

When she finished, the Pope looked at Von Meier. "The Holy Church asks that Miss Aldonzo's role in the robbery be expunged from the records. We do not want her prosecuted."

Von Meier nodded. "That can be done."

The relief that trickled through Darlena's body was quickly doused by a somber reality. The death of Thad and Papa left her life forever changed. "What about Cardinal Lastavis?" she asked.

"The Holy Church will deal with him," the Pontiff replied.

Darlena jumped to her feet. "You have to turn him over to the authorities for trial and imprisonment. He's responsible for Thad and Papa's deaths. He's a murderer."

Guista stepped in front, blocking her from towering above the seated Pope.

"There is a higher judgement than the legal courts of man," the Pope continued.

"You're going to let Lastavis go unpunished because it might blemish the reputation of your Holy Church?" she asked. "How can you justify such hypocrisy?"

"I assure you that Cardinal Lastavis will suffer for his actions," the Pope replied.

She turned toward Von Meier. Her eyes begged him for support.

Von Meier shook his head. "There is no evidence linking Cardinal Lastavis to Candalio or the murders of Thad Raphano and your papa."

Darlena whirled and sidestepped around Guista to confront the Pontiff. "What about the reputation of Thad Raphano? Lastavis vilified him as a radical who tried to kill you."

"Father Thadeus will be exonerated both within the Church and in public." The Pope clasped her hand. "You're still a child in life. As you gain more wisdom, you'll find that the sweet taste of revenge quickly turns bitter in the stomach. You'll face difficult personal decisions that force choices bringing both satisfaction and pain."

She yanked her hand away. "I'm not a child and it's not revenge to expect justice. I want Lastavis punished."

Guista started to reprimand her harshness.

The Pope silenced him with a wave of his hand. His voice remained gentle. "You have suffered a terrible loss. The loss is even more tragic because a leader within the Church apparently perpetrated the acts of cruelty."

The word "apparently" angered Darlena. She stalked to the door and then paused to look back at the Pope. "If you don't quickly absolve Thad Raphano of all blame, I will tell the news media everything. People need to know that Thad died trying to save your life. Since you won't publicly condemn Lastavis's conspiracy, at least correct some of the wrong he did. Lastavis blocked Bishop Baccalete's request for funds to restore the Bernini fountain at St. Luke's Church in Granople. Dedicate the restoration of the Bernini Fountain to the memory of Thad Raphano. No priest ever served his Church with more dedication or courage."

"Funding for the fountain," Colonel Guista said, "has already been provided by a devout French Catholic. The marble has been shipped to Granople."

Von Meier caught Guista by the shoulder. "Was the marble in freight cars here at the Vatican when the robbery occurred?"

"Yes," Guista replied. "But we thoroughly searched that freight car before it left."

"You searched it on Sunday, but the freight car did not leave until Monday," Von Meier countered. "We can assume the benefactor for the Bernini fountain was our jewel thief. He had Cardinal Sergio's drawings of the buildings and catacombs. His accomplice moved the stolen treasures through the catacombs to the railroad area and loaded them on the freight cars Sunday night after you completed your search. If we act quickly, perhaps we can intercept him before he leaves Granople."

Guista grabbed his radio. "We'll use the Vatican's large helicopter. I'll bring some of my most trusted men."

Darlena blocked Guista's path through the doorway. "I'm coming, too."

He tried to push her aside.

She battled to remain in the doorway. "If I stay here, I'm going to talk with the news media."

Guista glanced back at the Pontiff. The Pontiff nodded. "All right," Guista muttered. "But stay out of our way."

"The jewel thief will make the transfer to Brauder outside Italy," Van Meier said. "I'll call the police in northern Italy and tell them to put roadblocks at the French and Swiss borders and search every vehicle leaving Italy."

Twenty minutes later, the helicopter lifted off from the Vatican heliport, carrying Guista, eight Gendarmes, Von Meier, and Darlena.

She studied the grim-faced Gendarmes armed with automatic weapons. She suspected that they intended to kill Craig for desecrating the Holy Church. Guista would do whatever was necessary to protect the public perception of the Church.

How could she keep them from killing Craig?

CHAPTER 45

▼

Romano sped along the highway in the black Opel, his eyes straining to discern the make of cars on the hill ahead of him as he listened to Craig's voice on the cellular phone.

"The black Mercedes is a kilometer behind me, making no effort to catch up," Craig said. "I crossed into France ten minutes ago. I suspect Brauder plans to ambush me after I turn onto the mountain road another five kilometers from here. Try to disable the Mercedes but don't get into a firefight. I need your support in the mountains."

"I will deal with Brauder's men," Romano growled. He clicked off the phone. Listening on the dead German's telephone to the conversation between the occupants of the Mercedes and the men waiting in France convinced him that Brom Eidler was in the Mercedes, and that Eidler had tortured and killed Rita.

Romano's hands tightened on the steering wheel. Eidler would die for what he did.

In the Mercedes, the driver studied his rearview mirror. "I see the Opel now. It's catching up fast. Berner must have a problem with his cell phone that kept him from answering our calls."

Sitting beside the driver, Brom Eidler ran his stubby finger over the map spread across his lap. "Reynolds has to climb a steep hill eleven kilometers from here. I'll call Kusler. We can trap him between us.

The driver glanced back at the onrushing Opel. "Berner is pulling out to pass us. He must want to tell us something. But he's alone. Why would he leave Heinrich at Granople?"

"Give him your phone," Eidler said to the two men in the back seat. "I want him to block off traffic trying to enter the mountain road while we deal with Reynolds."

The driver pressed the button to lower the side window.

"That's not Berner!" shouted a man in the back seat.

The driver jammed the accelerator to the floor. The men in the back seat yanked their assault rifles from the floor.

Bullets from Romano's AK-47 ripped into the rear and side of the Mercedes as he roared past.

The bloodied driver slumped over the wheel. The Mercedes swerved into the middle of the road and careened toward the steep embankment on the side. Eidler grabbed the steering wheel. The car bounced off the steel guardrail and skidded to a stop. One man staggered out of the back seat, gripping an assault rifle, his face bleeding from shattered glass.

Eidler clambered from the car and stared up the road. "He's turning and coming back." Eidler grabbed the assault rifle from the man and crouched behind the front wheel of the heavy car.

The man scrambled into the back seat and over his dead partner's body, retrieved another rifle, and fired through the side window at the oncoming Opel.

Romano grasped the steering wheel with his right hand, shifted his head and left shoulder through the window, and braced the AK-47 on the outside door mirror. A burst from his rifle ripped open the hood and blew away the front window of the Mercedes.

A fusillade of bullets from the Germans shredded the front of the Opel as it bore down on the Mercedes. The Opel's front tires disintegrated. The windshield shattered, lacerating Romano's face with glass shards and blurring his vision. Pain seared his arm and shoulder.

The Opel swerved toward the guardrail.

Romano squinted through narrow slits, wrestled the car back into a collision path with the Mercedes, floored the accelerator, and emptied the AK-47 into the Germans' car.

Gasoline spewed onto the ground and ignited, engulfing the underside of the Mercedes in flames. The German in the back seat continued firing at the oncoming Opel.

Romano twisted the steering wheel, trying to swerve back into the center of the road, away from the Mercedes.

The Opel skidded sideways and smashed into the Mercedes. The impact drove the Mercedes backward, crushing Brom Eidler and demolishing the guardrail.

Both cars exploded in flames.

CHAPTER 46

▼

From the curving upgrade on the following hill, Craig saw the flash. The two cars plunged into empty space, tumbled in fiery death spirals, and crashed into the mountainside a thousand feet below. In previous robberies, Craig had been indifferent about the future of the men he used to help in the heist. Romano had been different. Beneath his crude, bullying persona, Romano had been unflinching in his commitments and an invaluable partner in the impossible robbery. They had formed a unique bond of kinship.

His mind swept away the thoughts and focused on the problem at hand. Kusler and his men would ambush him somewhere along the mountain road. The truck groaning up a steep hill would be an easy target.

Craig pulled onto the side of the road, yanked a large manila envelope from the glove compartment, and spread the detailed topography map on the seat. It would be better to hide here and make Kusler hunt for him. He had ten million dollars of currency and another ten million in easily transported, easily fenced jewelry and diamonds. Most of the money that Brauder had given him already resided in a variety of untraceable bank accounts. He would hide the paintings, elaborate jewelry pieces, and specialized Vatican treasures. Later, he would use a secondary dealer to negotiate with the Vatican and insurance companies to buy back the paintings and religious artifacts. They would gladly pay a substantial reward to the dealer for giving them the location of the missing items.

Von Meier would connect the deaths at Granople and the car crash with the robbery and launch a massive manhunt for him. But Kusler remained the immediate problem. Kusler's people would already be coming to find him.

Craig had studied the topography map earlier, picking out potential alternative remote hiding areas. He scanned the map, pinpointed the nearest possibility, oriented himself, and pulled out onto the highway.

His mind purged away all emotions. He still owned the treasures. They had to hunt for him. The looming specter of death became simply one dimension of the complex equation to be solved.

Craig drove another three kilometers, swung off the highway, and roared up a bumpy, twisting road. Exactly one kilometer from the highway, he stopped. He grabbed a leather pouch and plastic travel bag from a hidden compartment underneath the seat and paced swiftly into the dense undergrowth of the forest, counting his steps. He stuffed the pouch and bag beneath the decaying trunk of a fallen tree and methodically studied landmarks around him.

The pouch and bag contained two of the most valuable religious paintings, the Codex, the Gutenberg Bible, jewelry, and the stack of currency. If he had to abandon the truck, he could come back later to retrieve this fortune. If the police trapped him, he would negotiate his release for return of the priceless relics. Von Meier would refuse, but the Vatican would jump at the offer.

Craig ran back to the truck and continued the ascent, finally pulling onto a level area devoid of trees and dominated by a sprawling, deteriorating massive metal building. The topography map showed an abandoned foundry, a perfect place for hiding the truck if the doors could be opened.

A quick check told him the huge rusty, dented metal doors were beyond any hope of opening. Maybe he could hide the truck at the rear of the building beneath overhangs.

The sound of an airplane made him look upward. A single-engine airplane swept toward him. It passed overhead, banked, and came back again.

Damn Kusler had a spotter plane out looking for him. There was no place to hide now. Kusler would be here in a matter of minutes.

Craig climbed into the back of the truck, dug into a crate of produce, and pulled out a bundle of dynamite sticks and electronic gear. After locking the rear doors, he opened the truck hood, shoved the dynamite sticks into a previously prepared metal box, and attached an electronic igniter.

He jumped into the truck, shifted into reverse, and rammed the back end of the truck into the metal wall of the building. That would make it difficult for Kusler to break into the truck.

He threw the keys into the underbrush, grabbed the Heckler & Koch automatic, and reached underneath the steering column to attach four loose wires onto an electronic board.

His ears heard the roar of an approaching car.

They were already here!

Craig sprinted to the side entrance of the building and crashed through a window.

A quick glance outside told him two Mercedes had surged into the clearing. He ran through the dusty, shadowy building, dodging piles of rubbish and steel beams.

His mind churned through possibilities. He had spotted four men in each car. Eight against one, but Kusler would give first priority to securing the treasure. If he could reach the forest, he had a good chance of eluding them.

The sound of a Mercedes running along the side of the building made him stop. The car roared to the backside, cutting off his escape route. Kusler wanted both the loot and a final confrontation.

Craig's eyes scanned the area. The ground floor gave more maneuvering room, but the second level provided better positioning for a firefight. He couldn't risk being pinned down on the floor while they moved in from above. He scrambled up a rusted, broken stairway to the second level, ran to the window on the opposite side, and glanced out.

A metal roof covered the area directly below him. A partially collapsed conveyor loading structure stretched above the shed roof and extended to the lake. Thick forest bordered the opposite shore of the lake. The conveyor structure appeared to be the only possibility for escaping from the upper level.

He moved back into the interior of the building, squeezed into the cage of a derelict overhead crane, and waited for Kusler's move. Eight against one were improbable odds, but not impossible. Impossible doesn't exist.

"Reynolds," Kusler's voice called out. "We can blast you out of there, but neither of us wants to light up the neighborhood with gunfire. Let's talk a deal."

Craig surveyed the second floor structure for additional battle positions and checked the ground level for movement. The semi-darkness would initially work to his advantage.

Kusler's voice broke the silence again. "I'll let you live in exchange for the rest of the treasures. We have the truck, but I suspect you've split the loot and hidden some of the most valuable items elsewhere. Tell me where the rest of the loot is and we'll let you walk away."

Craig frowned. Had his pattern become that predictable? He stuffed the Sig Sauer inside his front belt. His hand wrapped around the Heckler & Koch automatic. Fifteen rounds in the magazine and another fifteen in the spare magazine.

That would definitely light up the neighborhood.

"We'll give you one of the Mercedes to escape in," Kusler called out. "You already have fifteen million of our money. We'll toss in another ten million, plus you can carry one bag of jewelry. We'll both walk away with no hard feelings on either side."

Craig smiled as he muttered silently to himself. "Come on, Kusler, I'm not stupid." He noted two silhouettes slipping in through side windows. He had already spotted a man prowling in from the rear. His catlike night vision had adjusted to the dim, shadowy interior, noting every beam, every potential hiding place, and every movement.

"I'm out of patience, Reynolds!" Kusler yelled. "This is your last chance."

One of the shadowy figures crouched beside a heavy milling table. The man would move again, going for a better position behind a stack of steel beams ten feet away. Craig shifted position and lined up the shot.

The figure darted toward the stack of beams. Craig fired three times. The figure never made it to the steel beams.

A hail of bullets clattered the steel frame of the crane. Craig rolled behind an overturned metal table.

Seven to one now, but they knew his location. Twelve bullets left in the magazine.

The sound of the truck starting up reached his ears. As expected, Kusler had told one of his men to hot-wire the ignition so they could move the truck before gunfire brought unwanted company. Kusler was very predictable.

It was time to introduce some unpredictability. Craig pulled a miniature electronic pack from his pocket. He pressed the red button.

The roar of the explosion shook the heavy metal doors on the front of the building and sent dust cascading everywhere. A figure jumped from behind a pile of steel rubble near the door, looking for a safer place.

A burst from Craig's Heckler & Koch knocked him down. But the man rolled out of sight beneath a large steel-topped table. Hurt but not totally out.

Seven bullets used, eight left. Craig scrambled on all fours to the brick wall of the huge kiln. Bullets splattered and ricocheted around him. He squeezed past the kiln to the other side and slid down among debris overflowing from a storage bin. The explosion in the truck cab certainly killed the driver and maybe an accomplice. That meant at least two are dead and one partially disabled.

With the truck engine destroyed and the back jammed against the building wall, Kusler couldn't move the treasures. He would be foaming at the mouth.

Craig pulled the cartridge case from the Heckler & Koch, stuck it in his jacket pocket, and inserted the full one. They had him boxed in now to a narrow area of the second floor. Kusler would bring all his men inside the building and launch an assault. It was time to exit the building through the window and try to reach the lake.

The metal roof of the building suddenly began reverberating from the whomp, whomp, whomp of a helicopter. Gunfire erupted outside the building.

Craig dodged and ducked his way to the window and swung out onto the narrow catwalk.

A big helicopter sat on the ground behind the two Mercedes. Vatican Gendarmes were spread around the partially cleared front area of the building. Several had sheltered behind the cars. Two others crouched among a pile of metal near the helicopter. All were firing at the building. One Gendarme sprawled face down in a pool of blood.

With Kusler and the Gerdarmes battling, this was the time to make a run for it. Craig edged along the crumbling catwalk toward the steel conveyor structure stretching across the shed roof and protruding over the lake. Portions of the walkway flooring along the side of the conveyor buckets dangled downward into space. The partially collapsed roof blocked the walkway in other places. He would have to jump from the catwalk to the conveyor structure, pull himself up into the housing section, and climb from bucket to bucket to reach the lake. One slip would send him tumbling onto the shed roof and probably through it to the floor of the foundry. If the fall didn't kill him, Kusler would. But the conveyor structure represented the only escape route.

Craig glanced toward the Gendarmes. They hadn't seen him.

The sound of breaking glass came from behind and to his left. Craig twisted sideways and saw an assault rifle and the head and shoulders of one of Kusler's men shove through an upper level window. The man swung the rifle barrel around to fire.

Craig's volley knocked him back through the window.

Bullets ricocheted off the metal around him. The Gendarmes had spotted him.

Craig leaped for the conveyor structure, dropping the Heckler & Koch as his arms stretched out to grasp a horizontal I-beam. His chest slammed into the metal, knocking breath from his lungs. He wrapped his arms across the top of the beam, pulled his body upward, and lunged inside the metal housing of the structure.

Bullets splattered against the outside wall of thick metal. He huddled down inside the protective bulk of a conveyor bucket, stripped off his jacket, and shoved the Sig Sauer automatic inside his back belt.

Craig scrambled along the conveyor buckets. Spasmodic bursts of gunfire hammered metal around him. The structure housing at the far end had collapsed, leaving the outermost conveyor buckets unshielded. He would have to jump from the final conveyor bucket to clear the dock below him, which meant exposing himself to gunfire.

His lungs sucked in deep breaths. He lunged from the housing into the next bucket, sprang from it to the outermost bucket, and crouched in its bottom as bullets splattered the metal. Craig clasped his hands on the upper edge of the bucket on the opposite side from the Gendarmes, catapulted over the edge, and plummeted toward the lake twenty feet below.

He splashed feet first into the lake. Frigid water shocked breath from his lungs. He fought his way to the surface and gasped in air.

Bullets sped across the surface toward him. Craig ducked underneath and swam for the forested area two hundred yards away. When he surfaced again, no one fired at him. The Gendarmes and Kusler's gunmen must be too preoccupied with each other to concentrate on a lone individual in the lake.

Craig stroked toward the distant shore. He had to reach it quickly and get out of this frigid water before it drained his energy and disoriented him.

The sound of gunfire diminished. Kusler and his men had probably retreated into the forest. The Gendarmes would not pursue them. They would concentrate on salvaging treasures from the truck.

Thirty more yards to the shore. His arms flailed like lead posts. The shoreline blurred. Craig continued kicking and stroking, gasping air into lungs shriveled by icy water.

His foot touched bottom. He staggered up in waist deep water and slogged to the shore. His body convulsed. Hammers pounded inside his lungs. His legs wobbled. He forced away the numbing impact of the cold water and kept moving toward the forest.

"Don't force me to kill you."

Craig knew from the accent that the voice was Von Meier's. He looked toward the thin, gray-haired man standing at the edge of the trees with a Ruger in his hand.

"Put your hands on top of your head and turn your back." Von Meier said.

Craig debated grabbing for his Sig Sauer. But Von Meier would get off two shots before he could fire back. Most likely, they would kill each other. Why kill the one man he respected? Plus, he still held a trump card. The Vatican would bargain for the hidden treasures. Craig clasped his hands behind his neck and turned sideways.

Von Meier pulled the Sig Sauer from his belt and threw it into the lake. "You've amazed me in the past, but robbing the Vatican exceeded anything I could have imagined. You must have known the impossible odds."

Craig turned to face Von Meier. "I hid some of the treasures, including sacred items especially important to the Vatican."

They gazed in silence at each other.

"Check, but not checkmate," Craig said.

The roar of the helicopter lifting off made both of them glance that way. Gendarmes were firing at the helicopter. But armor plating installed to protect the Pope during travel deflected the bullets.

Craig eyed the rapidly ascending aircraft. "Somebody just stole your helicopter. It was probably Kusler. He flew contraband before moving up in Brauder's organization."

Von Meier stepped back a few paces, kept his Ruger leveled on Craig, and glanced at the sky. "Darlena is in the helicopter. She killed Candalio when he returned to the Vatican and then exposed Cardinal Lastavis's plan to gain the Papacy. After I realized that you hid the treasures in the marble shipment, she insisted on coming, hoping to stop the Gendarmes from killing you."

The helicopter disappeared behind the trees.

"I know where Kusler is headed," Craig said. "Brauder set up the rendezvous for delivering the merchandise at a deserted ski resort that burned down. It has a runway, so Brauder could fly there in his jet. Kusler will dump the helicopter nearby and have them pick him up in a car. You have to raid the place and rescue Darlena. Brauder will take her back to Germany and ravage her for revenge against me."

"We don't have any legal evidence that Brauder has committed a crime," Von Meier replied. "We can't send police in after him."

"Then let me get her out," Craig retorted.

Von Meier shook his head. "You know that's not possible."

"If you let me go after Darlena, I'll show you where I hid the paintings and sacred relics from the Vatican. Maybe I'll manage to kill Brauder before his men kill me. Then you'll have everything you want. The Vatican will recover all its treasures. With me dead, the Vatican won't have to air their dirty linen in public. If I live through it, I'll turn myself in to you."

Von Meier's eyes narrowed. "Why should I trust you?"

"I hid the treasures in the forest nearby. I'll show you exactly where on the way out. Everything else is in the truck. I swear that's the truth."

Von Meier continued to grasp his Ruger with both hands and kept the barrel pointed at Craig's chest.

"Damn it!" Craig yelled. "Don't let Brauder ravage Darlena."

The skin on Von Meier's face tightened.

"Please let me rescue her," Craig pleaded. "Part of what I stole from the Ducote Chateau is still in a safety deposit box at a Paris bank. I'll give you the bank's name and the safety deposit box number."

"Letting you go after Brauder violates my principles of criminal law," Von Meier replied. He shifted the Ruger into one hand and pulled out a pair of handcuffs from his coat pocket. "But letting Brauder kill Darlena violates a much higher principle. Put these on. I'll remove them when we reach Brauder's hideout."

Craig clicked the handcuffs on. With the element of surprise, he might reach Darlena before Brauder killed him. But if Von Meier didn't intervene to help, they would be trapped inside Brauder's compound.

At some point, he would face a terrible decision. Kill Darlena rather than let Brauder brutalize her.

CHAPTER 47

▼

Craig crouched behind bushes adjacent to the burned resort house and studied the layout. Enough twilight remained to see silhouettes of buildings and landscaping. But the semi-darkness provided an array of shadowy hiding places. "That's Brauder's jet being refueled on the far end of the runway," he said to Von Meier. "It looks like they're preparing to leave. The only building with lights is the one over at the base of the ski lift. So that's the building I need to reach."

Von Meier pointed toward a wooden balcony on the lighted building. "I see a guard there and one out by the airplane, plus the man beside the fuel truck. How can you approach the building without them spotting you?"

"There's another guard standing over by the metal storage shed."

Von Meier squinted into the twilight. "I can't see him."

"He's back in the shadows," Craig said. "Between that one and the man on the balcony, they can see every approach. I'll take out the man at the shed first and then nail the one on the balcony."

Von Meier unlocked the handcuffs, pulled a gun from his coat pocket, and handed it to Craig.

Craig spun the chamber and scowled. "This is a Ruger thirty-eight. It only holds six bullets and takes two to stop a big man. I need an automatic with punch."

"I don't arm myself for warfare." Von Meier handed him another three bullets. "These are all the extra bullets that I have."

Craig had seen Von Meier borrow a Beretta 9mm automatic from the Gendarmes. With a fifteen round magazine and a muzzle velocity that would stagger a man with one shot, the Beretta would be a much more potent weapon. "I might get inside with the Ruger," Craig said, "but I'll never get back out. That's the idea, isn't it?"

"I'm already stretching way beyond legal bounds to do this much," Von Meier replied.

"Where Darlena's concerned, boundaries don't apply," Craig retorted.

He shoved the three spare bullets into his pocket, scanned the area again, and turned to face Von Meier. "If I don't reach her, you have to stop Brauder's jet from taking off. Don't let Brauder take Darlena back to Germany."

Craig plunged into the thin line of trees surrounding the ski resort.

CHAPTER 48

▼

Darlena sat on the edge of a bed, her hands bound behind her. Her body shivered from chill evening air coming through the open window. In a chair nearby, a burly man munched on a sandwich of thick bread filled with cheese and meat. He opened a bottle of beer, took a deep gulp, and leered at her with cigarette-stained teeth.

"How about a drink? A few beers will put you in the mood for the trip back to Germany. You'll be providing the in-flight entertainment." Partially eaten food dribbled from his mouth as he laughed.

Darlena turned away and stared at the drab walls of the room. Pain knifed through her neck and head. The blow from Kusler's Luger on the helicopter had opened a gash above her ear. Blood continued to ooze into her tangled hair. From Kusler's comments to Brauder, the Gendarmes had recovered the Vatican treasures. Kusler didn't say whether he killed Craig before the Gendarmes arrived. His silence on the subject gave her hope that Craig escaped.

She pondered why Brauder hadn't already killed her. Why carry her back to Germany? They didn't need a hostage. No one knew Brauder was here at the abandoned ski resort. Even if Guista knew, he wouldn't care. Guista would triumphantly tell the Pope that the treasures had been recovered and the woman who could embarrass the Vatican met an unfortunate death at the hands of the jewel thief's co-conspirators. Lastavis would be forgiven in the name of protecting the spiritual integrity of the Holy Church.

All hope of justice drained away, replaced by an escalating foreboding of what loomed ahead for her. She remembered a comment from Craig. "Dying isn't the worst thing that can happen to you."

The door opened and a husky woman walked in. "Go load the luggage on the plane," she said. "I'll watch our trophy."

The man guffawed coarsely and clomped out of the room.

Darlena had seen the woman standing in the entry corridor of the building when Kusler brought her in from the car. Now, as the woman strutted to the lone dresser in the room and pulled off the belt around her waist, Darlena realized how imposing she was. With a big-boned body both fleshy and muscular and an attractive face with thick lips, she oozed sensuality. Short blondish hair framed blue eyes that glowed like an alley cat stalking a meal.

The woman placed the belt and a Ruger Redhawk Magnum on top of the dresser chest and prowled over to stand a few feet away. Her legs spread apart in a haughty stance, the black leather mini rising high on her upper thighs.

"We have some time before the plane leaves, so we might as well get acquainted. I'm Groda Voight. You belong now to me." Groda smiled. "Your Italian prostitute Rita told us all about you before she died. Amazing how talkative a person can become with a little persuasion. She said you're Craig's woman."

The shift in tenor of her voice and the harsh glare in the woman's eyes sent a shiver through Darlena's body.

Groda's dress spread open as she unzipped it all the way to the bottom. She wore neither a bra nor panties. "Do exactly what I say," she growled. "I become very angry when I'm not satisfied."

Groda grasped Darlena by the breasts and massaged them as she pressed her backward onto the bed, leaving Darlena's legs dangling over the edge. She inserted her thighs between the legs and spread them apart. Her fingers began unbuttoning Darlena's blouse. "I want to see what Craig found so fascinating about you."

The clatter of gunfire echoed through the open window!

Groda shifted her attention to the window. The sound of more shots filled the silent night. Groda yanked Darlena off the bed, dumped her on the floor, and stomped her in the stomach, driving out all her breath and bringing her to the verge of nausea. Groda snatched the gun from the dresser and ran from the room.

Darlena heard the door lock. She rolled over onto her stomach and struggled to her knees.

Only silence outside now. Whoever had been firing had stopped. Groda would be back soon. She had to escape. But how could she escape with her hands bound behind her?

Darlena wriggled her bound arms downward toward her buttocks. If she could get her hands in front, she would have a better chance. She had done this numerous times as part of limbering up exercises for gymnastics, but never with her hands tightly bound.

She kept wriggling and twisting. Her wrists were almost below her butt now. She rolled onto her back and swung her legs upward to touch her shoulders. Pressure on her stomach increased the nausea. She wrestled her bound arms past her thighs, knees, ankles, and finally over the toes.

Darlena sprang to her feet and looked around, hunting for anything sharp. Her bound hands yanked open dresser drawers. There was nothing anywhere in the room. She bit into the rope with her teeth, gnawing and pulling to loosen the knots. The knots were too tight.

What could she do?

In desperation, Darlena kept tearing at the rope with her teeth.

CHAPTER 49

▼

Craig scrambled over the low stone fence and tumbled onto a patio abutting the building as a spray of bullets raked the wall and fence. He rolled over and fired a burst of shots from the Heckler & Koch A3G3 assault rifle taken from the guard that he strangled at the storage shed.

The man on the balcony staggered against the railing, but kept firing.

Craig's next salvo sent him tumbling over the railing to the ground fifteen feet below. The hefty A3G3, with twenty rounds, gave him equality with Brauder's gunmen. Eleven shots fired, nine left. He needed to conserve his bullets.

The crash of glass behind him! He leaped back across the stone fence and crawled on his hands and knees.

Bullets shredded the wooden flower boxes on top of the wall. Someone had come from the building onto the patio, pinning him down here at the fence. Another of Brauder's men would work around to his unprotected side, trapping him in crossfire.

Craig looked for better cover but saw none.

In the bedroom, Darlena heard footsteps coming down the hallway.

She lunged to the heavy dresser, pressed her shoulder against the side, and strained to move it. Grudgingly, the dresser slid across the wooden floor. She maneuvered the dresser against the door.

Someone unlocked the door and tried to push it open. A man cursed and began slamming against the door, inching the dresser away.

She ran to the window and glanced out. The ground loomed twenty feet below her. A metal drain gutter ran up the wall a few feet away. It looked sturdy.

Darlena twisted her hands, bringing the inside wrists together, allowing her to spread her palms apart. She climbed onto the window sill, stretched out to grasp the gutter, and swung out as the door smashed inward, knocking the dresser chest away.

She hung there, her fingers clinging to the metal and thighs pressing against the gutter.

Kusler's head poked through the window. He swung the gun in his hand around to point at her. Darlena saw animal anger consuming his face and eyes.

Shots shattered the window, knocking Kusler backward out of view.

Darlena twisted her head and saw a figure crouched at the stone fence.

"Run for the burned out building!" Craig's voice shouted. "Von Meier is there. He'll protect you."

Bullets splattered the stone fence. Craig disappeared from sight.

Darlena pushed away from the wall, twisted in midair to position her body for landing, and plummeted toward the sloping ground twenty feet below.

She flexed her knees, struck the uneven embankment, and rolled over to lessen the jolt of the impact. When she lunged up to run, pain ripped through her right ankle. She staggered and almost fell, but regained her balance. Half running, half limping, Darlena struggled toward the house ruins a hundred yards away. The air filled with the sound of gunfire behind her. Every step sent a shock wave of pain up her leg. Her ankle wavered on the verge of collapse.

The ankle couldn't support her weight any longer. She fell, clambered back to her feet, and made another ten yards before falling again. The burned resort house loomed twenty-five yards away.

Bullets splattered into the ground behind her, clawing toward her like a shark bearing down on wounded prey.

A figure leaped out of the darkness, scooped her up over his shoulder, and ran zigzagging toward the building ruins. They tumbled headfirst over a pile of burned wood and debris. Darlena heard the heaving of his lungs as he pushed her down against the ground and held her there.

"You're safe now," the harsh Dutch voice of Von Meier said.

Darlena tried to struggle up to look back toward the other building, hoping to see Craig running toward them.

Von Meier kept her pinned to the ground. "He's trapped. We can't help him."

"You can't let Craig die," she gasped. "He saved me."

"It's what he wanted to do." Von Meier worked on the rope binding her hands.

Back at the stone fence, Craig crouched low and listened to faint footsteps on the patio. There were no bullets left in the assault rifle. One hand gripped the Ruger thirty-eight and the other grasped the rifle by the barrel.

He flung the rifle. As the rifle hit the fence ten feet away, he sprang up. The gunman on the patio had momentarily shifted his attention toward the noise.

Craig put two bullets into the gunman's chest, and then ran to a clump of shrubbery, dove into it, and slid down an embankment.

Bullets decapitated the shrubbery.

Craig loaded his remaining extra bullet into one of the two empty chambers of the Ruger and assessed his situation. With a gunman hunkered down behind the cab of the fuel truck, trying to cross the open field to the burned resort house would be suicide. But he couldn't stay here. A gunman with an assault rifle could zero in on him from the upper windows of the building.

A strange calm settled over him. The certainty of dying didn't bother him. He had killed Kusler and most of the other gunmen. Brauder would kill him, but didn't have enough men left to risk going after Von Meier. With Candalio dead, Lastavis exposed, and her role in the robbery negated, Darlena could begin rebuilding her life.

Saving Darlena was his ultimate achievement. Not even the fires of Hell could take that away from him. But he would die fighting rather than wait here for Brauder to kill him.

Craig worked his way along the embankment to the edge of the runway. The fuel truck loomed a hundred feet away. Five bullets in a Ruger thirty-eight against a well-positioned gunman with an assault rifle made survival highly unlikely. Unlikely, but not impossible.

A slight depression for drainage ran along the side of the runway. Not much cover but it would have to do. He flattened out on the ground and crawled along the depression toward the fuel truck.

A figure appeared at the corner of the truck and sprayed bullets along the edge of the runway. Craig's two shots sent the man jumping behind the huge truck wheels.

Craig lunged forward a few yards and then flattened out on the ground and inched forward, his eyes straining to see any movement beside the truck.

It was too dark for the man to pinpoint his exact position on the ground. But Craig's catlike eyes spotted momentary movement along the wheels of the fuel truck. He lined the Ruger up with the end tire.

A silhouette lunged around the edge of the large tire, spewing bullets from the barrel of an assault rifle. Craig's three shots knocked the man backward to the ground. The assault rifle clanked onto the concrete runway.

Craig tossed away the empty Ruger and ran for the assault rifle. If the remaining men in the building chose to challenge his escape across the open field, the fallen gunman's rifle would make it a more even battle.

Bullets shattered the assault rifle as he reached for it. He whirled and saw a figure emerge from the darkness of the airplane wheels.

"I could have already killed you," the figure said. "But I wanted to give you one last look at what you walked away from."

Groda Voight stepped into the glow of the airplane lights. Her legs spread apart in her haughty, sensuous stance. The Ruger Magnum in her hand pointed at his chest. Her elbows tucked into her sides, pushing the unzipped dress away from her body. A smile illuminated her face and accentuated the intensity of her large blue eyes.

"Take a good look at what you could have had," Groda purred. "You could have had the money, the power, and me to share it with."

Even as the messenger of death, Groda exuded a magnificent sexual aura. Craig forced a smile. "You have a contorted concept of sharing. Most people call it bondage. Brauder will never let you run his organization."

"Brauder is dead," Groda retorted. "You killed Brom Eidler and Kusler. So I put three bullets in Brauder's stomach while he cringed in the rear of the airplane, afraid to join the fight. As of tonight, the Lubeck Bay casino has a new owner. I'll have the money, the power, and a hundred men groveling for my affections." A throaty laughter spilled from her pursed lips. "I'll screw all of them, occasionally in bed but mostly in their pocketbooks."

She moved her elbows, letting the leather dress fold around her. "You were the one man I really loved. Because of that, I'm not going to make you suffer. No bullet in the knee, no bullet in the stomach. One well placed shot between the eyes, so you'll die knowing I still love you."

Groda shifted the gun upward to point at his head.

Shots hit the ground near her. Groda glanced around.

A tall, silhouetted figure stood in front of the burned resort house, firing a revolver at her. From that distance, there was no chance of hitting her.

In the moment that Groda turned away, Craig lunged behind the truck and scrambled toward the rear. A bullet from Groda's gun ricocheted off the metal tire rim. Another shot whined past his ear.

Craig crouched against the rear of the truck. His ears heard her footsteps stalking toward him. He grabbed the fuel truck valve and twisted it open. Jet fuel gushed onto the concrete and splashed underneath the truck, spreading in all directions.

Groda Voight's steps came closer, almost to the back edge of the fuel truck now. Her voice called out. "I have a ticket in my hand with your name on it, Craig. It's a one way ticket to Hell."

His hand pulled a palm-sized cylinder from his pocket. "Check the ticket again," he replied. "It's got your name on it."

Craig popped the miniature phosphorus flare, threw it under the truck, and ran. The flash of fire billowed in all directions. Heat engulfed him, searing his back and choking his lungs.

He dove headlong into the ditch. Flames lapped the air above him. Smoke blinded his eyes. His lungs gasped for air and found only searing heat. He scrambled on all fours along the shallow ditch, feeling his way with his hands and sucking in a thin layer of air close to the ground.

A deafening roar flattened him into the muddy bottom of the ditch. Heat scorched his back and legs.

Craig lunged ahead. His feet slipped in the mire, sprawling him facedown in mud. Hot smoke seared his lungs. His mind blurred. He clawed the ground with his hands to keep moving.

The intensity of heat diminished. The blur of his eyes partially cleared. His lungs sucked in acrid but oxygen-rich air. Smoke billowed above him, but there were no flames.

Craig staggered to his feet and looked back. Fire engulfed the demolished truck and airplane. Groda Voight had received an early introduction to the fires of eternity. If there is a Hell, she would soon be running it. The Devil would be no match for her.

The hairs on his arms were singed. His clothes smoldered. The burns on his hands stung but didn't look serious. Craig staggered across the field toward the resort house ruins.

Darlena limped into the field, wrapped her arms around him, and kissed him. "I saw the fire erupt and thought you were dead," she gasped between kisses.

The caress of her lips on his face soothed the pain and swept away his exhaustion. He clasped his hands around her thighs and lifted her up so they were eye to eye. "I would have done anything to get you out of that place. I've loved you from the moment I saw you exercising on the stone fence that morning after the train riot."

Even in the semi-darkness, he saw her emerald eyes glistening.

"I love you more than any man I've ever known or ever will," Darlena replied.

Von Meier stepped out of the shadows, the Beretta 9mm automatic dangling in his hand. "Craig Reynolds, I'm placing you under arrest for robbery of the Vatican. You'll be returned to Italy for trial."

Craig lowered Darlena to the ground and moved away from her. "I'm no longer a threat to you. My jewel-thieving days are over. I made a promise to take my sister Joan back to the United States. I won't fight you, but I'm not going to prison."

The Beretta remained pointed down. "I don't want to kill you," Von Meier said. "But I will if you try to leave. Turn around and let me handcuff you."

Darlena stepped toward Von Meier. "Please let him go. He destroyed Brauder's organization. Without his help, the Pope would be dead and an evil man would be ascending to the Papacy. Craig chose not to kill you. He chose not to kill me. He's promised you that he'll never rob again. I love him. Please don't take him away from me."

Von Meier's eyes remained focused on Craig. "He's a criminal. I don't have a choice."

"You do have a choice!" Darlena blurted out.

"Turn around and put your hands behind you," Von Meier said to Craig. "You haven't killed any people during your robberies. The courts will give that and what you've done today some consideration. They may shorten your sentence."

"Put down the gun," Darlena said in a terse voice.

Von Meier frowned at the snub-nosed revolver gripped in her hands. "Is that the gun I took away from you?"

"While you were in the field firing at Groda Voight, I rummaged through your satchel and found it." Her hands trembled but kept the gun pointed at him. "I lost the only other man I could ever love. I lost Papa. I won't lose Craig. Drop your gun."

"Don't, Darlena," Craig said. "I promised Von Meier that I wouldn't try to escape if he let me rescue you."

Von Meier turned to face her, his gun still pointed toward the ground. His finger remained wrapped around the Ruger's trigger guard rather than on the trigger itself.

They stared at each other, his eyes unblinking; her eyes round and unyielding.

"Don't, Darlena," Craig said again. "Give him the gun."

She shook her head. "I'm begging you, please let Craig go."

Craig stepped between them and faced Darlena. "If you help me escape, you'll face criminal charges. You won't be able to go back home to Luguri. You won't be able to coach gymnastics. I can't do that to you."

Darlena bit down on her lip. "I won't let him kill you."

"He's not going to kill me." Craig glanced toward Von Meier. "I won't resist. Do what you have to do."

Craig grasped the barrel of Darlena's revolver, eased it from her grip, and tossed it onto the ground in front of Von Meier. His arms wrapped around her and pulled her against him. "Go back to Turin and become Italy's best gymnastics coach."

"I'll wait for you," Darlena gasped. "No matter how long. I'll take Joan to the farm at Luguri. She'll be happy there." She stretched up and kissed him on the lips.

Von Meier stood motionless, the Beretta still dangling in his hand. "You could have bargained with the Vatican and walked away by telling them where the other treasures were hidden. You chose instead to risk everything by coming here to rescue Darlena. But that does not change the reality that you have committed serious crimes."

Von Meier's eyes shifted to Darlena. "Before my wife died, she told me that I needed to remember that the legal system works best when law and compassion are partners. If Helga were alive today, she would say that you've already paid too high a price for the misdeeds of others. Allowing Craig to leave is wrong. Adding to your pain is a greater wrong."

Von Meier shoved the Beretta into his coat pocket. "I'll tell the authorities that Craig died in the inferno with Groda Voight. You're free to go."

Darlena hobbled over to him and hugged him. Tears filled her eyes and wet both their cheeks. "Thank you. Thank you so much. Papa once told me that great men do what is right, not what must be done. I didn't understand what he meant until now. I will never forget your kindness."

Von Meier looked at Craig coming up beside them. "I'm doing this for Darlena."

Craig extended his hand. "You're an exceptional man. The only lawman I respected."

Von Meier clasped his hand. "Don't disappoint me."

"You have my word." Craig put his arm around Darlena's waist. "Plus, my wife would never allow it."

EPILOGUE

▼

The *Charlotte Observer* carried a feature article on the success of local North Carolina gymnasts in regional competition. It credited the success to the coaching of Darlena Wainwright, who established a gymnastics school here fifteen months ago. The article described her as, "a young woman with boundless energy and a mesmerizing presence when she steps onto the gymnastics floor to instruct or demonstrate."

Ms. Wainwright, after praising the efforts of her young team in winning the bronze, had boldly predicted, "These girls will compete for the gold next year. I owe that to them. I owe that to my husband, who provided funds from his investment company to sponsor this gymnastics school. I wish Craig could have been at the tournament, but he was on a business trip."

On page seven of the newspaper, a short article announced the death of Cardinal Lastavis, currently on health-related leave from his responsibilities at the Vatican. Cardinal Lastavis fell from the balcony overlooking the seaside cliffs at the villa of a relative. Italian Police declared the death an unfortunate accident.

Perhaps God is too patient with evildoers and content with providing punishment years later in the bowels of Hell.

Sometimes a little push is needed to speed up the process.

The End

978-0-595-43924-
0-595-43924-1